FIRST VICTIM

A NOVEL

NICHOLAS DEL GANDIO

SLEEPING GIANT

Sleeping Giant Publishing, LLC
www.sleepinggiantpublishing.com

First Edition paperback printing 2016

Manufactured and printed in the United States of America

1. Crime – Fiction. 2. Suspense – Fiction.

ISBN: 978-0-983-52773-2
Library of Congress Cataloging-in-Publication Data

For Nick, when you passed away, I knew I had to finish what you started and get this book out there. This is for you, my love. You did it!

FIRST VICTIM

A Letter From The Author's Wife

Dear Reader,

I am writing this letter to share with you the story of an amazing man, husband, and father, as well as the author of this book. Unfortunately, my husband suddenly passed away from a heart attack before final edits, let alone success in publishing it. Because he was so passionate about his story and getting it out for everyone to read, in honor of him, I present it here in raw form - the way he left it the day he died.

Writing *First Victim* was so cathartic for him. He never told anyone about his father, not even his closest friends. My husband was a perfect example in proving that you do not have to be a product of your parents. It was important for him to share with others, that despite being born into a horrible situation, one can still overcome, and create a wonderful life. I believe that from a very young age, he took what he knew about his father, and used that information to make a vow to himself. That vow was to do whatever it took to become the polar opposite of the man his father was, which is exactly what he did.

Nick Del Gandio was the most kind, caring, and loving man I have ever known. As a pharmacist, he made it his life's work to take care of everyone he met. He always went above and beyond the requirements or expectations of his job by caring for, and about, all of the patients who sought him out. Often times, he would become so close to his patients, that they would become dear friends of ours. He helped his patients in so many more ways than any ordinary pharmacist would. He had so much passion for his work, and for helping people.

Nick was not only a great pharmacist, but he was the greatest friend a person could have. He kept his friends near and dear to his heart. Some of his friends, up until the day he died, were friends made in kindergarten, grade school, high school, and college. In addition, he made friends wherever he went. People were so drawn to his infectious personality. He had kind eyes, and an even kinder heart. He would do anything for his friends, because he loved them dearly, and they most certainly loved him back.

Of all the people my husband ever met, or loved, I was the luckiest. I was fortunate enough to spend twenty years of my life with Nick. He swept me off my feet, and chose me to spend his life with, and oh, what a life we had! We dated for two years, and led on to get married, buy a house, and have two kids. In later years, we moved across the country and built our dream home in Las Vegas. We had a wonderful marriage, and we couldn't have been happier. We had the perfect life together.

Nick was a wonderful husband, which he was proud and confident about. When we talked about having kids, however, he was not so confident. He didn't know what being a father entailed, because he never had one. For good reason, he was terrified of being a dad, but I knew in my heart that he was going to be the best. True to himself, he read all the books and learned whatever he could about being a father. As soon as he held his baby, all of that went out the window. Love completely overwhelmed him, and all his paternal instincts took over. I couldn't have dreamed of a better father for our two beautiful kids.

Nick was taken away from us much too soon. Our lives will never be the same. We miss him every single day, but I am so thankful that he chose me to share his last twenty years with. I am thankful to him for giving me our beautiful children. I am thankful that he showed me what a real man is, what a great father is, and for teaching me how to be a better person. Most of all, he showed me what real love is. I will continue to raise our children the way we had always planned. I will honor my husband, the love of my life, for the rest of my days. Until we meet again.

Prologue

My identity has never been important; however, my story is. For the protection of my family and myself I must remain anonymous. I have legally changed my birth name to remove any association that could be made between myself and New York City's acclaimed Tape Measure Rapist. The situation into which we were catapulted between 1969 and 1970 has required a life lived in sort of a self-imposed victim's protection program. I say self-imposed, because the authorities offered no assistance to us after the guilty plea was entered. Not even a crumb came our way; they just left us to fend for ourselves. Not even an obligatory, "Everything will be all right." Nothing. The stigma that is forced upon family members of serial criminals has not been properly addressed by either society or the authorities.

The federal witness protection programs in place across the country are designed to protect witnesses and the families of witnesses who testify at the trials of those who have committed heinous crimes against society. What is often not addressed is the backlash that occurs to the immediate family members of the perpetrator. I was not witness to his crime spree, yet for my entire life I have had to deal with the circumstances he created. I was an innocent two-year-old boy when he struck out against society, yet it was my family and I who received the life sentence. It would have been appropriate and welcome if the authorities had given a shit about the family he left behind. We should have been relocated with new identities after the torment came to an abrupt end. Instead, my family was abandoned after the sentencing, sent back to our original four-room apartment in Brooklyn to exist amongst everyone who had firsthand knowledge of our crumbling lives. We had to deal with the aftermath for many years to come.

It's been over forty years, and Robert Maseano still walks the same ground as I do. To the disgrace of the New York State justice system, he was wrongly spared from death. I'm sure there would have been more satisfaction for us if he had received death as a sentence. It would have been more satisfying for me, anyway. But it was not in the state's plan for us to be vindicated that way. I have lived most of my life in the shadow of my father and his past. My goal has always been to avoid him and his legacy, as I tried to fabricate a normal existence with my broken but recovering family.

I lived my life on the streets of Brooklyn, economically forced to remain in the same first-floor apartment where Bobby Maseano formulated his plans. The authorities never looked back, never wondering how that young lady he was married to was going to survive. How would she be able to pay the bills, feed her small child, and move forward without a helping hand from the state? There are, in every case, more victims than those who have the ability to testify in a court of law. There is always a "first victim," and in Bobby Maseano's case, it was me.

Decades have passed since his incarceration, and I am now confident that the only characteristics we share is the love of the New York Yankees and maybe a good long pull on a Marlboro. The genetic predisposition theory of violence and criminal behavior has nothing to do with me. There is no weakness in my moral character, no propensity toward violence, no compulsion for sexual dominance--or any other deviant behavior, for that matter. I have never been incarcerated or in any trouble with the law. I have never had any issues forming concrete relationships with friends, have never become antisocial, have never deviated from the normally expected path in life set for me by my protectors.

I have, however, gotten a few speeding tickets. That's it, nothing else. You can check my records. Bobby Maseano should know that I have certainly checked all of *his* records.

The wounds have healed over time, but they have never gone completely away. I have had him in my crosshairs many times and yet by the grace of God, I chose to let him live. I've seen his Rochester home, I've seen his white Chevrolet Sierra parked in the driveway, and I have seen his wife and other kids. I have his email address and his phone number. I know where he works as a landscaper, I've seen him manicuring lawns and trimming front yard bushes. I have seen him interact with people who obviously don't know his true character or his past. I wonder if his new wife knows. If I decided to talk to Nancylee, would she be shocked by what I had to say? Does she know that she lies down at night with a serial rapist? I wonder about the answer to that question quite often.

I have seen the newspaper articles and all the police reports. I have seen his face a thousand times, in crowds, on the streets, in clubs, at the ball fields, and at the morgue. Nightmares work that way. They leave an indelible imprint in your gray matter, and it's there for life. Nightmares sometimes become memories when you don't have any real memories to recall. Bobby could have been anyone. He could have been the baseball coach in the park teaching kids how to play the game. He could have been any of the fathers in the auditorium at school awards ceremonies. He could have been any of the fathers helping their sons get their first car street-worthy. Bobby could now be the spoiling grandfather that only the lucky kids have. Then again, he was none of them. I know his life. I know his circumstances and I know

3

his story. I know his past and I know his future. Be thankful that the evil spliced into the helix of his DNA has not yet surfaced in mine. If I had it my way, his life would have ended years ago. I, his son, would have sent him to his Maker to be properly judged. I wait for the day he is judged by the hand of God. It should be a spectacular event.

Chapter 1

It's Sunday morning somewhere around 10:00 a.m. Under normal circumstances I would still be snuggled up between my wife's breasts, trying to work myself in a little deeper. There is simply no other place I would rather be then tangled up with her in bed. For me, weekends are made for family, especially when the kids are already wide awake and ready to go. My plan is always to spend at least part of the day watching a few ball games with my son and sometimes my daughter when she's in the mood. Mornings are just not a good time to take in a ball game.

We have been living in a well-populated area of the Mojave Desert for nearly four years now and it's been, to this point, impossible for me to remember to catch east coast baseball games so early in the morning. It's unnatural for me to watch baseball before lunch. I have spent my entire life watching the Yankees at 1:05 p.m. and now in the desert, the games are winding down about this time.

Sure, I catch the highlights on ESPN or Sports Channel, but it is not the same. I receive all the score updates on my phone. I have a few apps that help me stay fully informed. Every time the score changes, the damn thing goes off, bleeps, or buzzes, forcing me to respond. I try to keep up on the current scores when I'm at the hospital, but it's not easy. Hospital policy restricts personal cell phone use, because the frequency waves at which the phone operates can interfere with some of the cardiovascular-monitoring equipment. Technically, administration has banned the use of cell phones for personal use, even checking emails, especially when there are cardiac patients anywhere on or near the main nursing unit. There are always cardiac patients on the unit. My office, located adjacent to the critical care unit, is the most widely used satellite in the hospital. I just can't work a twelve-to-fourteen-hour day and not get the updates. So when no one is looking, even I break the rules. Of course I have the games recorded at home, but watching a game well after the fact just doesn't do it for me. I usually scan through the recorded games looking for plays that are going to make the highlight reel.

My waking moment this morning is due to a collection of diesel engine roars and crashing noises outside my front door. As my sleepy brain awakes, my initial impression is of a war zone, like explosions and gunfire somewhere in the South Pacific. I was captivated by Laura Hillenbrand's *Unbroken* last night before I fell asleep with her book flopped on my face. The intense images that formed in my brain from her carefully descriptive words have not yet left me. My thoughts quickly gather and turn back toward my morning's reality. None of my vivid thoughts are real. I am safe, not in the South Pacific, but rather in a suburban area of Las Vegas.

I stumble out of my bed and make my way through the master bathroom to the east-facing window, where I know I can view the source of the thunderous noise that reminds me of the South Pacific. There is no traffic on this street. There's no reason for anyone to be here unless they live here. There should be no major activity here on a weekend morning, anyway. At least not without some advance notice. There are only four homes on the cul-de-sac and I know one thing for sure: I'm not the one responsible for the commotion. I have to find out who is responsible for the violation of the rules and regulations. If anyone were to voluntarily violate the rules, it would be my next door neighbors. I'm almost positive of that, and it turns out I'm correct.

The initial assault, as I peer out of the window, is a blast of early morning sun rays directly into my eyes, which constricts my pupils, further limiting my view. It takes a few minutes, constantly shielding my eyes from the sun's blinding rays, before I'm able to focus on three bright yellow trucks with blood-red lettering. Red Rock Landscapers has fully assaulted my neighborhood and is operating in full force, attacking the caliche rock with massively loud jackhammers.

The main issue I have is with my family, and how in God's name the barrage of jackhammers, diesel engines, and crashing boulders directly outside their windows didn't wake them from their obviously impenetrable sleep? How would they wake in an emergency? What about the fire alarm? Would that wake them up? I'm not sure, because the noise level outside is significant and the three of them are lying in their beds, sound asleep like it was the dead of the night. Not even a twitch to signify any brain function. Nothing.

Thanks to Red Rock Landscapers I'll be sure to catch the game today. These early September games are all-important as the Yankees get poised for another spectacular October. First place again, and it always feels good. Boston's in third, Baltimore's in second. I usually don't worry about anyone else in September besides Boston. The Red Sox are just a thorn in my ass every year, and they never go away quietly. It does, however, make the end of the season more exciting, and I always remain focused on the standings until the Yankee clinch is announced. I can then shift my focus to the postseason. That's what I wait for all year long. My team is the perennial favorite and can never be counted out. Occasionally they falter and lose a series in the postseason and that really pisses me off. I'm still struggling with the Boston four-game sweep, after the Yankees won the first three in 2004. That one really hurt.

I enjoy watching the games outside in the backyard with my family. I have a comfortable setup under the palapa, which is a constructed hardwood structure with a straw roof that serves as a covering for the outdoor kitchen. I invested a significant amount of money in the whole setup, especially the sound system, mainly because I intend to broadcast Yankee victories over the block wall and invade the entire space of my neighbor's backyard. I only do this for his complete enjoyment. I enjoy his dismay as I crank up the volume flooding the surrounding area with John Sterling's voice "Theeee Yankees win, theeee Yankees win, theeee Yankees win." Life's always good heading into October. You see, the neighbors happen to be Red Sox fans, and I hate the Red Sox.

Lisa, my beautiful wife, interacts with the neighbors more than I do. She doesn't hold the whole Red Sox rivalry against them as much as I do. The girls are part of a group of four who regularly meet for lunch at which I'm sure they have some good laughs at the expense of each other's husbands. It's all good, though. I don't really mind being the brunt of a few jokes. I have thick enough skin, and I probably earned some of the jokes anyway--I can't speak for the other husbands. Their friendship keeps Lisa busy and out of the department stores and, most importantly, off Facebook. It's a great comfort to me that while I'm at work, Lisa has good friends to spend time with and have some quality adult interaction with. I've seen firsthand what spending every waking minute with the kids at home can do to an otherwise patient, intelligent woman. They have the capability of turning her brain to mush, and they have accomplished that mission several times over the years.

Lisa has been nurturing a newfound love for baking and decorating cakes. Some of her creations are spectacular and are worthy to be presented at the finest bakeries. She's well on her way to mastering turning sugar into art. She makes cakes for birthdays, holidays, and nearly all other special occasions. Lisa has made cakes for July 4th, Halloween, Christmas, and even a giant cheeseburger cake for Father's Day. My daughter Rose, and son Joseph are sous chefs whom Lisa has personally trained. They enjoy the creative process and spending time with their mother. Good-quality creative time spent together is priceless from my point of view. The house always smells like a piece of recently baked goodness, always drawing you in and always making you feel welcome.

My wife and I are well aware that our kids will leave the nest someday, but they will always return for nicely cooked homemade meals and fresh-baked desserts. We make a conscious effort to have as many meals together as possible, because this is our family time, where we can all just sit around and catch up. If we stay true to this now, it may carry on through their teenage years and hopefully into adulthood. The aromas will always be familiar, and those memories will always be calling them home. I have to admit, our lives are pretty awesome these days. I have a wonderful wife, two spectacular kids, and three dogs: Maggie, Millie, and Melody.

Looking back over the years, I can appreciate all the effort that was poured into giving me the best possible life by my mother, Ann and my grandparents, Teresa and Leonard. Their undying contributions of love, support and guidance have made me who I am today. All the hard work they have done on my behalf for all those years has provided me with the ability to be the kind of father to my own children that I always wished I had.

My life did not start off smelling like roses. There were no silver spoons in my mouth when I was born. If there was a smell, it would have been that of rotting sewage. It was more than a rough start for us back then as a young family living in Brooklyn. There was barely enough money to pay the rent and put food on the table. We were just getting started in life and the rug was pulled out from under us, almost from the very beginning. My mother was just starting to figure out how to raise a little boy who was entering the terrible twos. It was hard enough to raise a family with two parents, and now she was faced with doing it alone. How would she be able to manage life by herself? My father, Robert L. Maseano, somehow had morphed into a serial criminal, and the path of destruction he left behind was almost as wide as Manhattan itself.

Chapter 2

My biological father Robert L. Maseano, or Bobby, as he was known to friends, family, and coworkers, has not been a part my life for over forty years. I would like to think that the only ties that link us are the love we share for the New York Yankees and a good pull on a Marlboro. Although I have no firsthand knowledge of this, the stories of his undying dedication to that team has always resonated with me. I have wondered over the years how he was able to nurture a loving connection with a baseball team and yet not have the means or capability to develop and maintain a caring relationship with his wife, family, child, or anyone else for that matter. Bobby was able to disassociate himself from his actions and sever all ties with his victims, his family, and even me--at the time his only son.

The Health Insurance Portability and Accountability Act of 1996, better known as HIPAA, prohibits me from obtaining his mental health records from any of the prisons or hospital facilities to which he has been remanded. Bobby is protected from me under this rule, as it defines his privacy following the new national standard. However, this rule is really of no consequence to me at this point in my life. I know Bobby Maseano is a sociopath. Let me divulge some stories of his life and failures; then tell me if I'm not right. I know Bobby did not learn from negative experiences, because I know he had many throughout his early life. He has demonstrated this through countless crimes and atrocious acts against women. Was there ever a sense of responsibility or accountability for these acts? There was never any accountability to my mother Ann nor to me. This I do have firsthand knowledge of. I have lived it my whole life.

Bobby Maseano was unable to form any meaningful relationships prior to his incarceration. Every relationship he coerced people into failed and evaporated. He was left alone to sink into his own delusional psychosis. I have read the reports which described his inability to control his sexual appetite. Multiple counts for the same charge leads me to believe that he had a significant dysfunction in impulse control. His moral sense was also nonexistent. He could not have been a moral, scrupulous human being and be charged as he was. I know his behavior changed, but only after he was removed from the streets of Brooklyn and Queens. I personally have never heard or read a regretful word from him. I am guessing that Bobby was also a failure emotionally, never connecting with anyone, not even his mother, on any meaningful level. The complex web of circumstances that constituted his life was all about him, and was a continuation of his self-centered existence. Bobby manifested his sociopathic existence through his criminal behavior and the individual heinous acts, mostly upon defenseless women.

Bobby's work history supports the diagnosis of sociopathy. He was never able to hold a job for an extended period of time, regardless of the responsibilities he most definitely had at home. His decisions to abruptly open a fish market in downtown Brooklyn and close it almost as quickly also support the sociopathic theory. Bobby never showed up to work at the fish store, not even once. The money he borrowed was hard-earned by my grandfather, and he pissed it away as if he had not a care in the world. Bobby wasn't able to work at supporting his family because he had impulses and desires that needed servicing. The pull toward deviance was of gravitational proportions. His crimes were aggressive and violent, executed without regard for the pain and emotional stress he was inflicting. The sexual assaults were high-risk both to his victims and himself. Bobby's thought process was flawed, consumed by impulses and compulsions to act upon these women with the violence of an unrestrained animal. Bobby Maseano's punishment, which was imposed by the Supreme Court of Queens, New York was unjust, because today he still breathes the same air as his former wife, his victims, and myself.

This life-altering situation was his doing, not mine, yet I paid dearly for his crimes. Bobby Maseano may have paid restitution to society, but he has never paid any to me. It doesn't matter to me how many years he's been incarcerated, how many jailhouse fights he has been in, how bad his living conditions were, or even whether he has suffered a lifetime of pain for the crimes he has committed. I'm sure there were fellow inmates at Matteawan and Franklin who unknowingly vindicated me every time they took a piece of his ass. I know that they didn't look favorably upon him or his crimes. In the hierarchy of prison society, it's the sexual predators who usually find themselves inhabiting the bottom of the barrel. Knowing this gives me a sense of gratitude for all he has undoubtedly endured. The fact is, there is still more to pay. Every breath Bobby takes until his last one, he will be ing. There may have been court orders, incarcerations, a divorce, and serious jail time, but I am his blood, his creation. I am his son, and he owes me for the life he had left me with. For forty-two years we have been strangers, nothing to each other. I wouldn't know him if I walked past him in the street. It's probably better for him that our paths have not yet crossed. I was his first victim. He needs to know this, understand the severity of my ordeal, and someday be held accountable to me, then God. Good luck with either encounter.

I have lived in his Grim Reaper shadow and have paid for his violent and vicious crimes for far too many years. The shame he had cast upon me was unfair and unwelcomed. Bobby chose his path in life, and yet it was the innocent who suffered the consequences of his actions. From an early age, I reluctantly assumed the responsibility of being the "man" of the house. How can a child be the man of the house? That's not right. That's not the way my story should have played out. I was only seven or maybe eight when I realized that if I had any chance at a normal life, a chance of ever becoming a non-victim, a chance of ever not feeling persecuted because of him, it would have to come of my own doing. I had to rise above the humiliation of having him as my father. This is not what an eight-year-old boy needs to be thinking about. Everyone knew his life would be spent caged for the salvation of his other victims and for me, his offspring. Bobby Maseano stole possessions, innocence, and purity from many people in his life. Society may forgive him one day, but I will not. I can't and I won't. Ever.

Ann, my mother, naturally became my hero. She never left me. She comforted me when I was upset, sad, confused or when I couldn't make sense of the life situation my father had cast upon us. Ann had more balls than Bobby ever had. Ann was at times visibly weak, but she never cracked. I remember wiping her tears as they streamed down her warm, loving, and always glowing face. The face of an angel, her face, should never have shed one tear for my father's misguided indiscretions. With every swipe of my hand, her tears raced down my fingers into my palm and I clenched them tight into a fist, heightening the hatred I had for him. At times she thought of giving up, but she never did. She took on both parenting roles with a vengeance and succeeded with insurmountable tasks. I don't know if the sacrifices she made for my benefit could ever be repaid. She split herself in half, taking on unfamiliar, unwanted burdens and struggled, especially with the fatherly duties. After all, she wasn't a good baseball player and couldn't take me camping, hiking or fishing. She didn't do any of the outdoor activities that I craved so much. She couldn't throw or catch a football, wrestle with me, or show me how to play music. But she never gave up, and she was tenacious in her fight for us to just survive. Ann never wavered in her conviction that I must turn out as normal as possible under those horrifying circumstances. Ann is an unlikely hero, one who would never have assumed the role had she not been thrust into it. She was a young mother who didn't sign up to take on both parenting roles. Bobby Maseano wasn't evil enough to steal her away from me, although I know he tried. This is yet another failure in his miserable life.

Tell me where it was written that he had the right to leave his son to grow up and spend a lifetime repairing the shitstorm he left hind. My mission in life became, and is still to this day, protector of my mother and my family. She protected me from him in my early life, and I protect her now as she enjoys her senior years. I still accept the challenges of this role today, careful to be by Ann's side for every difficult situation, death, or drama that life places before us. We survived together in the wake of his destruction and will always continue to do so. Bobby Maseano has no power over us anymore. We know that this life is of his creation, and the punishment he received is not consequential to us. Early on, we committed to each other and formed a cohesive unit. We will continue to thrive in spite of him.

Bobby Maseano's legacy was a burden that was left for me to realize over the course of my early years. I was forced to carry his legacy throughout my young life, all the while trying to make sense of it. In the beginning, I made excuses for him in my childish thoughts. I have told myself stories about what went wrong with him and why my situation was different from that of most other kids my age. I never fabricated the same story twice. Well, maybe I told the story of how he died a miserable death a few times, just for shits and giggles. Still I wondered: Where was the disconnect? Where was the short-circuit? What was the chemical imbalance? Was there a deficiency in a neurotransmitter? If so, which one? Serotonin, dopamine, norepinephrine? Were there any outward signs in his life that could have been acted upon to prevent the pain and suffering he caused to so many people? Were there medical interventions that could have been launched? And if so, why weren't they? What was his young life like before he met my mother? Was he molested as a child? Was he verbally, sexually, or physically abused? There are reasons he turned out the way he did; I just don't know what they are. I may never know.

I have little, if any, recollection of his parents. I didn't even know their names for most of my life. I can't refer to them as grandparents, because they were as much of a mystery to me as he was. I don't have any feelings about them, especially not any hatred. I hope Bobby had the chance to question his parents about the point in his life when he made the wrong turn. Did he ever find out where he crossed over and landed on the wrong side of the tracks? It might have been as simple as "turn right here" and he turned left. Could it be possible that the answer is as simple as a wrong life turn? Were his parents involved in his life? Did they purposely neglect the warning signs of his mental issues? There had to be warning signs; there are always warning signs. Many times warning signs are not recalled until years later. Did he ever discuss this with them? Did he ever recall any specific instances, even many years later, in which he was able to pinpoint the triggers of his deviance? I often looked for signs of deviance in myself. Would my destiny be similar to his? No, definitely not!

Certain questions always arose in my mind. Was there a genetic link that would lead me down a violent, deviant, or criminal path? The endless array of stories a young boy can develop in his mind is staggering. The truth is these stories and complex ideations never go away. I am forty-four years old now and they are still there, lurking in the background for me to wrestle with, sometimes winning and sometimes losing. They live on in my psyche, although I have figured out how to suppress them over time. "Time heals all wounds" is a cliché and may hold true in some instances, but, time has not healed all the wounds he has inflicted. The difference now, forty-plus years later, is that I no longer blame my existence for his crimes. The situation he created was his and his alone. Bobby Maseano chose it, and he deserved the outcome.

I realized at an early age that despite not having a father to raise me, guide me, teach me, and nurture me, I could succeed, but I was going to have to do extra work. I have succeeded because of the strength of my character and the conviction in my soul. I was going to succeed as a son, husband, and parent. I was always willing to do the extra work. There's a funny thing about having children, they need you from day one. Somewhere along the way, Bobby must have missed that memo.

On March 3, 2001, I became a father for the first time, and for the first time in my life I experienced a fear that was beyond my control. I was honestly scared as hell. I didn't really have any tools. I couldn't pull anything from my memory banks and had no points of reference. There was nothing in my memory which I could tap into and extract the things I wanted to do the same as my father or the things I wanted to change. There was just nothing. I counted heavily on my wife Lisa and on my natural instincts to be there for our little girl while I figured out how to cope with my new reality. I read a few self-help articles on the topic, hit a few daddy support websites, and with Lisa's help managed to be adequate at my job of being Rose's dad. I did all I could to bond with this precious little bundle, and at first I did not feel the response I was looking for from her. It was pure devastation. Was I not giving her what she needed? Could this be my biggest failure? I felt I was going to fail her emotionally, as had been done to me so many years ago. This inadequacy would eventually leave me, but only after much struggle. I began to do what daddies do best for their daughters: just be there, strong as a rock. I had to do what I thought was right and learn from my mistakes. I mostly supported my wife in her efforts and allowed my daughter to become an extraordinary young girl, then a young lady. Good job, Daddy.

My thoughts of Bobby's life only recently became relevant again. It was shortly after the terrorist attacks on the World Trade Center, in New York City on September 11, 2001. On that horrific day, Rose was barely six months old, innocent and helpless. I was at work in Long Beach, New York when the first plane hit. I remember tuning in the radio and hearing of the tragedy. What a terrible accident, was my first thought. The whole world changed when the second plane hit the other tower. In a split second the situation went from being a probable accident to an unimaginable act of terror. I was physically only a few miles from ground zero, but my heart and mind were thousands of miles away, with my young family wrapped in my strong arms, sheltering them from all the evil in the world. Rose and Lisa did not have to be so close to this type of horrific act.

I sincerely apologized to Rose when I finally arrived home for having brought her into this crazy, fucked-up world. That was the first time she ever heard me curse. I held her tight, my wife at my side, and we prayed for everything to be better the next day. The roar of our Air Force jets boomed over our home and for my precious little girl, sleeping was impossible. A revelation occurred for me just after the second plane hit. I realized that I possessed the true instincts of a protective father and husband. I clearly remember doing anything and everything to get home and protect them. I made a promise to Rose that night, as the horror played over and over relentlessly on the flat screen behind me. I would get her away from this madness as soon as I possibly could, even if that meant leaving family and friends and relocating to a different and hopefully safer part of the country, somewhere that's not an enormous terrorist target like New York City. As a protective father, having my wife and daughter only a few miles away from Ground Zero was too close. We had to leave for more peaceful surroundings. We had no choice. I wondered what my father would have done in the same situation. Would he have done everything humanly possible to get back to me and protect me from the evil that exists in the world? I don't know for sure but my best guess is that I would have been the least of his concerns.

My son Joseph was born three years after Rose, on March 31, 2004, and at that moment I began to experience the pressure of being a new dad all over again. I was not only a daddy again, but now I had to be a daddy to a little baby boy. Shit, I had just figured out how to handle a little girl and now this, a baby boy. It started again, the unsettling fact that I had no point of reference from which to draw wisdom. Now, with a baby boy, there is going to be more pressure to get it right. There will always be issues and concerns which I don't have answers to. I utilized some of the tools I'd developed after Rose was born and applied them to raising my son.

There was no turning back now, and I quickly realized that after the first few months, boys are extremely different from girls. Not the obvious differences: I mean there's a different level of learning, a different way of interacting, a different way of loving them. The amount of love is the same, it's just in a different way. The way I see my son is more like I'm looking at mini-version of myself. We both have all the same parts. I knew from day one that he would develop into a strong, charismatic, intelligent young boy and be fearless in the world. I'm still working on making him fearless, though.

When I look at my daughter, it's like I am looking at the face of an angel, not something I helped to create. I just knew she would evolve into a fun-loving, strong-minded, intelligent, down-to-earth young lady. In many ways she's a lot like my mother, Ann. Rose hasn't hit her teen years yet, but so far so good. Rose, don't worry, Daddy will be ready for those years also. I'm ready, for sure. I have created my own points of reference now and I feel that I can handle myself as a man, husband and most importantly, a father.

Chapter 3

Every Sunday back in the late 1960's, between April and October, at or about 1:00 p.m., the Zenith television, housed in a well-worn maple-colored console cabinet, would be tuned to WPIX Channel 11. Its dial had seen much use through the years and was severely abused, sometimes held in place with Scotch tape. It was a lucky day when turning the knob to the station you wanted to watch actually brought the picture into focus on the first try. Perched atop the console sat an indoor antenna which often required some adjustment, simultaneously coordinated with tuning in the channel to get the best picture. Aluminum foil loosely wrapped around the top of the rabbit ears would increase the surface area of the antenna, thereby bringing in a perfect ture. Sometimes. This was not an easy achievement, and often became a two-person job, one holding, wiggling, and stretching each rabbit ear and the other person carefully turning the knob. It didn't matter though; whatever it took to get the game on was what was going to be done, even if someone had to handhold the antenna the whole three hours, even throughout the commercials.

At that time, Bobby was a fixture at the apartment of Ann's parents in an area of Brooklyn called Bensonhurst. He'd be taking in a game, chugging down a few free cold beers, waiting for the usual afternoon Italian feast.

Sundays were special back in those days. The neighborhood was comprised mostly of Italian-Americans, and Ann's family was no different. The block became absent of life about this time of the day, because everyone was inside enjoying their Sunday afternoon meal. Some were recovering from overstuffing themselves and some were getting ready to eat, but everyone was getting ready for the Yankees game. The scenes were pretty much the same, no matter whose house you were in: the ladies and young girls gathered in the kitchen stirring the sauce, gently rolling homemade pasta, making the meatballs, cutting the garlic bread, opening the gallon of homemade wine, and plating a spread of antipasto. This always included hard salami, sharp provolone, olives, roasted garlic, and sweet fried peppers. Some of the girls, like Ann, were in charge of cleanup, washing, and drying all the preparatory dishes and bowls. Females resided in the kitchen until all the final details were perfected, and the men, the good-for-nothings, just sat there in front of the console, fighting over whose turn it was to get up and change the channel or adjust the antenna. The ladies did all the work and the guys did all the eating and sleeping. That's how it was back then, and there didn't seem to be anything wrong with it. The girls took pleasure in preparing all the food and the guys took pleasure in devouring it; then they would all pass out.

When mealtime arrived, Ann's mother Teresa would call into the living room for the boys to come, always wanting them to hurry and enjoy before her food turned cold. Bobby wondered why in God's name the pasta was ready at the same time the game was starting every week. "How does that happen?" After calling a several times for the boys to come and eat,, Teresa would send Ann to physically fetch them. Ann didn't like to confront Bobby when the game was on, but at this point she had no choice. Ann didn't want to show her mother in any way that she was afraid of Bobby, so she strolled into the living room and kindly asked everyone to come in the kitchen. Bobby usually responded pleasantly as long as Leonard, Ann's father, was still in the room. Leonard always exited the room first, drawn by the traveling aroma making its way down the short corridor. Then Bobby's demeanor would change wickedly and he would snap at Ann, saying in a muffled violence, "There's no good reason why she wouldn't let me eat in front of the television and watch the game. There's fucking plastic on everything anyway. What's the fucking difference where I eat?" When Teresa walked into the room to see what the holdup was, Bobby became as polite as could be.

Ann finally realized how easily he bounced between personalities. Bobby's physical and verbal actions unsettled Ann. One time, Bobby gently kissed Teresa on the cheek as he passed her by and warmly said, "I was just on my way in." Ann followed Teresa and Bobby into the kitchen, rubbing her left wrist gently with her right hand as she tried to dissipate the pain inflicted by Bobby's slightly assaulting grab. "Son-of-a-bitch," were the only words she was able to whisper to herself. Ann tried to convince herself that what just happened was just a one-time occurrence. Bobby had never laid a finger on her before. She had never seen Bobby act that way, and she had hoped she would never see it again.

Teresa was actually quite fond of Bobby. Maybe it was because he always praised her cooking, or maybe because he occasionally helped her out around the house. Sometimes, Teresa would even allow Bobby the honor of meatball detail. Making the meatballs for Sunday dinner was more of a privilege than a chore in Teresa's home. Most Italian women would simply not trust a man to even come close to the meatballs or the sauce. The fact that Teresa allowed Bobby to help her in the kitchen was seen by Ann as an event or acceptance, sort of a bonding moment. Bobby was always willing to help out with anything that needed to be done, and he too saw Teresa's allowing him to help with the meatballs as a sign that she was someday going to fully embrace him as part of her family. Until now he was just married into the family and there was a lot of work left to do before he would be fully accepted.

Bobby often gorged himself to the point of collapse. The food-induced coma that ensued was typical and common, at least among the men--some lessons are hard to learn. There was definitely a palpable decline in energy levels after Sunday dinner as compared to fore. Dopamine and serotonin released at full throttle, and a welcomed calm began to set the mood for the rest of the afternoon. The blue-and-white paisley print button-down shirt was relieved of its duty. The top button of the black polyester slacks forcefully came undone and Bobby pulled up on the floor with a plastic-covered couch pillow for a few minutes' rest. There he lay in his now-exposed wife beater undershirt, hand slightly tucked into the elastic waistband of his open pants. The customary low-level snoring began to commence and Ann sarcastically said to herself, "How lucky can one girl get?"

Ann knew that once Bobby made his way to the floor, he would be there for hours-the king of the castle, or so he would like to think. It didn't take long for Bobby to fall into a state of intense relaxation bordering on sleep, but never progressing to a full REM. Any success he managed at fighting off the impending slumber was because he had to catch the rest of the game, even if it was through one opened eye.

Although Teresa and Leonard had almost accepted Bobby, the relationship had not fully developed, but it was on the way. Teresa held onto her reservations about him and was determined to stand by her convictions until she could be proven wrong. Leonard, on the other hand, was more willing to accept him into the family. Leonard found it hard to see character flaws in anyone. He always gravitated toward the good in people, often to a fault. There was always something holding Teresa back, and she approached her embracement of Bobby Maseano cautiously. Ann, on the other hand was all in, hook, line, and sinker.

Ann enjoyed some hours of comfort, because for that short period of time, maybe four to five hours, which included game time and nap time, her family was intact and she knew exactly where Bobby was, on the floor where everyone had to step over him to pass to the other rooms. No one ever rested on the couch. Everything, all the priceless heirloom pieces of discounted furniture, were dressed with plastic slip-covers back in the late 60's. Even the dog preferred the floor.

Ann had no cause to worry about what Bobby was doing, where he was going, or where he had been. The games provided some hours of much needed peace and quiet for her. There were some exhilarating games that went into extra innings when the score was tied at the bottom of the ninth. These were better games for Ann, and she looked forward to them. It didn't matter whether the Yankees won or not, at least to Ann. The longer the game went on, the more peace she had in her life. This was not the case on weekdays.

After a short while and as soon as Bobby gained more control of his wife, he began not to come home at the end of his workday. This started small, with an occasional late night, but it quickly progressed. One night he staggered in hours late and ignored all of Ann's probing questions. Ann said, tears swelling in her eyes and anger growing in her heart, "Where were you? I expected you home hours ago. The baby has been crying non-stop for hours and I'm almost out of diapers. I didn't know what to do with him!"

Bobby, offering no answers to her questions, stated, "Your mother is right around the block. Why didn't you call her or take the baby there if you needed help?"

"I can't run to my mother's house every time the baby cries," she explained. "I need you here, on time, to help me."

Bobby's response, which was becoming customary, said, "I will get here when I get here, and not a minute before. I'm working long, hard hours all day and I need to unwind before I come home to you and all this shit."

Ann silently asked, "What the fuck do you think I'm doing here all day? I'm not sitting on my ass listening to Elvis all day."

Occasionally Bobby would go out with the guys from work, usually to Cobblestones Pub on Queens Boulevard. Cobblestones was a favorite spot of the guys' and Bobby was 1 accepted into the mix. It really only took him buying a couple of rounds of drinks and he was in. Not one of the other drivers ever turned down a free drink. As long as Bobby had money in his pocket and he was buying, he was welcomed.

Cobblestones was appropriately named after the ancient floor which had been masterfully installed in the mid 1920's. The antique bar had old-world charm with a well-worn decor. The bar itself was crafted out of solid oak and adorned with a solid brass foot rail, which ran the full twenty-two feet from one end to the other. The walls above the bar were home to two large highly-polished brass lion heads that had been converted into tap beer dispensers. The cobblestone floor had developed a shiny patina after all the years of hard-soled shoe traffic polishing the stones' surface. Overall, the bar was as original as any the guys had ever seen, and the craftsmanship was noteworthy. The entrance doors were nearly ten feet tall, made of some kind of solid wood, and were finished with black paint which had chipped and scratched over time. The handles were three feet long, also made of solid brass and shaped like the lion-head adornments on the inside but on a much smaller scale. The building itself was a three-story semi-attached brick structure that would qualify for demolition under normal circumstances. However, that building had been protected as a city landmark. This does not mean that improvements didn't have to get done. It just meant that the inspectors would look the other way periodically unless there was a major violation. Cobblestones had evolved into a hot spot for locals and the industrial workers in the neighborhood and was responsible for a few broken marriages.

The bricks were exposed on the inside as well as the outside, keeping the erosion of this landmark as even as possible. The staircase which led up to the second-floor bathrooms were slightly tilted to the right. The combination of a cobblestone floor and leaning staircase, combined with alcohol intake, made for many eventful journeys to the upstairs bathrooms. Women would often twist an ankle, especially when wearing heels which were a few inches too high. There was no shortage of men to break the fall and the ice at the same opportune time. The railing was itself solid, but was only loosely mounted to the wall. Some screws hit the studs and some obviously did not. For some reason, navigating the stairs became easier the more drinks that were consumed and the later the night dragged on.

The original owners of the building ran liquor through the doors during the prohibition years. The facade varied in those days, but it mostly posed as a tobacco shop. Patrons would come in for smokes, mostly hand-rolled dirty tobacco, and walk out with a fifth or two under wraps. The owners were not worried about the quality of the smokes. At that time there was little money in the tobacco business and plenty of money in liquor. Judging by the vast quantities of large empty whiskey jugs set on the high shelves, alcohol was the business to be in. No one knew anything about the availability of grain alcohol back in those days. It was the best-kept secret in the hood. Hell, even some of the cops, out of uniform of course, went in for smokes and a drink. That's what made the world go around in the 20's, 30's and now the 60's. Alcohol, smokes, and an occasional drunk blonde.

Chapter 4

My mother Ann was a lady, beautiful on the outside and delicate on the inside. Her lightly colored face contrasted nicely with her wavy strawberry blonde, hair, which stopped at her shoulder. She always presented herself as well-dressed, put-together, and magnetic. Her sensitive soul added to her overall attractive nature. The routine was hot rollers at night to have waves or tight curls in the morning, depending on the diameter of the roller she chose. It seemed slightly odd to me at times, the way she would parade around the apartment with rollers in her hair. I still don't know how she was able to sleep in those rollers without them burrowing deep into her head. Ann went through a lot of unnecessary primping for her curls to be just right. I remember marveling at how she was able to walk, without a hitch, in high heels. It appeared unnatural to have the heel of her foot six inches higher than her toes, but she managed to properly navigate the halls and looked graceful clicking across our worn vinyl floor.

The years we spent together were learning years for both of us. I observed everything and internalized all events as life lessons, so that I might be able to use her teachings someday when I needed to be guided by experience. I watched her interactions with people, friends, neighbors and family, and this taught me communication skills, which I found to be very useful in later life. I watched her emotions materialize, then dissipate, for what seemed to be no apparent reason. Although not fully understanding the magnitude of her highs and lows, I tried to be sensitive to her emotions, to comfort her when she needed someone to lean on and to be somewhat firm when she needed that as well. It sounds funny that I would have to be firm with my mother at such a young age, but in certain situations I was the voice of reason. I'm sure that because of her I've developed into a different person than what the genetic map had planned for me.

We were a team and on some level became friends in the process. We just needed each other and more importantly, we were physically and emotionally there for each other. She navigated a fine line between parent and friend. There is a different level of comfort that can be obtained from a friend than from a parent. To fill any voids that existed, we created a mechanism by which we were able to deal with each other's emotional needs. I would talk to her about things that a boy would typically not share with his mother. I had to utilize her as a mother, father, teacher, counselor, disciplinarian, and friend. It's something that can be understood only by another boy who was solely raised by his mother. There are many reasons for me to be a mama's boy, and I'm proud of each and every one.

Through the spring of 1984, there had been no serious callers for Ann. We had had many years together without any outside interference from the opposite sex. There was no one she was very interested in nor anyone whom I approved of. When there was someone of interest she always looked for my approval and I rarely gave it. Ann was mine, and I was not willing to share her with anyone--not until I was ready. The natural separation was inevitable, and I was completely aware that it was happening. I'm sure Ann felt it as well. The length of time we spent apart widened over time. I had baseball, school, friends, and eventually girlfriends. She had work, friends, and family. I'm sure it was a lonely time for her as I knew, even then, that I was an inadequate substitute for a male companion.

We often discussed lonely feelings, the emotional abandonment, the fulfilling path in life we were aimlessly searching for, the one that would lead us to higher ground. There must have been immense fear involved in being a single parent and raising a son back in those days. I was in tune with it, but as I grew older, I developed a fear of broaching the subject. It was working, and she had a good grasp on the responsibilities she had inherited. I was not prepared to disturb in any way what we had built. I tried my best to be there for her, always conscious of her emotions and never intentionally stepping on her sensitive soul. I'm sure I did, at some point as we grew together, but I was as careful as I could be with the testosterone that now started to consume me. I proceeded with caution, succumbing to the reality that I was going to be a man someday soon, and would have to remain dedicated to protecting and caring for her as she had done for me all the years of my childhood. We had created an uncommon bond, begun by the incarceration of Bobby Maseano, one that will never be broken for any reason. Not ever.

Bobby was gone for a very long time. The years passed by, seemingly like the weeks of a month and I was growing up, starting to have a life of my own. My mother made sure there were many conversations about how to treat females. What level of respect there should be and if it's not there, just walk away. Never raise a hand to a girl. Never use language that is offensive, because words can be as damaging as any other weapon. Always proceed with caution and develop mutual respect for each other. Care for any female as if it were she, Ann. Ann's guidance was precious and priceless. She had been the defining force in my life, and I am a better man today for her actions and words. Ann's words were as piercing as a 9mm slug, and they have never left me. I can only hope that I am able to dispense this wisdom to my own son. If I am successful with Joseph and he becomes the man I expect him to be, we will have completely succeeded in breaking the cycle which was laid before us. I relish the fact that I have lived the lessons that my mother taught me and I know I will enjoy a sense of completeness as I watch my son become a well-respected, honorable young man. I have full confidence in him and fully expect him to live a worthy life.

As I became an adolescent there were a few friendly first dates for Ann, but only when I supported it. I'm reminded of one which actually included me and a not-so-pleasant walk on Canal Street in Chinatown, New York City. The narrow Chinatown streets were decorated with colorful advertisements in what seemed to be symbols instead of letters or words, obviously to attract Chinese patrons and not cans. There was barely a legible word to be read anywhere, at least not an English word. There were a massive number of immigrant Chinese people living and working in the area, and the majority of the business was generated from the locals. The most appropriate mode of transportation was a bicycle, because navigating a vehicle down the overcrowded streets was nearly impossible and considered hazardous at best. The locals were a force to be reckoned with, numbering nearly one hundred thousand in a two-mile radius, all seemingly congregated on Canal Street. Chinatown was a city within a city, providing safety to the Chinese immigrants who congregated in this area of Manhattan.

The date started off well enough, but quickly deteriorated as we braved the perimeter and then entered the heart of Chinatown. Canal Street was somewhat repulsive to us as we navigated around the enormous amount of trash that had collected on the sidewalk. The homeless population of Chinatown resided in the alleyways between the endless rows of take-out restaurants. Makeshift cardboard shelters were strewn out along our path, as the homeless population trickled out from the alleyways to the curbs, looking for discarded morsels of food and beverage. The lasting memory of that evening was that out of all the homeless street dwellers we saw that evening, none of them were Chinese. I was sure I would never take a date of my own down Canal Street.

In front of Lucky's Take Out Kitchen we gawked at the Chinese food being prepared in the kitchen, which was barely visible through the grime of adherent grease that obscured our view, almost to our benefit. This was a scene that you can go a whole lifetime without seeing twice, and you'll be better off for it.

At first, I was amazed at how fast the chef worked his tools, how well he controlled the ladle that flipped the fried rice, and how some kind of sauce was squeezed from the bottle held at shoulder height, never once with regard to measurement. I clearly remember the treat of the street-side window which allowed us to admire the chef and take in the culinary show. The chef wore his Chinese take-out chef uniform, white pants, and a white Fruit of the Loom-type tee shirt. The tee shirt had started its life white, but now lived pale yellow with just a hint of white, mostly on the back where the grease had less of a chance to adhere. I was sure the tee shirt had never been washed. It probably could have stood up tall all by itself without a problem. I don't know for sure how old I was at that time. I couldn't have been more than nine or ten, but I was clearly old enough to remember an unimaginable occurrence.

As the greasy cook tossed the contents of his wok and the flames peeked out from under a place I was unable to see, a bead of sweat ran down his face and clung to his chin for what seemed to be a full minute. Then it happened, gagging us simultaneously, as if our stomachs were screaming at our eyes to close. A single drop of sweat flew from his chin with no chance of missing the twenty-four-inch wok and landed dead center into someone's fried rice. Then it happened again: drip, drip, drip. The horror of what we had just witnessed led us to the conclusion that this could not be a coincidence. What are the odds that we were witnessing the only sweat drops to ever fall off a Chinese cook's chin directly into someone's dinner? We waged that this is a common occurrence, and although we had been having a decent time walking around Chinatown up until this point, dinner would not be had in this part of Manhattan--not that night, and not ever. Why should we even consider ever coming back to Chinatown? It was dirty as anything we'd ever seen. The streets smelled of week-old urine. The shops were full of fake merchandise, like a "leather" pocketbook for $5.00. And now every grain of rice, every piece of sweet and sour chicken, and every egg roll, in my mind, would be soaked in the sweat of the Chinese cook. That first time became the last time we ever considered eating in Chinatown. This was the first and last date with that guy.

Ann quickly became frustrated with the dating scene. In some odd way she was content with her nine-to-five job at the phone company and with her family and friends. There were obvious gaps in her happiness, but she was able to fill them with hand-selected individuals who supported her. She was always good at nurturing relationships; she just chose not to nurture any with men at that time. Ann preferred to spend her time nurturing relationships that lifted her up. Men in general had a way of dragging her down. Ann invested countless hours being a good friend and a great mom. That was time well-spent.

Living in Brooklyn was always a social event. Everyone was fairly friendly, and it didn't take long to develop strong bonds with neighbors. The apartment where we lived was in good condition, and modern for the late 60's and early 70's. The appliances were all new from Sears and although they were not top-of-the-line, they surely served us well for many years. New apartment appliances were a strong determining factor as to why Bobby and Ann had rented those rooms, because they didn't have any spare money to purchase new appliances. The paint colors that Bobby had applied to the walls warmed the apartment and offered a welcoming atmosphere. The bedrooms were painted in soft earth tones which contrasted nicely with the brightly colored bedding and window treatments Ann had picked out. The living area had new wall-to-wall carpeting, and the furniture that had been purchased with the money from their wedding gifts fit perfectly in the space. Ann had done a spectacular job at decorating on an extremely limited budget. It would not have been possible for her to leave the apartment after Bobby was arrested. She had a nice place, the rent was fair, it was fully decorated, and it was very close to her parents. Ann unknowingly had the infrastructure in place to prevent a full and catastrophic collapse when Bobby was finally arrested. She worked hard to get past the fact that everyone knew why her husband was a serial rapist. It took a long while for her to get over it, but she eventually did.

Chapter 5

St. Mary's Mother of Jesus Church was located just around the corner and up one block from Ann's apartment and was a well-populated gathering place for mass. The mostly Roman Catholic residents of the Brooklyn neighborhood made it a ritual to be at one of the Sunday morning masses, regardless of their activities during the week. Let's just say that just as God rested on the seventh day, so did the members of the organized crime families. Most of the Italian men in the neighborhood were sure to make it to one of the services. Some were there for godly reasons and some were there merely to ask for forgiveness for the illegal work they had done the previous week. It made no difference which side of the law you walked on from Monday through Saturday. On Sunday, everyone was there, holy, and welcomed. The church, and especially Father Devlin, never turned anyone away because of the mistakes they had made in life, even if that meant that they sometimes had to take a life. It was just family business, and it had no place in Father Devlin's heart. Doctors were the same as yers. Grocery clerks were the same as surgeons, and made men were the same as altar boys.

The old church was packed when Father Devlin presided, and all in attendance listened intently, hanging on every word, if you could believe that. The way he delivered the mass was unparalleled, if you compared him to any other priest in the parish. He was quite young for a priest, somewhere around thirty-five or so. He was nearly six feet tall, with a pale white complexion, brownish freckles, and a bushy red mop of hair. He could often be seen walking the neighborhood streets checking on the young ones, me included. His specialty at the time was showing up where there was potential for some good old-fashioned wrongdoing. Father Devlin seemed to be everywhere all at once. If we wanted to smoke a cigarette on the corner, there he was and out went the cigarette. If we were planning to steal something from the candy store, he would be turning the corner heading straight toward us. We would never run away from him, as we all thought he had some kind of divine intervention going on. If we were not doing well in school, cutting class, or being disrespectful to a nun or teacher, he would somehow show up at school and sometimes appear in class. He never really said too much about the wrongdoing. His presence was enough to curtail all the illegal activity, and we morphed into little angels right before his eyes. Father Devlin never saw the bad in any of us. If he did, he never mentioned it. He always gave us the benefit of the doubt. We were all angels when he was around. After all, he did have a direct line to the Big Man upstairs, or so we believed at the time.

Father Devlin was everything to that parish. He was the priest everyone went to for confession. He was an extremely busy man at confession time, especially in that neighborhood. If you were going to be married or needed to baptize a baby, he was the first choice on everyone's list. The other priests were lucky to get last rights and funeral services, or they might have been out of a job. He organized the school basketball league and started intramural wiffle ball leagues, all done to simply keep the kids off the streets and out of trouble.

In his infinite wisdom Father Devlin also came up with the concept of "Parents without Partners." There was a large consortium of parishioners who were newly divorced, with young children. Ann was in that boat. This combination of circumstances was not conducive to creating a strong social life. Single parents faced with a lack of support would often be relegated to staying at home and tending to the broken family. Father Devlin organized an opportunity for single parents to meet in the church basement on a biweekly basis with the main purpose of socializing and forming new bonds within the community. He had the means through strong community donations to transform the basement into a lounge where adults, all in similar situations, could gather and gain support from each other. The DJ would play soft easy-listening music at an appropriate volume that did not compete with the conversations that were taking place. The volunteers who staffed the basement kitchen served finger food and drinks. Father Devlin managed to supply fairly acceptable wine for the events, and the edge was quickly removed from most after the first or second glass. Tables and chairs were set up for gathering, and the nights progressed well past the midnight hour.

Elderly ladies of the community donated their time to tend to the children up in the church who were brought to the gathering. Father Devlin was sure to promote this opportunity including the children. If the children couldn't attend, then neither could the parents. The quiet room in the main church was located just to the left side of the oval Italian marble altar and close to the exit doors. This room was an enclosed, soundproof area and was built so that young children and infants could attend mass services and not disturb the entire congregation. It would now double as a makeshift nursery and babysitting station during the meetings. There was tremendous support from the community for this program, and I'm sure the support was not simply because Father Devlin asked for it. This community was not immune to the nearly 40% divorce rate that existed in the late 60's through the early 70's. "Parents without Partners" was Father Devlin's mission to bring singles together, relieve the pressure of meeting new and exciting people, and observe the repair process, as he knew that most wounds would eventually heal.

After much hesitation and deliberation, Ann, and a couple of friends, Maryann and Felicia convinced each other to give the new church program a try. They had nothing to lose and possibly something to gain. Months had passed, yet they still had not ventured out, giving one excuse or another. The girls grew bored with their usual routines, but fear of the unknown was sometimes paralyzing. The bar and club scene for socializing had been intriguing in months past, but was now growing tiresome, and any newfound excitement would be a welcome change in each of their lives. The decision had finally been made, wardrobes had been selected, and a commitment to each other had been sealed. None of the three girls would break from the group and go off and leave the others to fend for themselves. They all had serious trust issues with men which would not be resolved with one night out and a few glasses of wine. The anticipation of some time being spent with other adults, whether male or female, would force out some adolescent emotions in the ladies, and they all welcomed the change from their usual Friday nights at home.

Ann wore black slacks slightly belled at the bottom, black heels, and a black-and-white silk print blouse with her diamond heart pendant appearing just above the neckline. She thought the diamond heart would show off her loving nature and would maybe fend off some unwanted advances. Her strawberry blonde shoulder-length hair framed her face, and she felt good about herself. She hadn't felt good about herself in a while. Her appearance was well put-together, and she felt better about her attire than she did about her expectations. She told herself over and over again not to have high expectations. It's just a night out. Just go out with the girls and have a few drinks and a few laughs. Ann was anticipating people-watching more than anything else. Maryann was one of those people who could pick a person apart from across the room. She had no filter, and her tongue often fired soon after the first taste of alcohol.

Maryann was the catalyst, and Felicia soon followed. The constant barrage of verbal assaults on anyone and everyone lent itself to a night of good comedy. Ann, on the other hand, was much more subdued, more of an introvert in uneasy social situations. She was not one to aggressively start a conversation and was often the first to drift away to isolation. The evening started off well enough. All three walked to the church, strutting down the block with surprising confidence. They fed off each other that night, and their collective confidence began to rise as each met at Maryann's house promptly at seven on the last Friday night in October. The slight chill in the air was braved by the ladies, because they knew the warmth the wine would provide would soon follow.

Maryann was her usual comedic self, blasting on every presented opportunity. She must have finished off a whole bottle of wine in the first hour or so. When this occurred, all bets were off and you had better get out of her line of fire. Maryann seemingly abused everyone in the basement of the church, short of Ann, Felicia, and Father Devlin. Everyone else was fair game, and she satisfied herself almost to the point of passing out. Felicia was only slightly more reserved and polished off nearly three-quarters of her own bottle. She obviously held her wine better than Maryann, but not well enough to keep her blouse buttons fully engaged. Ann reminded Felicia that she was in the church basement and needed to keep her clothes on. Ann had her usual glass or two and remained the sober, responsible, designated chaperone for the rest of the evening. When she wasn't babysitting the two fools, she did allow a nice gentleman to strike up a conversation.

Bart Stein was his name, and he was certainly out of place in a Catholic church basement. It was rare to hear a Jewish name in that area of the Brooklyn, especially in the confines of a Catholic church. It's not like it never happened, it was just odd, and Ann certainly quired. Bart was not a drinker, and when he offered Ann another drink, they both declined to Coke on the rocks. Bart was about five foot eight inches and well-built for his age. It was obvious to Ann that Bart still worked out, or had done so for much of his younger years. Bart proudly sported a full head of nicely groomed salt-and-pepper hair, slightly more to the pepper side. Ann commented on how nice his hair looked and he seemed genuinely appreciative of the fact that she had noticed. Bart was a gentleman the whole night, and he even handled Maryann and Felicia well, just enough to keep them at bay while he made sure to get in as much face time as possible with Ann.

The night ended with two slow dances between Ann and Bart. MaryAnn and Felicia sat back-to-back, each supporting the other so neither one fell over. As they strolled from the dance floor for the final time that night, Bart made an offer to drive all three ladies home. He had plenty of room in his 1970 Buick Skylark and plenty of muscle to get the ladies home in sports car style. Ann gracefully declined, explaining that they lived close by and would be fine to walk home unattended. Maryann and Felicia accepted immediately. Once again, Ann became the voice of reason. Bart was eager to obtain Ann's phone number, as his attraction to her was apparent. Ann conceded and offered her phone number to him, something she normally did not do. Bart gratefully accepted it and after writing it down on a white paper napkin, placed it securely in his wallet for safekeeping. Bart walked the ladies up the split-level marble staircase to the exit door of the church. He once again offered to drive them home and Ann again declined. Of the three ladies, Ann was the only one with a stable gait as they made their way through the parking lot and veered right around the rectory, heading home. One block remained to navigate, and they would make it home without major incident. Maryann was first to be guided into her apartment, followed by Felicia; then Ann walked herself home. This was the perfect sequence, since Maryann verbally shared her feelings that this new avenue created by Father Devlin would elevate them from the sorrows of their recent destructive relationships. She practically screamed it all the way home. Ann was sure that the whole neighborhood was tuned into Maryann's boisterous comments about the night, all the way from the church to her apartment. Felicia and Ann were happy to get Maryann home safe and sound and equally happy to give their ears a break.

Ann, happy to be safely back in her apartment after a much-needed night out with the girls, began her usual ritual of unwinding before settling down in bed. She kicked off her heels, gently folded her slacks and blouse, washed the makeup from her face, and breathed deeply as she stared at herself in the bathroom mirror. She fondly reflected back on the time she had spent with Bart and hoped that giving her phone number to him wasn't a mistake. She trained her thoughts on the evening and on the good time, trying to avoid the usual thoughts that infected her mind nightly. No matter how greatly improved her days had become, the night always recalled the events that had come to define her.

Bobby had been physically gone for nearly a year, and Ann was no longer married to the man, but in her late night thoughts he was always there. She couldn't control her thoughts, and she couldn't control the grip that Bobby still had on her. It didn't matter whether she had a boring night at home watching Johnny Carson on television or a night out with the girls, meeting new people and becoming excited about living life again, Bobby always came back before she closed her eyes and attempted to fall asleep. Sleep was often elusive. Bobby Maseano remained an ever-present obstacle, even though he was now remanded to the custody of the New York State Department of Corrections. He was physically over one-hundred miles away, locked up in a cage which Ann knew she would never see, yet in her thoughts and nightmares he was right there by her side, breathing the devil's breath on her tender neck. The monster never really goes away.

Chapter 6

Asylum Road was a gravel-surfaced, unpaved stretch in the low hills of Beacon, New York. The road was intentionally unpaved, and the facility fully supported the policy of not filling in the six-to-twelve-inch craters that infected the two-mile, almost one-lane path to the south gates of Matteawan State Hospital. The south gate entrance was for New York State Department of Corrections vehicles only. The visitor entrance was located through the front-facing north gate. The north gate entrance was impeccably landscaped and offered a warm and inviting first impression. The facility was a state-run insane asylum, whereas the main entrance appeared to have been landscaped by the same people who facilitated the landscapes at the best of the Hilton hotels. There did not seem to be any expense spared in maintaining the acres and acres of gardens, trees and shrubs. To the common eye it would appear to have been an extremely pleasant place to have to do your time and pay your debt to society. The outward appearance was that of a country club and not a facility that imprisoned the criminally insane. It certainly did not present like Riker's Island or The Bronx

House of Detention. Looks can be deceiving, and at Matteawan, they certainly were.

New York State's most criminally insane were transported there from all over the metropolitan area and for some of those maniacs, the last breath in the free world was taken just outside the south gate. A majority of the vicious, sadistic, and insane inmates would certainly die there. Most of the large transport vehicles were reconditioned New York City school buses that had long since been retired from the duties of transporting the city's youths. There was not a trace of the innocence of school bus yellow to be found anywhere on the vehicles. The reconditioning of the buses included the installation of bulletproof glass for the front windshield, the driver's side window, and the front double doors. The rear doors had been removed and replaced by steel panels and the area converted into a security well for the rear guard. Most of the side windows had been replaced with 12-gauge steel, cut to the exact size of the original opening and held in place by reinforced welds to make the new panels impossible to kick out. The remaining side window openings were replaced with bulletproof glass and steel bars which were mounted directly to the reinforced frame of the old bus.

The battleship gray exterior was the backdrop to the jet-black block letters painted on either side: New York Department of Corrections. The rear of the bus clearly warned drivers to keep back 200 feet in case of emergency braking. The front grill had been replaced with steel battering rams, also mounted directly to the frame. The cabin of the transport vehicle had a bulletproof window to the driver's left side and a solid cage enclosure that could be locked shut in the case of an emergency, making the cabin essentially a self-contained isolation chamber. In the event that a prisoner attempted to overtake an armed guard, the driver would remain relatively safe and in physical control of the vehicle, at least for a short while. The tires were skirted by panels of formed metal, making the sidewalls somewhat puncture-resistant. This was a vehicle that had been designed to never lose an inmate, and to date there had never been an escape. There had been a few attempts at escape, but all had failed. All of the escape attempts ended quickly and with lethal force.

The front exit doors operated simultaneously and had to be activated by the use of two keys. The driver had one key, and a heavily armed guard had the other key. The system of opening the door had worked flawlessly since its inception in June of 1967. The procedure that was in place at the time was the result of an attempted hijacking of a Department of Corrections van which resulted in the death of two inmates and one guard on a transport from the Bronx House of Detention in October of 1966. At the time, the guard was not armed and offered little resistance to the hijackers. The attempted hijacking resulted in three unnecessary deaths. No prisoners were released, and the surrounding community of Beacon, New York remained safe from the inmates on their journey down Asylum Road. The situation could have turned out a lot worse, if it had not been for the response of corrections officers from the facility, who responded quickly to the distress calls from the driver. New York State Department of Corrections top officials looked at the attempted hijacking very seriously and formulated a two-year plan to change and implement new policies and procedures. Officials committed to the modification of the transport vehicles to better protect the corrections officers and the public as a whole.

The new procedure commenced as follows: The armed cabin guard would call, "All clear to open," when he felt secure that there was no possible breach of his weapon space. This was defined as having no prisoner within 10 feet of the tip of the 12-gauge shotgun when it was pointed in any and all directions. This was possible because the maximum number of prisoners to be transported at one time was limited to 20. The seats were strategically spaced so as to have ten prisoners capable of sitting in the rear behind the guard and ten capable of sitting in the front. The guard had the entire center of the bus in which to move about and take control from any direction. The rear space was well-contained, and the inmates were held at bay behind steel bars. Most of the guards could be seen standing in the same position, back to the bus's steel sidewall, shotgun locked and loaded, muzzle pointed sky-ward. They were ready for the unpredictable nature and behavior of the future residents of the insane asylum.

The prisoners were shackled by the wrists to the seat directly in front of them, which of course was bolted down to the steel floor. Ankle shackles attached directly to the purposefully positioned fasteners un-der each seat. Minimal movement and absolutely no talking between inmates was strictly enforced. Any sudden moves, except those that were in line with the jerking movements of the vehicle, could be and often were seen as signs of aggression. Prisoners rode the final two miles in pools of their own sweat, tears, puke, and urine and they did so, heavily medicated and in silence. The buses had to be disinfected daily, hosed off inside and out, but the repeated assaults by various body fluids had embedded the stench in the core of the metal, under the tight spaces between the metal and the bolts and in the hollowed-out spaces between the original bus and the armor plating. The jerking trip down Asylum Road and the putrid stink of the Department of Correc-tions transport vehicle was often the last memory of the free world for the criminally insane prisoners. For many, once the bus entered the south entrance preliminary gate, life was over, and the process of de-caying and dying began.

The south gate of Matteawan was guarded by four heavily armed of-ficers, two of which were perched twenty or so feet up above the com-pound in guard towers, covering the courtyard with state-issued rifles. Two drug- and bomb-sniffing officers from the facilities in house K-9 unit were on duty twenty-four hours a day. There were a total of six highly trained German shepherds which were rotated through the entry gate with each arriving vehicle. As the chain-link gate electronically opened from guard tower, one of the transport vehicles would be au-thorized to enter into a thirty-yard-long and fifteen-yard-wide area that was contained between the twenty-five-foot electrified chain link fenc-es topped with the customary ringlets of razor wire on all sides.

The inspection of the vehicle prior to being granted permission to enter through the main gate was extensive and invasive, usually consuming close to thirty minutes. The dogs paced back and forth, frantically at first with the anticipation of finding something of trained interest. As apparent disappointment set in, the K-9 officers slowed their pace and almost appeared somber as they slowed further, then finally halted and fell to the ground in exhaustion. The well-trained K-9s were first to signal an all-clear by lying down on the ground, snout resting softly on a folded paw. This absence of agitation in the K-9s signaled that there was only a minimal chance that contraband had gone undetected. Once the human officers completed their search, the vehicle would be waved through. The prisoners remained bound to the bus substructure, and tensions always rose dramatically throughout the search. Neither the dogs nor the human guards reacted to the agitated patients unless they absolutely had no choice. Now that the inmates had breached the preliminary gate, they were considered patients of the hospital and wards of the state. It's a matter of nomenclature whether they were referred to as inmates, or patients. They were still prisoners of the state. It would be hard to imagine any of them feeling like a patient rather than a prisoner. None of the men acted like patients and none of them wanted to be medicated like a patient. Most tried to refuse the doctor's attention, but New York State did not leave that choice up to the incarcerated. They would all be medicated before they proceeded any further into the facility.

Thorazine had revolutionized the treatment of the criminally insane. It had effectively established the chemical restraint capability in the asylum, seemingly upon initial contact at the intake ward. Since the mid-1950's Thorazine had been the drug of choice for the psychiatrists in all asylums. It had proven to be a highly effective sedative and was used upon admission to take the edge off the patients who had just arrived at the gates of Hell. Thorazine was a weapon, and it had become an effective tool for combating schizophrenic patients and their often violent out-lashes or psychotic behavior. The chemical cage was an added layer of protection for the doctors, guards, and other patients. The goal of therapy was to chemically provide a level of remove in the scrambling, narcissistic thoughts that were racing throughout the minds of the deteriorating patient population. A welcome side effect was a slight-to-moderate sense of sleepiness, which often nipped in the bud physical aggression towards the staff and other inmates. Properly medicated patients, in the upwards of 800 mg per day range, could lead a somewhat normal existence in Mattewan, while being a cooperative incarcerated patient.

The patients were not released from the bus structure until the vehicle had entered through the main gate. This didn't happen until all the required inspections were competently completed and the vehicle arrived at the intake unit. The restraints that bound the patients to the vehicle would be released electronically by the two guards onboard, but for now the shackles remained fastened and intact.

One by one, the prisoners emptied the vehicle and asylum life began with a medical examination and pharmacological intervention. Once the new admissions had exited the vehicle, the enormity of the facility became overwhelming to most. To see the main building's roofline from this distance, one had to look straight skyward. Most inmates left the vehicle with heads held low, glancing at the shackles that bound their shuffling legs. The intricately carved columns that terminated just under the facade of the massive rear portico replicated hair flowing across an angel's face. Detailed woodworking and quality craftsmanship were not spared on the facility which was constructed in 1892. The intricate woodwork was all hand-carved, utilizing thousands of skillful man-hours. The results of their efforts would function better as fine artwork than as support columns for an insane asylum. It could be quite disturbing to watch the severely insane come into immediate conflict with the movement of the angel's hair which was carved in extraordinary detail into the wood. Hair flowed across the angels' faces from right to left in synchronicity with the easterly winds. Delusional thoughts would often awake the wood carvings, and the sculpted faces would begin to take form and life. Disturbing conversations had been documented between patients and the sculptured wood columns. Murders and suicides had arisen from the relentless nature of the words on this architectural masterpiece, and there are stories of instantaneous breakdowns and complete psychotic episodes upon first glance of the sculptures. The carved faces had been known to "speak" to the subconscious mind and inflict further agitation. The doctors were prepared with the first doses of Thorazine almost immediately. There was a constant battle between reality and delusion, which continued and propagated throughout the entire length of incarceration.

The large bronze plaque adjacent to the twelve-foot solid hardwood double swinging doors read as follows:

The Asylum for Insane Criminals
Established in New York, 1892

The massive dark red brick buildings that make up the full campus were designated into two basic areas of classification. The asylum resided on about one-third of the campus. The remainder belonged to the lucky criminals sentenced to the Fishkill Correctional Facility. Lucky, yes lucky, not to have had pleaded insanity in a court of law in the state of New York. An electrified chain-link fence adorned with rows of razor wire separated the asylum from the correctional facility, and the two populations never commingled. The general population were housed in cell blocks A - D, and did not take kindly to their insane campus mates. Many of the patients in the asylum had perpetrated crimes against women and children. As demoralized as a prisoner can be throughout the length of incarceration, there was usually a common theme inside. Everyone hated rapists and those who had committed crimes against children. Most prisoners seemed to be able to recall their own morals when it came to rapists. They forgot how heinous their own crimes were, and the thought has always been that nothing was worse than being a rapist or a baby killer. They fed on the hatred that existed and would spend nearly every waking hour plotting to kill or torture rapists. Crimes had a hierarchy in prison. Among heinous crimes, rape and sodomy were clearly high on the list. There was no protective custody there in the insane asylum, just higher and higher doses of Thorazine: submission by chemistry.

Some of the more notorious criminals who had been remanded to the asylum and had served extensive sentences or died on the inside are George Metesky, the "Mad Bomber'" Izola Ware Curry, the woman who stabbed Martin Luther King Jr. while he signed books at a Harlem bookstore and Robert Maesano, "The Tape Measure Rapist," who faced one hundred and five years if convicted on each of the seven counts of first degree sodomy. Bobby only received twenty-five years for his crimes. Ann and I received life.

Chapter 7

There were beyond twenty initial charges against Robert Maseano. Due to fear and the fact that his known victims were not co-operating with the Brooklyn and Queens District Attorneys' Offices, the final count of first-degree sodomy charges had been dropped to seven. The immense fear injected into a rape victim is beyond comprehension, and the details of the traumatic event often are agitated by that self-destructive fear. Cooperation with the authorities is one of the last thoughts the women are trying to process at that traumatic time. The flood of emotions clouds the senses, and as the brain pools with a rush of neurotransmitters, clear thought becomes nearly impossible. The physical violation of a person's body develops into a violation of the mind and soul. The walls close in and the psychological torment begins all over again. The run of emotions plays games with the attempt at a logical thought process. The victims, in these cases women, harbor a strong fear of males in general for a prolonged period of time, possibly forever. They develop anger at both themselves and the assailant. How and when will the recovery and healing process begin? What will other people think of them now? How can they go on with their lives? How can they deal with the shame they are feeling? How can they live a normal life after being the victim of a rape? It is a relentless cycle of the unconscious brain trying to protect the fragile psyche. It is a battle that can be won, but it is often a long and emotionally damaging experience.

Robert Maseano, a seemingly gentle, well-loved, and jovial man from Brooklyn, New York, was now tagged the "Tape Measure Rapist." He had violently attacked scores of women throughout Brooklyn and Queens. At the age of twenty-three, while living with his wife Ann and his young son, he morphed into a sadistic rapist, and by all accounts it happened overnight. Ann and her baby boy were the furthest thoughts from his mind. He was rarely ever home, and when he did set foot inside his door it was with incompetent excuses of working overtime or going out with the boys for a few drinks after work. In reality he had no "boys," only acquaintances who tolerated him when he invited himself into their inner sanctum. He didn't have any real friends to speak of, at least none that would have his back when shit hit the fan. This group of guys were all family men, coworkers, and they had nothing in common with him other than the place they worked. Maybe they talked together about baseball and the Yankees, but that in itself does not make for any lasting friendships.

Bobby was unable to do the work that was necessary to see any project succeed. He had squandered a twenty-thousand-dollar loan from Ann's parents, Teresa and Leonard, which was intended for him to buy a small fish market, and that money was never repaid. Bobby had proven himself over and over not to be a motivated employee of any business. It was nearly impossible for Ann to believe that he was now working overtime for a delivery company and that he was so stressed out from all the work that he needed to unwind with a few drinks before coming home. Ann knew Bobby was lying; she just didn't know to what magnitude.

FIRST VICTIM

Ann had questioned Bobby many times in the past about his whereabouts, and his erratic responses made her increasingly more ful. The tone and temperament that he displayed when being questioned was becoming cause for major concern. This person did not seem like the man she had married just over a year ago. Bobby, always unstable, was becoming explosive. Ann did not anticipate the first backhand to her face as Bobby violently exclaimed, "Don't ever ask me again where I'm going or when I'm coming home! It's none of your fucking business. Are we clear on that?"

Ann's only response was to fall to the floor, tears streaming down her face, and sob, "Bobby, I hate you."

He quickly recoiled in a panic. "Oh my God Ann, I'm so sorry. I didn't mean it. Let me see your face."

"Get the fuck away from me or I will call the police," Ann yelled. Bobby knew he couldn't have the police there. Not after what he'd been doing. Bobby Maseano certainly knew what he'd been doing. Insane or not, he knew enough to avoid the police and try to cover up his tracks. Bobby also knew that his wife Ann was now becoming the enemy.

Bobby had already checked out as a parent, barely acknowledging his young son's existence--never changing a diaper, never offering to participate in a feeding, never rocking the crying baby to sleep. Bobby was gone. He had also checked out as a husband and provider. The chemical imbalance in his brain had taken him over and had consumed his every action and movement. His language changed, becoming abrasive and abusive. Bobby became offensive to be around. Yet strangers never saw this side of him. He was cunning enough to always maintain the nice-guy image when he was around friends and neighbors. As long as he maintained this façade, Bobby knew that people would not believe that he was capable of doing the things he was in fact doing. As Bobby's aggression became more visible, Ann feared for her own safety and that of her helpless child.

51

Money, jewelry, and collectibles appeared in odd places around their apartment without reason or explanation. Ann found a wedding ring in Bobby's sock drawer while she was placing his clean laundry in its proper place. She found a diamond tennis bracelet in a half-empty carton of Marlboros which was hidden in the end table on Bobby's side of the bed. There were earrings at the bottom of a shaving mug, hidden under the soap cake. Ann's continued searches yielded silver coins and even small gold bullion bars. "What the hell is going on here?" Ann said out loud to herself at this last discovery. The obvious answer in her mind was that Bobby was stealing from the parcels he was supposed to be delivering. She had thought maybe that the stress of providing for the family, losing the fish store, and paying the bills was the reason he was hiding the unexplained items around the house.

Bobby was clearly a thief in Ann's eyes. Ann hoped that a thief was all he had become. She feared that there was more to it than that. Had she made a mistake in falling in love with Bobby? How would she get out of this relationship? She had speculated that she knew him well, and only now did she realize she didn't know him at all. They had dated for four years before they were engaged to be married. She should have known him well in that amount of time. How would she protect herself and her baby boy? Too many questions and no concrete answers. Ann had lost the desire to continually question Bobby about his whereabouts. She never mentioned the items she found around the house, never asked where they came from or to whom they belonged. Ann wanted to know, but then again maybe she didn't. How do I get out of here? Ann fought back and forth with herself. *Where would I go? What a mess this has become.* What a mess our lives were--and there was no obvious way out.

Bobby often went hot off the handle, but only when Ann was alone and vulnerable. Ann wanted to know why. *How does he manage to control himself at certain times? How does he turn it on and off?* Conversations with Gracie, our upstairs neighbor at the time, were relaxed and mostly normal, as they had always been. Bobby was the life of the party, so to speak, when Gracie came down from her second-floor apartment for a hot cup of coffee or just to chat. Brooklyn neighbors get together for coffee, to chat, or for any other reason at all.

Ann could not rationalize away the changes in his personality, and those changes certainly couldn't be explained, at least not yet. Ann's main responsibility was to protect herself and her young son at all costs. The devious lies were astonishing, becoming so frequent and his speech so incoherent that after a few months, Ann quit even engaging him in conversation. Everyone else seemed fine to engage with Bobby. He was well-liked on the block, talked to everyone, and even played ball with the older kids in the schoolyard when the weather was nice. Could all of this be in Ann's mind? No one else had seen the changes. No one made any comments, at least none that she had heard. How was he able to switch from a normal fun-loving guy to a sadistic and heinous abuser? The stress was wearing her down like the erosion of a mountaintop. Ann eventually collapsed under the weight of the destruction of her marriage and her family, never really knowing the magnitude of the evil that resided with her in the small two-bedroom apartment. Worse times were coming.

Sodomy was the main charge and the one that would yield the most jail time, possibly life. There were also charges of burglary and robbery. These, however, paled in comparison to the weight of the sodomy charges. The charges of burglary and robbery resonated with Ann as an explanation for the pieces of jewelry and coins that she had discovered stashed throughout the apartment. Ann had known for awhile that Bobby was stealing, but she was too frightened to say anything to anyone. At that point, Ann did not even confide in her parents, though she had always been the type to tell them everything. They knew there were problems, but they attributed the tension to money issues and the stress of raising a young family. Ann and Bobby were a young couple trying to make it, and that in itself was stressful, her parents rationalized with each other. Teresa suspected there was something deeper going on with Bobby, but she had no proof, only suspicions. Teresa, having no verbal filter, told Ann in no uncertain terms to keep her eyes and ears open to all possibilities. But there was no way for Teresa and Leonard to save Ann and her young boy from what was about to unfold.

The plea agreement that was reached at the culmination was guilty by reason of insanity. Bobby had claimed that he suffered from amnesia, which is a loss of memory due usually to brain injury, shock, fatigue, repression, or illness. In reality Bobby did not suffer from any of those symptoms. According to Dr. Daniel Schwartz, the psychiatrist who was consulted at the time, amnesia is a gap in one's memory, or the selective overlooking or ignoring of events or acts that are not favorable or useful to one's purpose or position.

None of that actually existed. None of the speculations were true, not even a little. There was no brain injury, no shock or fatigue, nothing. Family and friends even denied the presence of any major stress. This was just a ruse to get his ass off the fire and out of the en. Would the insanity plea work? Could Bobby fool the justice system just as easily as he fooled scores of women? Could a sociopath appear to be insane and have a judge and jury believe it? And if so, what would be the consequences of the plea deal? Surely he was not getting off, not with positive identifications by the victims! Not with the female heroes who had been his victims but now would serve as his executioners.

The decision to plea out with an insanity defense was the handiwork of a state-appointed attorney, Marvin Kornberg. Bobby's counsel urged him to reach a plea agreement. Bobby made the decision easily when the District Attorney's office attacked him with the possibility of one hundred and five years if convicted on all counts for the maximum penalty.

Bobby Maseano was a man who had no documented history of mental illness and had never overtly displayed sexual indiscretion toward females, yet was being held accountable for seven counts of sodomy in the first degree. There should have been many more counts. Many more victims were terrorized to the point of impending silence. These women would rather spend the rest of their lives trying to heal from the pain that had been inflicted upon them than to face Bobby again and relive their ordeals face-to-face with their attacker in court.

The preliminary identifications were made possible because of the skillful sketch work of Detective Helen Pastore. Pastore was a fifteen-year veteran of the NYPD and had been the lead detective, assigned to many sex crimes against women in Brooklyn. Detective Pastore had a soft, warm, engaging way about her. She possessed a warm smile, deep blue eyes, and was easy to feel comfortable around, almost from initial contact. Rape victims need a warm smile. Their world is cold and threatening in the first few days after the attack, and a kind smile on a female detective's face takes some of the defenses down, in only for a short while. These women need many things after the attack, and a warm smile certainly helps. It puts them at ease most of the time and increases the chances that some of them will be willing to discuss the putrid details of the attack.

Victims are forced to relive what they most certainly want to forget. Many preliminary police interviews take place in a hospital emergency room, where the clinical environment adds to the coldness and uncertainty of the situation. Who knows how many times in their lives they will relive that torture? Detective Pastore had the ability to tease out the unimaginable details of the worst offense that can be perpetrated against a woman. Maybe it was Pastore's flowing blonde hair. Maybe it was her lightly freckled face, or maybe it was her unimposing size at barely 5 foot 2 inches. Whatever it was, she was the best the NYPD had for compassionately extracting the details needed obtain solid information and get the manhunt underway.

Detective Pastore was full of compassion, and when she was with a rape victim it was really all about them. It wasn't just a job at that point. She was feeling the pain, wiping the tears, both the victim's and sometimes her own. Helen Pastore was a strong, vibrant, and compassionate woman first and a police officer second. She always found the human element in her cases and always considered the victim's emotional state before attempting to gather details. She could only imagine what it would be like to be violently attacked like these poor women had been. It made her sick to her stomach, literally.

Forcing composure upon herself, she first befriended the innocent victims as they lay there looking up from the confines of a hospital bed, at what was more than a police officer doing a job. This woman cared about the victims, probably a little too much. She was often reminded of that by the other detectives and by everyone else who knew how invested she became in the lives of these women. She consoled the victims, and the families, too, when they were present, and assured them that she would do everything in her power to catch the bastard and not stop until he was behind bars. Family or other forms of support are often missing from the emergency rooms in these situations. There are unrelenting feelings of being dirty, ashamed, and alone. Will the victim's family understand? Will they look at her differently? Will her family disown her? It had to be her fault. Because of the shame the victims feel, their families are often never informed. Detective Pastore's initial weapon in the sex crime war was a #2 pencil and a sketch pad. She would wait all night to get something out of a victim that would be good enough to get her pencil and pad together.

She had talent with a pencil and pad and was effective at listening to the women's descriptions and translating it into a composite drawing. She didn't hear just the words; she heard the emotion and was able to transform that element into a cheek, a chin, an eye, or a mouth. Details were drawn from her emotional connection, because she was able to actually hear what someone was saying underneath all the emotions. She had worked this talent far too many times in the recent past, and her skill level had greatly improved.

Detective Pastore was assigned to her first case primarily because she was female. She knew and understood that. The thought from NYPD brass was that the victim would respond more favorably to a sensitive female officer. This turned out to be the correct move. It was a complete bonus to the NYPD that she had a creative pencil. Detective Pastore was dispatched to Victory Memorial Hospital's emergency department at 6:45 p.m. She arrived accompanied by Detective Giovanni Nardi. The young lady lay motionless in her hospital bed, curtain drawn closed and the light only dimly lit above her head.

Nurse Nancy Lawless intercepted the intruding officers stating, "Detectives, she had a horrible night. Please don't wake her, not now anyway. She's lost a lot of blood and probably won't wake for another hour or two."

"Blood?" questioned Detective Nardi. The detectives were not expecting to hear that this young girl had cut her left wrist in the bathroom of her apartment just before calling 911.

"It was mostly a superficial wound but she did catch a small vein. It could have been a lot worse for her if she had pushed any harder on that blade," Nurse Lawless said. Her left wrist was wrapped with white gauze and she honestly looked peaceful resting in that bed. "She's lightly sedated and has been coming in and fading out for the past few hours."

"Mrs. Lawless, we really need to talk to her," Detective Pastore pressured. "We'll sit here for hours if we have to. We need to know what happened to her while it is still fresh in her mind," Pastore added.

"This is a hospital, detective, not the police station," the nurse said, with the first sound of frustration in her voice. "You can wait if you have nothing better to do, or you both can come back tomorrow. Don't worry, she'll still be here," Nurse Lawless concluded. The nurse huffed as she exited Emergency Room One, leaving the detectives and expecting them to respect her request to return tomorrow. "They'll get tired of hovering over her. It won't take too long," she commented to herself as she left the detectives.

After about two and a half hours, the girl woke up with a startled look on her face, as if she didn't know where she was exactly. Detective Pastore's face was comforting to the confused woman. The details that the young lady offered to Detective Pastore were surprisingly clear, considering she had just awakened from a chemically induced sedation. The details were explicit and heart-wrenching. Detective Pastore tied her long blonde hair in a loose ponytail while trying to keep her composure. She concentrated on the details of her suicide attempt more than on the details of the rape that preceded it. Detective Pastore worked her questions in, trying not to shut the fragile girl down. Pastore had to get her to describe her attacker's features if she would be willing to recall any in clarity.

Detective Pastore managed to engage the girl long enough to produce a sketch of a white male with prominent dark eyebrows, brown wavy hair, high cheekbones and big blue eyes, and wearing a light colored ball cap. Pastore knew the sketch wasn't accurate and she thought it probably didn't even come close to what the attacker really looked like. Her pencil performed as sporadic as the victims thoughts and words. The drawing had little resemblance to anyone the NYPD had information on. Pastore thought her initial sketch looked more like a cartoon character rather than a rape suspect. There was more detail in the girl but she refused to cooperate. She was emotionally and psychologically shutting down and she was locking the detectives out completely. Pastore could almost see the girls self defence mechanisms activating. She was trying to lock the details of the man's face away and soon no one would be able to bring those details back to the surface. Detective Pastore pleaded with the young victim to open up and describe her attacker, but the girl had sunk so far into her misery to be of any use to the police. She just wanted to die.

Chapter 8

The brown paperbag wrapped corrugated box that Bobby had lifted from the warehouse belonged to the delivery route of Dennis Adams. Dennis was not a large man, barely reaching five foot, five inches tall. If he weighed one hundred and fifty pounds on a particular day, that meant that he had had a huge meal the night before. He was physically weak and emotionally fragile. If there was anyone in the company who was picked on and treated unfairly by his coworkers, it was Dennis. He was the object of many childish pranks. Dennis never formally complained about any of the other drivers and internalized all the trauma they inflicted on him, just as he had done his entire life. He had handled it in grade school and in high school, and he was handling it now on the job.

He was once traumatized when three unidentified employees entered the men's room a few minutes after he entered a stall. When the men noticed that he had gone into a stall to do his business, they came up with an immediate brainstorm. Two of the drivers soaked paper towels and entered the stalls on either side of Dennis. Standing on their respective toilets, they reached their arms up and over the top of the metal divider and simultaneously began to squeeze the water from the soaked paper towels directly onto Dennis's head. While Dennis was in panic mode, searching for the source of the cold liquid that had soaked his head, the other driver, who was perched low on the floor in front of the stall door, reached in and grabbed Dennis's shoes. With one clean, smooth motion toward himself, he was able to gather both of Dennis's shoes, his work pants, and even his boxers, all of which were all collected around his ankles. The three idiots fled the men's room and remained unidentified. Dennis' clothes and shoes found their way to the trash receptacle on the left side of the sink. He remained in the men's room naked from the waist down and soaked from the waist up for an embarrassing twenty minutes until he eventually located his clothes in the trash.

Dennis had been driving for the company for nearly five years at the time of the incident. He started soon after graduating high school. He knew he wasn't college material and didn't apply to any schools, not even Queens Community College. He had a squeaky-clean file according to his human resource manager, although he had a few parking tickets over the years and one speeding violation; that was it. Dennis Adams was distraught by the missing package, and he knew from the first minute he noticed its disappearance that his job would be on the line if the package did not resurface. He also knew that any one of the other drivers could be responsible for messing with him. They had all been involved, at one point or another, in playing games with him. It just became so commonplace that the joking around didn't bother him anymore, until. However, this time the guys had gone way too far. Dennis knew that not one of those sons-of-bitches would come forward and speak out in his defense. He was one man, on an island by himself.

Bobby, on the other hand, had tried to become social with the other drivers over the past couple of weeks. He was somewhat accepted and was sort of invited to be part of the group that would often get together at Cobblestones after work. The watering hole was where tight bonds were formed and working friendships solidified. It made no matter to Bobby or any of the drivers that Dennis was facing termination for the missing parcel. Bobby Maseano was cold and calculating, and this package was not going to be returned under any circumstances. He knew that for certain.

The manifest that was handed out to the drivers by Harry Carson, the dispatcher, was always spot-on. Mr. Carson, as all the young drivers called him, was an elderly black man who had been with the company since its inception in 1965. He was highly regarded by the younger drives mostly because he had great stories from his former life in the military. He had a special way of telling stories and they always turned out funny. The old man, Harry Carson, was just fun to be around. He had a way of guiding those boys and keeping them focused on their jobs. Harry had performed nearly every function for the company, from driving to making photocopies, but now that the years had caught up to him, the job of driving safely for eight hours a day was considered beyond his capability. Once he returned from lower back surgery, his job description had been changed to that of dispatcher. He was fine with the change, because the back surgery provided only partial relief from the pain he had been suffering from for the past ten years. Even in his advanced age the company valued his loyalty and tion. The personal days he used for his surgery were the only days he had taken off in the past three years. The company authorized his three-week post-surgery recovery time, but Harry returned in less than two. Harry was a company man, and management knew it.

There hadn't been an error on the delivery manifest in years. The manifest for each driver was handed out just prior to their entering the warehouse, so each driver could witness his truck being loaded and verify that the manifest matched the truck's inventory before it was loaded. This routine became tedious at best for most drivers, and only a halfhearted effort was put forth to actually do a proper tion. The drivers all knew that their job depended on the manifest matching the truck's inventory and that the company would take a missing package very seriously, especially if it was valuable. It just had never happened before. Complacency set in quickly among the drivers, and now Dennis would probably pay with his job.

Some drivers changed from their street clothes into their uniforms in the employee locker room which was located on the second floor just above the dispatch room. For the most part they were a good group of guys who did their jobs and who liked to have a good time when they could. From management's perspective everyone seemed to be getting along just fine with each other. Then there was the outcast, Dennis Adams. Stories about who got laid the night before or stories from the night out at Cobblestone's often bounced around as the guys dressed for the day. Dennis would try to engage in conversation with stories that everyone knew were false. He always told racy tales of fictitious sexual escapades. No one believed his stories, but they did start the day off with some comic relief and made him more of a target. As the drivers finished up the tasks in the locker room, they flocked to the break room for a cup of coffee and maybe a danish, bagel or donut. Little time was spent there, because the break room was only the size of a large walk-in closet, just big enough for a folding table, six chairs, and a coffee pot. It was more of a pit stop area instead of a break room. The next and last stop before the warehouse was to see Harry Carson to obtain their work schedule for the day.

The delivery trucks were all white, with the painted graphics "REA Express Trucking" in red-and-black block lettering on either side of the vehicle. They were lined up in numbered parking spots just outside the warehouse doors. There must have been enough room for sixty vehicles outside. Daily operating volume was usually handled with fewer than twenty vehicles, but there was room for expansion. There were four main loading docks, all in full operation during the morning rush. The loading docks serviced about five trucks each in the morning during the loading process. The loading dock and warehouse crews wanted to get the trucks loaded and out on the road as early as possible. These same trucks had to be loaded in the late afternoon for the evening deliveries. The earlier the trucks got out in the morning, the earlier they got back and reloaded. The warehouse operation worked like clockwork. Everyone knew the routine, including the drivers.

Everyone knew that at some point there could be an error on the loading dock, but it hadn't happened since the new systems had been implemented. Smart money for the drivers was to let the expert dock hands load the cargo and go. That's it, just go. Yes, there were screw-ups at the facility, but never did a package get lost or misplaced. Maybe a shipping label misprinted, or maybe the address was unclear due to poor handwriting. Having the incorrect zip code was sometimes a problem. A few deliveries had been made where the client was not charged or they were overcharged, but never an error with a package on the loading dock.

All the drivers, including Bobby, knew that most of the packages were insured to some extent. Some were insured for fifty dollars and some were insured for twenty thousand. None of the drivers knew the value of the individual packages. REA Express Trucking made sure that information on package insurance was kept strictly confidential. They could have been delivering rare and priceless coins, jewelry, gold bullion, or dirty underwear. No one knew, most of the time. Most merchants covered their product or parcel with a fair amount of insurance, covering at least the net cost. Very few merchants would risk not having any insurance coverage so, if something should happen and the package vanished or was damaged, it was covered.

Bobby moved his truck out of space number ten and was second in line at the loading dock. Once the truck in front of him was loaded, locked down, and had pulled out Bobby backed in and the loading process commenced again. The packages were called off by the loading dock hand, Jimmy Hansen. Jimmy had done his job flawlessly every morning and again in the afternoon for three years now. He was extremely accurate in his processes. It just so happened that Jimmy was the nephew of one of the main owners of the company. Bobby acknowledged each package that was called out, barely glancing at his manifest. Bobby always responded in the affirmative and gestured as if he were checking off with a pencil on the manifest. This was the same false gesture he repeated for all his packages.

Jimmy was a tall, lanky kid with a red pimply face, maybe nineteen years old. He could have been a basketball player but had some coordination issues. He often tripped over his own size thirteens. He mostly worked on weekends, holidays, and on breaks from Hofstra University, where he studied marketing and finance. He had been there for the three preceding years and had always done a decent job. No reason to doubt him today. *Why bother*? Bobby thought. They get it right every time. Once the truck was loaded, Jimmy yelled out, "Hey Bobby, you can lock your door. You're all loaded. Forty-seven for you!"

"Got it, Jim. Thanks, and I'm out. See ya later," he added as he walked toward the end of the loading dock. Bobby acknowledged the forty-seven packages, but once inside the truck quickly realized his manifest totaled only forty-six.

Bobby had signed for all forty-six packages, closed and locked the drop-down rolling door of the truck, and departed REA at exactly 7:15 a.m. He headed out of the parking lot, making a quick right turn, and headed toward the Brooklyn-Queens Expressway. Bobby knew traffic would be heavy at this early hour, and making his way to his farthest stop would prove to be as challenging as ever. Traffic was always heavy on the BQE during morning rush hour. Construction on these ancient roads never seemed to get completed. If by some act of God a project was completed, the city started another just a few miles down the road.

The BQE, like all New York City highways, takes a beating every winter. The ice-cold winters, inevitable snowfall, and severe icing conditions force the necessity for constant salt spreading. The plows that clear the snow in order to keep the roads open eat away at the surface of the roads, leading to the summer potholes that define New York roadways. Some of the holes are big enough to lose a whole tire inside the cavity. This cycle continues on a yearly basis and is a major source of frustration for commuters and commercial vehicle operators. Road rage incidents are frequent due to the poor driving conditions which are a major cause of accidents on the roadways. REA Express Trucking supplied its drivers with educational materials for managing the stress of navigating the New York roadways. Although the material was a mandatory read, it rarely did any good. Some drivers found themselves in accidents and altercations on almost a daily basis. There was a sign in the warehouse that informed the drivers how many days they had gone without an accident. It most often read, "Zero days."

The actual unlisted package was a small parcel addressed to P and J Jewelers in Brooklyn, New York. This little package would not be arriving today or any other day, Bobby laughed to himself. Bobby was not on a Brooklyn route this morning. He had been to four stops and made all four deliveries uneventfully when the call came over the CB radio asking all active drivers to perform an inventory check on the remaining packages in their trucks. The command was bellowed loud and clear, and the instruction was to look for a missing package addressed to P and J Jewelers. "The route this package should have been on is 327, belonging to Dennis Adams," called the dispatcher. "All drivers are to report back to dispatch after a full inventory of remaining on-board parcels."

Bobby was the fourth or fifth driver to radio back into patch. "This is Bobby," he said with an evil grin on his face.

"Go ahead, Bobby," Mr. Carson responded from dispatch.

"There are no extra packages on my truck. All my packages are accounted for and all match to my manifest. Should I continue on my route or wait?" Jimmy obviously did not remember calling out forty-seventh package for Bobby, nor did he remember calling out numbers to any of the other drivers except when he was announcing packages for Dennis Adams.

Mr. Carson said, "Continue on your route and report to dispatch when you get back."

One by one each driver dutifully called in on the CB radio. All drivers stated that the package was not on their truck. Each and every affirmation was negative. Only Bobby knew where the package was, and he wasn't telling or giving it back.

Bobby pulled his truck into a parking space almost directly in front of the United States Post Office on Queens Boulevard, just outside Jamaica. Inside, he took a self-stick address label and wrote Robert Maseano, 2416 83rd Street, Brooklyn, New York 11214. He proceeded to peel off the original label and stick his own address label exactly where the original was just removed. He then reinforced it with clear packing tape, which was supplied by the post office clerk. Bobby was confident that the label would not fall off. He blacked out the return address, went to the back of the line, and waited for service. He paid the $4.25 fee to the heavy Hispanic female post office worker and then headed back to his truck. There were more deliveries to make, and he had to get back to the warehouse at or about his usual time. Bobby did not want to attract any additional suspicion.

The package arrived at Bobby's apartment building two days later. The mailman left the package on the floor behind the outside door, in front of the inner half-glass door which was locked for ty. This door was accessible only by ringing the bell located just under the mailboxes and the buzzer system in each apartment, or by a tenant's key. It was common for the mailman to leave large parcels for a tenant in the hallway. The four-family house had a bank of four modest-sized mailboxes. Anything larger than a carton of Marlboro would not fit into the mailbox opening. Bobby was sure his neighbors would be snooping around the package to see if there was a hint of what was inside. Bobby was careful to have this package unmarked except for the address label he wrote out. The package lay on the floor untouched by any resident until 6:45 p.m. when he returned home from work. Bobby had not detoured to Cobblestone's that night.

Mailing the package to himself was a complete success. Retrieving the untouched package was also successful. Examining its contents would be the next challenge. Ann was already curious about the box, because she had noticed it in the hallway when she returned home a few hours before Bobby. Ann was sure not to touch the box, but she immediately recognized the handwriting on the post office label. This didn't make sense to her. Why would Bobby mail a package to himself? What was going on here? She knew she couldn't ask him about it. She just looked the other way and paid no attention to him or the package; she sure hoped he would believe she wasn't paying attention.

Bobby picked up the package and tucked it under his left arm, holding it securely, like a running back holding the pigskin. He reached into his right front pocket to retrieve his house key. He couldn't ring the bell; he was trying to go undetected. He managed to get the key into the lock of the half-glass door and once through, he proceeded quietly to his apartment door. He eased the key into the deadbolt lock and turned to the right, then pushed the door open. He entered quickly, proceeding directly to the bedroom. He entered, closed and locked the French doors. Bobby carefully hid the package in the bottom drawer of the men's chest, then exited the bedroom and headed toward Ann, who was putting dishes away in the kitchen. "Did you see that package in the hallway when you came home?" Bobby questioned.

"Yes," Ann replied.

"Why didn't you take it inside?"

"The last time I took in and opened a package for you, I got slapped across the face. That's why I didn't take it inside," she said in a slightly abrasive tone.

"So, you are finally learning how to be a good wife. Good job, Ann. It's about time," Bobby concluded as he turned and walked away, heading toward the living room.

Ann, as usual, was searching for a good excuse to get out of the house and a way to avoid any confrontation. "Bobby, I'm taking the baby and going to my mother's house for a little while," Ann said suddenly. Teresa and Leonard lived just around the corner. "She needs help baking cookies for Sunday."

"Whatever. And make sure you take your son with you," Bobby yelled.

"Like I would leave him alone with you, you crazy fuck," Ann muttered to herself. "Of course, Bobby. I have him in the carriage already and we're almost ready to go." What she really wanted to say was we're getting the fuck out of here and we're never coming back.

The minute Ann and the baby were gone, Bobby retrieved his package and proceeded to unwrap it, like a five-year-old child on Christmas morning. The outer brown wrapping was tossed aside onto the tile floor of the modest bedroom. The inner packing tape was cut in a clean, straight line directly in the middle of the upper flaps. Newspaper filled the box, serving to hold the small cartons in place. The smile that came to Bobby's face was as if the Yankees had just won another World Series. He let out a joyful scream, then quickly hoped that the upstairs neighbors had not heard his sounds of joy. Bobby was a different man now, in both clarity and demeanor. He had just unwrapped his biggest payday ever. One by one he extracted the cartons from the brown bag. Six brand new Rolex watches! Four Submariners and two Day-Dates--and they were spectacular!

When Ann returned home a few hours later, somewhere around 10:30 p.m., there was no sign of the box, the packing, or the merchandise. Bobby walked up behind her with renewed confidence. He put his right hand on her right shoulder, leaned across her back to her left cheek, and gave her a kiss. Then he walked silently away. Ann's blood curdled and tears began to slowly roll down her face. She knew what Bobby was doing. Ann knew that today her life had changed, and not for the better. She also knew that it would all be over soon, and was not in denial about her situation any longer. She knew the box contained stolen merchandise, and she was ready for him to pay for his crimes, and she was ready to get him out of her life forever.

Ann feared Bobby so much that she just kept her mouth shut. She never discussed the package with him. She would, however, be willing to discuss it with the police if they would just come, ask questions about him, and save her. Up until now there had been mysterious coins, jewelry, money, and even worn panties stashed in various areas of the apartment, but mostly in his men's chest. Ann knew Bobby would not change his hiding places. He always hid the important stuff in the men's chest. After all, it *was* a men's chest. Why would Ann need to go into a men's chest, anyway? Ann wanted to tell her story to anyone who would listen; fear strangled her into silence, but in her head she was screaming for help.

Chapter 9

Bobby woke early Saturday morning, instantly consumed with only one thought: pawn the Rolex watches. *Who would be willing to pay even a fraction of the retail value of these fine instruments?* The economic atmosphere in Brooklyn in the late 60's, early 70's hadn't been especially good. Most families were just scraping by, making barely enough money to pay their bills and put food on the table. It was a blue collar neighborhood, and a Rolex on the wrist of a bus driver or postman would raise some eyebrows. Bensonhurst was more of a Timex neighborhood.

The majority of Bobby's friends bought their watches at the local drugstore, which had some decent inexpensive watches for sale for around ten dollars. Most had plastic bands, and some even had a digital display. They worked just fine. Bobby was sure that no one that he personally knew was going to pay three hundred or more for a hot watch. Three hundred could feed a small family for two months. Three hundred bought a lot of pasta around there. Feeding the family and paying the bills was all that was important. Nobody gave a shit about what kind of watch you had on your wrist, if your kids didn't have food in their mouths. Most people around there probably had never even seen a Rolex up close. Bobby was looking to get a few hundred dollars for each watch, which were clearly worth a thousand or more each, he guessed. Even with the prospect of a great purchase, Bobby thought that if he showed these watches around the neighborhood, everyone would know they were stolen. He didn't need or want that. It was bad enough that Ann knew he had stolen merchandise. Ann did all she could not to let on that she knew Bobby had stolen watches in his possession. But he knew she knew.

Ann waited for the opportune time to sniff out the package and inspect its contents. There were plenty of available times, because Bobby was never home. He was up and out on weekdays at about 5:00 a.m., driving or taking the trains into Queens. On weekends he was up and out early, to only God knew where. Ann knew not to ask. She just let him leave. She had plenty of time to find the package.

Bobby had hid the package in what turned out to be the first place Ann looked: the men's chest, of course. Where else would she look first? The package was found in the third drawer Ann opened. She reached in deep into the bottom drawer, careful to disturb as little as possible. Bobby had things folded and stacked just so. Any deviation from his just-so ways would be a problem for Ann. There could be no rummaging through Bobby's drawers; he would surely know things had been tampered with.

Ann extracted the package with a surgeon's skill. She took two steps backward and sat on the edge of her meticulously made bed. She carefully unfolded the brown paper bag, reached into the bottom, and pulled out a small green box marked with the Rolex crown. Ann recognized the symbol from an ad she had seen in *Vogue*. Ann lifted the edge of the green box to peek inside, and the box revealed a brilliant silver-colored watch with a black face and gold bezel. She just about passed out. The first thought she had wasn't where did Bobby get these watches, nor who did they really belong to. Her first thought immediately following her examination of the contents of that green box was, Why would Bobby hide these watches in such an obvious spot? Could he have been setting her up? Could she put the package back exactly as she had found it? Would Bobby know that Ann had found the watches? What would he do to her if he found out she was snooping around in his men's chest?

There were so many other places he could have stashed the watches. Bobby could have stored the package in the basement, in the storage locker assigned to their apartment. Bobby knew Ann would never go down there by herself. It was dark, damp, and spooky, even for a grown woman. The enormous boiler that was housed down there was old and made hissing and banging noises. Ann was afraid to go down to the locker even when Bobby was with her. The storage locker would have been perfect, Ann thought. Bobby had full access. It was dark and secluded. There was almost never a time when more than one person was at the lockers together. Gracie and Sonny, one of the neighbors who lived on the second floor rarely ever came to the storage lockers--maybe at Christmas time for the decorations and the tree, but that was about it. Annette and Steve, who also lived on the second floor, had some cheap artwork stored in their locker. They never went down to the basement to remove any of it. Annette was severely overweight, probably closing in on five hundred pounds. If she ever were to make it down into the basement, she would never make it back up, not without an oxygen tank anyway, or having a heart attack or something. Steve was retired and never left her side, and he was lazy as shit anyway. Ann thought again, *Why not the lockers? Why not?*

Bobby knew Ann had been in the men's chest. He had folded the brown bag over itself, and when he placed it in the bottom of the drawer he positioned a two-inch piece of black thread in perfect alignment with the left edge of the bag. The right edge of the bag was pressed tightly up against the inside corner of the drawer. He observed the thread closely as he finished perfectly placing the package inside; then he slowly closed the drawer, watching the thread the whole time to make sure it remained in position. A perfect trap had been set. Ann would never see that thread and when she didn't, Bobby would know she couldn't be trusted. Not with this. Not with anything.

Bobby was right; Ann never noticed the thread. She was careful to put everything back perfectly, except the thread. Bobby knew. Even though he was furious about Ann's snooping, he had more pressing issues than having to deal with her. Ann was lucky that day. Bobby never mentioned the security breach of the chest. The issue just faded away from Bobby's mind as he became consumed with selling those Rolex watches as soon as possible. Bobby needed cash, and the Rolex watches were just how he was going to get it. He knew he had to get to 18th Avenue and in to see Carmine Mancini.

Carmine Mancini was a made man. He owned, but did not operate, Alba's Pastry Shop on 18th Avenue, just off 75th Street in Brooklyn. Carmine was a big man, and his personal bodyguards were nearly twice his size. He was never seen in public without at least two bodyguards. You could pick Carmine Mancini out of a Brooklyn crowd in a second. He was the only man in the fine wool suit, white custom-fitted dress shirt, and fancy-colored silk necktie. Carmine was a good-looking man, with dark brown slicked-back hair and a few facial scars which he had acquired in his quest to climb the mafia ranks.

Carmine was well-known in the neighborhood. He was well-known for many different reasons. Let's just say Mr. Mancini kept the neighborhood safe. If he didn't want you there, you were, well, just gone. He had a reputation for controlling everything from local businesses to the garbage collection. He had a hand in a few local auto body shops and two cement mix companies--one in Brooklyn and one on Staten Island. He seemed to have connections in the insurance business, and his body shops profited handsomely. If you wanted to open a business in his neighborhoods, sure as shit, Carmine or one of his goons would come knocking. Rarely did anyone refuse Carmine's requests. Protection was important in Brooklyn, and Carmine provided it. It was never an amount that would choke the life out of a business, just enough to stay on the right side of the man.

Carmine protected all who needed it, if you know what I mean. He certainly protected the Italians. He even protected the Jews. He did not mess with the blacks, though. There were so few blacks in the neighborhood, it just wasn't worth his time and energy to mess with them. He didn't seem to be interested in their money for some reason. There were only a few Jewish business owners back then, and they quickly learned who was in charge. Orders were rarely spoken. Carmine merely made requests and everyone responded. It's actually funny how many of NYPD's finest professed a love of Italian pastries and a good shot of Italian espresso. Everyone from uniformed patrolmen to high-ranking NYPD officials were frequent customers, and they never paid. Never. Carmine never took a dollar out of a cop's hand for anything.

At times, Carmine would be out there mixing in with the public, but only on special occasions like the feast which took place every September on 18th Avenue. The feast spanned from 75th Street all the way to 65th Street, closing down the entire avenue between those ten blocks. People came from every borough, and were allowed to enjoy and support the local Italian economy. Even blacks and Jews were welcomed there. The take from the week-long summer feast was in the millions, and every vendor was happy to pay the participation fee to the committee of church-going members who answered only to Carmine Mancini. Carmine always enjoyed a few degrees of separation from the dirty work. Who is going to suspect the church of being organized under an organized crime family? No one, that's who. I can tell you one thing for sure, if anybody did suspect any organized crime activity was occurring through the church they would never talk about it. It went with them to the grave.

Carmine had been known to give out free sausage and pepper hero sandwiches and pastries to the neighborhood kids and future wise guys. He liked the future wise guys. They made him feel like he owned the whole city. There might have been a time when he actually did own the whole city. The more free food and pastries he gave away, the more everyone loved him, and the more loyal they became. He expected loyalty. That was something that could never be compromised. No one ever got a second chance.

If Paul Massillo were still alive he would vouch for Carmine's power over the streets and how seriously he took loyalty. Paul got caught dipping his stick into Carmine's niece. He was doing her months before Carmine found out about it. To this day no one knows how Carmine found out about Paul and Nicole. Carmine was so fucking mad his veins nearly popped out of his neck. Carmine Mancini summoned for Paul. Of course, Paul did not lie about it. He told Carmine that he loved her and wanted to marry her someday. "You should have kept your dick in your pants until that day came," Carmine exploded. Paul did not say a word in response. Nicole pleaded with her uncle for mercy telling him how much she loved Paul and how they were going to get married. After much deliberation, Carmine agreed to spare Paul's life, but he would have to go away, far away. Carmine instructed Paul to pack his bags and be ready to leave for Italy in the morning. Paul respectfully thanked Carmine for sparing his life that night, and after collecting himself proceeded back to his apartment. Nicole was physically restrained from leaving with Paul and forced to stay with Carmine. Paul pulled his Lincoln Town Car into the driveway, put the car in park, shut the headlights off, then the engine. Then just like that, without warning, he caught two high-caliber shots to the left temple. No words were spoken, and there was no altercation. There was just two silenced shots and Paul slumped over toward the passenger seat. Paul was going far away all right, but it would not be to ly. Carmine had the beat cops, the lieutenants, and some say even the captain. Fuck, he could have had the mayor also. Nobody knew for sure except Carmine and the mayor. I don't know for sure, but it seemed like Carmine and his boys all got special treatment on just about everything. He "owned" the city councilman, the borough president, and the district attorney. Carmine had a full arsenal of high-priced attorneys, and he had them ready to fight every ridiculous charge anyone could manufacturer. He was untouchable for a long while. Carmine was a businessman, a made businessman who had shit-loads of money and power. Judging by the fleet of Cadillacs, Town Cars, Corvettes, and the occasional Ferrari, the pastry business was very profitable. He had a personal parking spot directly in front of Alba's. No one ever took his spot. There was never a time when a car was parked there that he didn't own. If there was a car there, it was Carmine's, and it was parked there to make a statement. He would sometimes stand outside Alba's and welcome his customers, friends, and the local beat cops, always surrounded by two, maybe three block-head bruisers. Though they had no power, they could sure take a bullet if they had to. Carmine was a popular man. He never overdid his local celebrity, but he never ran from it either. It seemed that he had more worshipers at the pastry shop than Jesus had at the church.

Carmine was a busy man who never did anything for himself. All business orders were silent, meaning few if any words were used. An upward tilt of the chin or an affirmative nod could start a war. All the boys watched him intently. They knew what he was saying, and he didn't ever have to utter a word. That's how things get done or undone in Brooklyn, with the simple nod of the head.

Bobby knew he had to get in to see Carmine. Carmine would be interested in those Rolex watches for sure. He probably had a few of his own, but once he saw them he wouldn't be able to pass them up. Carmine would understand their value and surely want them. But how? How could he get word to him? Bobby had been to Alba's many times for pastries. Everyone had been to Alba's. The pastries were made in Brooklyn, but made the way they were in Italy. Only the finest ingredients were used, and nearly everything was imported from the old country. The pastry display cases viewed like works of culinary art, perfectly lined up and glistening thanks to well-placed bright white lighting. That's what they were, and everyone had to have a dozen, especially on Saturday or Sunday. The line could be clear around the corner at times. How would Bobby Maseano, basically a nobody, get in to see the man? It's not like Bobby could just walk up to him and say, "Hey Carmine, I have six stolen Rolex watches. Would you like to buy them and maybe give them away as Christmas presents?" This was going to be a lot harder, and even Bobby knew that. Bobby, in his mind, had solid connections to the mafia, but in reality he had none. He might have known some people who knew people, who were connected, but he himself was a nobody on the streets, and he knew it. Italian people from Brooklyn all know somebody who knows somebody who is made. Big fucking deal. That doesn't get you in. It may get you killed, but it won't get you in.

Bobby Maseano knew that day would be a challenge, to say the least. He was unsure of how he was going to proceed or what he was going to say when he arrived at Alba's. He thought furiously about how to jump-start a conversation with the boys at Alba's. Most people just walked right by the soldiers, never uttering a word. They never broached conversations unless they had to or were told to. He thought for hours as he drove his 1967 Mustang around Brooklyn, heading to Alba's. The drive normally took about ten minutes if you weren't worried about getting your ass blown off. If you were worried, then it could take a couple of hours. Bobby finally found a parking space on 75th Street. He was so nervous he was barely able to park the Mustang in the tight spot. The overwhelming pressure of approaching men who were known to be organized crime family members nearly made him sick to his stomach. He sat in the Mustang for what seemed to be half an hour after he parked, trying to calm his nerves and desperately trying to halt the profuse droplets of sweat that were forming and running down his face. He began to breathe slowly, concentrating on decreasing his heart rate. In through the nose and out through the mouth. In through the nose and out through the mouth. Sweat dripped down his back, between his legs, and pooled somewhere just under his balls. This was as intense a situation as Bobby had ever been in. He wanted to call the whole thing off, but there was no other plan. Carmine was just inside Alba's with the money, and he was Bobby's best and only option. *Some best option,* Bobby thought to himself. *He is going to fucking kill me, then take my watches. Or maybe he'll take my watches, then kill me. "What the fuck?*

Bobby disembarked the parked Mustang, not because he was ready to face Carmine Mancini, but rather because his balls were soaked in his own sweat and he was getting more uncomfortable by the minute. Bobby adjusted himself, then aired out in the cool afternoon breeze until he was somewhat dry. He grabbed the brown bag with his trembling right hand, then swiftly and firmly tucked it under his left armpit for safe keeping. Bobby made his way around the front of the Mustang to deposit two dimes in the parking meter. The last thing he needed today was a parking ticket. Bobby backed himself away from the car. He was oddly surprised at how much traffic there was on 75th Street. After filling the parking meter, he proceeded to slowly stride toward the corner, allowing the breeze to continue drying his sweat-soaked shirt and pants. There was an obvious loss of confidence in his stride. He turned right onto 18th Avenue and marveled at two black Cadillacs and a 1965 Corvette. He wasn't sure what year the Cadillacs were, but he knew for certain that the Corvette was from 1965. Bobby had dreamed of owning a 1965 Corvette and living that high lifestyle. *This is my time* Bobby thought. *I deserve the fast Corvette life.* He had to forcefully remind himself to focus on the task at hand and sell the watches--just sell the watches.

Chapter 10

When Bobby showered in the morning on that Saturday, Ann knew he was planning to be out for the whole day and probably the whole night. She rarely questioned him at that point. She just wanted him to go and leave her and the baby alone. That would be the best thing he could do for them. Just let him go without saying a confrontational word. Ann was defeated, emotionally and psychologically. She was sure Bobby was up to no good, and her overall concern for him was fading. Of course, she had never been able to prove it, and even if she could, she would be too afraid to confront him. Bobby Maseano was a lot of things, but stupid was not one of them. He had not made any major mistakes yet. What legitimate business could Bobby have out on the streets of Brooklyn? None, she speculated repeatedly. Ann always had it in the back of her mind that one day he would make a serious mistake, and leaving the house with the six Rolex watches may just be the mistake she needed him to make.

Ann lay on the left side of the queen-size bed as the baby began to squirm in the bassinet, waking from his late-morning nap. Ann felt

Bobby's presence and peeked through squinted eyes as Bobby dressed and adjusted himself in the built-in mirror of the men's chest. She watched him open the bottom drawer and remove the package as if he were handling a nuclear warhead. Careful and quiet as he could be, he successfully completed the extraction and was poised to leave. A final backward glance at his family, and he walked out the door without a word. Bobby closed the bedroom's French doors to minimize the possibility of waking Ann and the baby. *Whatever we are to him at that point, we are definitely not a tight and normal family,* Ann thought. She guessed that if glances could kill, at that moment both she and her baby would be dead. She felt the negative energy shoot through her, and all she could do was pray that the baby did not fully awaken. He didn't. He lay in his bassinet, starting to move around, but still asleep. "Sleep, baby, sleep," Ann repeated to herself. "Just stay asleep."

Ann had to try to sleep when the baby was down. So it appeared relatively normal for both of them to be taking a late-morning nap. The baby was still waking frequently during the night, and Bobby was no help at all, even when he was home. Bobby never offered, and at that point Ann rarely asked for help. She knew she wouldn't get any assistance from him, and most of the time she wanted him as far away from the baby as possible. There was a lot of faded trust and even more dissolved emotions. Ann had lived her recent life in the dark, never knowing what Bobby was doing, where he was going, or who he was with. Ann had always suspected that there was something not right about him, but she had married him anyway. She always made excuses for the odd behavior. Ann would check the men's chest soon after tending to the baby.

Nothing came before Ann's baby. Once the baby was fed, changed, and content, Ann decided to open the drawer of the men's chest and see firsthand if the six Rolex watches were gone. They certainly were gone. Bobby was gone, the package was gone and so were her hopes of a normal family life. Ann peered down at her precious little boy and asked, "What the hell do I do now?" Obviously she didn't expect an answer, but a little help would have been just right at that ment. Ann went into the baby's room and searched the dresser drawers for an outfit. She dressed him in blue-and-red overalls over a plain white long-sleeved tee shirt. She slid on white socks which covered him to the middle of his calves and placed on his white Pony sneakers. Ann added a miniature size New York Yankees cap, and he was ready to go. She took the baby into the bathroom with her and placed him in a baby seat that would keep him busy while she showered. She left the sliding glass shower door slightly open so she could see him and he could see her. Ann donned a floral print blouse and chocolate brown slacks, then applied her basic make-up in an expedient manner. Once complete, she was ready to take the baby out for the afternoon. But where were they going? Ann had no specific destination in mind, but she knew she had to go. She heard small children playing outside her apartment window. She didn't hear or see any adults. She decided to leave, even though there was basically no protection for her on the street. She convinced herself that the initial fear of leaving the apartment was just her mind playing tricks on her, but she would rather have seen some adults around to come to her aid if the need arose.

Ann knew she had to go. She strode in double time, pushing the baby carriage for blocks. She tried to clear her head and make sense of the landslide which had become her life. Eventually and reluctantly, Ann came to the realization that she needed help. Ann knew she had to go to her parents, Leonard and Teresa, and talk about the recent events that had materialized in her life. She didn't know what type of reaction she was going to get from them when she explained the story. Ann hoped that maybe they would be sympathetic, but feared they would be angry with her for not listening to their advice when they warned her to get away from him and definitely not to marry him.

Ann reflected back in time as she struggled pushing the carriage up and over a high curb, realizing that Teresa was right when she said something like this would happen. Leonard was the quiet, more supportive parent, always telling Teresa to mind her business and to watch what she said in front of Bobby. Would Leonard continue to be supportive? Would Teresa want to keep the baby with her until all this got sorted out? The tears streamed down Ann's face as she approached the four-family apartment building. Ann had hiked nearly a mile, pushing the heavy baby carriage, before she arrived at her decision to turn tail and ask her parents for help. Her parent's apartment was just around the corner. It had never taken Ann so long to get to them. Ann wondered why she was so hesitant to open up to them and ask for help. At that moment, she realized what her biggest fears were. What if this was not the only time he had stolen packages from REA Express Trucking? What if he was involved with drugs? What if he was connected with the Mafia in some way? What if he had killed people? What if? That was the hardest part. The uncertainty was eating at her insides. She was starting to lose her mind. She was sure of that.

Ann cradled the baby in her arms after carefully removing him from the harness of the carriage. She hugged him tight and kissed his face twice. She left the carriage just inside the front gate of the whitewashed, all-brick house. There was no way she could manage the carriage up the front steps without help. Confident that the carriage would be safe where she left it, she proceeded to climb the steps to the front door. Ann was weak from draining emotions, and the baby seemed to have doubled his weight in the past hour. Either that, or she had lost half her strength. She entered, pressed the doorbell and nervously waited to be buzzed in. Once through the second door, she just had to go down the hallway to the right to reach the apartment. Simultaneously, as Ann and the baby arrived at the apartment door, Teresa opened it. The tremendous smile on Teresa's face quickly dropped to a distraught frown. Teresa almost immediately sensed that Ann was stressed, and not in her usual way. That, combined with the tear tracks of black mascara still moist on her face, made it an easy sis. "Ann, what's wrong? Is there something wrong with the baby?" Teresa asked quickly. This was an obvious first question, as Ann was still cradling the toddler as if to say that there was something indeed wrong with him. It was always about the baby. Above all else, the baby always came first.

"No, Ma, the baby's fine. The baby is the only thing that *is* fine in my life right now," Ann said.

"Give me that baby and tell me what is going on," Teresa demanded. Before Ann could say a word, Teresa bellowed for Leonard, and he came sprinting from the front dining room.

"What's wrong over here? What's going on? Give me that baby," Leonard pronounced with uncharacteristic authority. The baby was in his arms before anyone could object, and he wasn't giving him back. Leonard and the baby made an instant connection. The sight of his grandfather or even the sound of his voice seemed to be music to the baby's ears. He wanted only Leonard, and the baby always got his way. Grandpa supplied the love and admiration that the baby craved, the love and admiration that Bobby was incapable of manufacturing. Even at a tender age under two years, the baby soaked up Leonard's love like a dehydrated sponge soaks up water.

Ann took a seat at the kitchen table and immediately began tearing up. Words were missing as she choked up at the sight of Leonard holding the baby with such caring hands. "Why doesn't my husband have that loving feeling for that beautiful boy?," Ann said softly. "No matter what happens to me, my baby will always be safe," Ann internalized the statement.

Teresa interrupted the tears and her mind's wandering with an abrupt, "Ann, you better start talking, or I'll beat it out of you." Teresa was always the firm, strong willed, direct type.

With that, Ann began collecting herself and was soon able to form words again. She began to tell her mother how her young marriage was rotting from the inside out. "Bobby says he is going to work," Ann began. "He leaves the house at crazy hours. Sometimes, he leaves at 5:00 a.m. Sometimes he doesn't leave until 8:00 a.m. He comes home whenever he wants and never gives me an explanation. He doesn't even care enough to lie to me. How fucked up is that?"

"Watch your mouth in my house, young lady," Teresa demanded. Ann complied and apologized for her foul mouth.

"Bobby received a package the other day," Ann explained. "It was a box wrapped in brown paper. Like from a brown paper bag. He addressed it to himself and mailed it from Queens." Teresa looked puzzled. Ann explained again. "Bobby went to the post office and wrote out an address slip to himself."

"How do you know that, Ann?" Teresa wondered.

"Ma, I recognized the handwriting. He wasn't smart enough to disguise his handwriting. He took the package to the bedroom when he came home from work and tried to hide it in his men's chest. Mom, when I looked inside the bag I saw six new brand new Rolex watches. My husband is a thief."

Teresa, not having a clue about how expensive a Rolex watch could be, chuckled and said, "Those are expensive, aren't they? What are they, like a hundred dollars each?"

"No, they're like a thousand dollars each, and Bobby had six of them," Ann replied. "Where does a REA delivery man get six brand-new Rolex watches? He steals them, that's where he gets six Rolex watches. Ma, you don't understand, there's so much more."

Leonard, still cradling the baby, asked, "Has he ever hit you or the baby?" He waited, expecting an answer he didn't really want to her.

"No," Ann lied, not sure why she had just lied and covered up for Bobby again. Ann felt the full weight of defeat collapse her shoulders as she realized she was still covering up for a man she wanted nothing to do with anymore.

"If that son-of-a-bitch raises a hand to you or my grandson, I'll kill him myself," Leonard said.

Ann, shocked by the out-of character statement made by her father, abruptly said, "Dad, I will never let him hurt my son. I would die for my son." Leonard reluctantly believed her, but not completely.

"I think he is out trying to sell those watches as we speak," Ann started. "Ma, what am I going to do if he gets caught with those watches? What if he tries to sell them to the wrong people and gets himself killed? I really can't deal with the way he's been acting. I have to get away from him."

"Ann, it takes a village," Teresa responded.

"What does that mean?," Ann questioned, with a puzzled look on her face.

"It means that it takes more than a mother to raise a child," Teresa explained. "It takes more than a mother and father. It even takes more than help from grandparents. It takes a whole village. You will always have help, as long as your father and I are alive," Teresa assured Ann. "And we'll see if we can still help out a little from heaven, when we're gone." Teresa caressed the side of Ann's tearful face. The words Teresa spoke to Ann at that moment were strengthening and rejuvenating. For the first time in about a year Ann felt that no matter what Bobby was doing, no matter what signs she had missed, no matter if he got caught or even if he turned up dead, she and the baby were going to be taken care of by her family and the rest of the villagers.

Leonard, with baby in tow, stumbled away from the kitchen and headed toward the living room. He made an abrupt yet calculated stop at the phone on the wall. Leonard picked up the receiver with his right hand, rested it between his cocked head and shoulder, and began to spin the clear plastic dial. Seven spins, some short and some long. Ann could hear the clicking of the dial as it returned to its initial position each time a number was dialed, but she couldn't make out the number. Leonard struggled with the twisted cord, all tangled up from recoiling after being overstretched from the kitchen to the living room. Leonard walked from the kitchen to the living room as he always did when he made a phone call. Almost out of earshot, Ann heard only the first word Leonard spoke, "Nardi?"

Detective Giovanni Nardi of the NYPD answered the phone as he always did, "Nardi." That was it. No other identifying ment. Nothing. He never announced to the caller that they had reached the 62nd precinct. He never stated his title, "Detective." Just Nardi. Leonard was glad to hear Nardi's voice today. "Hey Nardi, it's me, Leonard," he began.

"Hey Leonard, how are you? How's that beautiful baby boy? I have to get over there soon and see him again," Giovanni Nardi ed. "When's his birthday? It must be coming up soon, right? It's gotta be a few months since I've seen him. He must be huge by now." At first, Leonard could not get a word in edgewise. Nardi was obviously excited to hear from his older cousin.

They hadn't spent enough time together lately, and the excitement caused Nardi to have diarrhea of the mouth. Leonard abruptly and loudly interjected, "Nardi, listen. Ann has some trouble with Bobby and I need to talk to you about it. It's real important. We think he's involved in something illegal. He had some watches and we think he stole them off his truck," Leonard explained.

"What kind of watches?"

"Rolex,"

"Really, Rolex, those are expensive."

"That's what I heard. I don't know for sure, because I've never seen one, but that's what I'm hearing."

"Okay, how do you know they're hot?"

"Where would Bobby, a fucking delivery man, come up with six Rolex watches, if he didn't steal them?" Leonard responded with another question.

"Holy shit! That's like six grand in stolen merchandise." Nardi said as if he just realized the magnitude of the accusations his cousin was making. "You really got him with six Rolex watches?" Nardi asked, looking for confirmation.

"Sure do," Leonard replied. "Ann is beside herself and we don't know what to do or where to go from here. We really need your help."

"I'll be there right after my shift tonight. I'll be there about eight. That good for you? Hey Leonard, want me to bring donuts?" It's not very often that a police officer makes his own donut jokes, but Nardi is definitely a special case.

"Nardi, don't you think that it's a little fucked up that you make your own cop and donut jokes?"

"Nah, when I get there I'll tell you one about the police officer, the rabbi and the priest who go into a strip joint," Nardi said jokingly.

Leonard cut Nardi off, "Nardi, please, this time it's real serious. Get here as soon as you can, please."

"I completely understand," Nardi replied, dropping the joking tone from his voice.

Chapter 11

Detective Giovanni Nardi pulled up in front of his cousin's apartment building in an unmarked silver Crown Victoria at 8:15 p.m. It was only a short drive from the 62nd Precinct, which was just a few blocks away on Bath Avenue. Ann and Leonard were sitting together on the front stoop waiting for him to show up. The anticipation of his arrival had sparked an uncomfortable restlessness in Ann. She became claustrophobic in the four-room apartment and had to get outside into the open space. "Air, Dad I need some air. Can we go sit outside and wait for Nardi?"

"Of course, I'll grab you a sweater." Leonard sat with Ann and tried to make conversation unrelated to their unfortunate position. This proved to be no easy task, as Ann was clearly consumed by the new trauma in her life and by her own negative thoughts. Nothing her father had to offer in way of conversation could break her train of thought. Eventually, all conversation halted and they both just sat there, sinking into the swamp of shit Bobby had dumped on them.

FIRST VICTIM

Nardi surely looked the part of an NYPD detective. His black trousers were complemented by a loose-fitting and severely wrinkled white button-down dress shirt with the top two buttons open. Blackish-gray chest hairs peeked out of the opening at the neckline. His mostly blue tie was pulled down about four inches from his Adam's apple and, judging by the stain toward the bottom of the tie, he drank his coffee black--and so did his tie. His long sleeves were shortened by at least two rolls from the cuff, then pulled up to just above the elbow. His gold detective's shield was clasped to his belt on his left side and his issued .38 special revolver was holstered under the same left arm. Nardi was an imposing individual at just over six foot one and pushing two hundred and fifty pounds of mostly muscle. He was still a good-looking man, even though his face had begun to reveal age and stress-related wrinkles.

Detective Giovanni Nardi had wanted to be a police officer since he was a little boy, and Leonard knew he was a damn good one. Leonard was a few years older and wiser than Nardi. Leonard had known that when Nardi's dream of playing baseball for the Yankees failed, he would go straight to the police academy. He had applied straight out of High School.

Nardi wore a confident and deliberate expression, and this quickly became somewhat worrisome to both Leonard and Ann. They had never witnessed Nardi in any sort of official capacity. Family outings, Sunday dinners, weddings and funerals mostly—that's when they had always seen him. This was a different Nardi approaching them as he made deliberate eye contact with his cousin. He was clearly in his true element. Nardi gave his greeting with the customary kiss on the cheek to both Ann and Leonard, and then it was down to business. The questioning began on the stoop under the pale yellow illumination of the streetlights. All three shared the same step. "Ann, tell me from the beginning what your concerns are and let me try and help you," Nardi began. Tears again began to trickle out of Ann's still-bloodshot eyes, and the gravity of her situation became apparent to Nardi before Ann was able to form a complete sentence. "Let's all stay calm and just talk to me as your cousin, not as a detective," Nardi said, trying to calm Ann. "I'm here to help you.

Ann began describing the behaviors that Bobby had been displaying, which had been slowly appearing during the past year or so. "He wasn't always like this," she started. "Nardi, you know him, right?"

"Ann, I can't investigate this for you and judge him also," Nardi said. "Just tell me your concerns, and we'll go from there."

Ann cleared the few remaining tears that were still trickling from her eyes, took a deep cleansing breath, peered over at her father, then back to Nardi. "When Bobby started to work for REA Express he had a set schedule," Ann said.

"What's REA Express?" Nardi asked.

"REA is where Bobby works now."

"I thought he bought a fish store," Nardi remarked with a confused look on his face.

"He did buy a fish store in March. The money my parents loaned him didn't last more than three months. He never went to work. He missed deliveries, pissed off customers, and lost two large catering hall accounts that were turned over to him as part of the deal. Can you believe it? Within three months, all the money my parents gave him to cover startup costs was gone." Ann accepted a consoling hand from Leonard, as if he were telling her it would be all right. "I feel horrible about the money he lost. It wasn't even his. How am I ever going to repay that money?"

"Ann, forget about the money and stay focused on the current situation for now," Nardi instructed.

"There are bigger problems here than the twenty grand he wasted," Leonard interjected.

Nardi tried to refocus Ann by refining his line of questioning to be more direct. "Tell me about REA."

"Well, after losing the fish store, Bobby was fortunate enough to get a job delivering packages for REA Express Trucking," she explained. "The company is based somewhere in Queens. Actually, I think it's in Long Island City. The starting pay was decent and Bobby promised me he would do good there. You know, because it's not a lot of pressure like owning his own business."

"So it started off good?"

"It did, it really did. Bobby was up and out of the house every day for the first two or so months, and it seemed like he actually was going to stick with this job. Bobby told me that everyone important at the company liked him and that he was doing a great job for them."

"What was the turning point?" Nardi asked. "When do you think things changed?"

"It was a Friday night. I think it was a Friday night," Ann said. "Anyway, Bobby called and said that he wanted to go out with some of the guys for a drink after work. He actually asked me if I would mind him doing that. I didn't mind at all, in the beginning. He was on-track and I thought he was doing fine at work so I said to myself, why not? That was a big mistake. That one night out with his friends quickly became a ritual. One night became two nights, then three nights, then four. When I started to object to him being out all night, almost every night, he decided never to ask again if I cared if he went out or not. My son and I became irrelevant from that day forward. Something changed in him. Like Dr. Jekyll and Mr. Hyde. I began to notice that he was off-schedule."

"What do you mean, off-schedule?"

"Well, Bobby began leaving the house at different times in the morning, and when he did come home, it wasn't in line with his usual pattern. Sometimes he would be home early and sometimes he would be home late. Some days he didn't wake up at all to go to work. There were days he took the train in and other days he would drive into Queens. There was just no routine. That's what first bothered me. There was a complete breakdown in his routine. Something was clearly off."

Nardi began to write some notes on a small spiral-bound notepad that he pulled from his back pants pocket. He scribbled his jumbled thoughts in his pad, like puzzle pieces that just didn't fit together properly. So, too, were his written-down words, jumbled and confused. The pieces just didn't make much sense. The words Nardi was jotting down did not describe the Bobby Maseano he knew. Lazy, uncaring, unfaithful (with a question mark), abusive, cunning, and deliberate.

Nardi was determined to find some answers for Ann and Leonard. He had established new character flaws and had noted the change in personality, as Ann had described it to him. "This is not the Bobby I know," Nardi whispered to himself. "What's going on here?". Nardi had been at Ann and Bobby's wedding. They had spent time together watching baseball games on Sundays. They had even taken in a few games at the stadium. They had shared the love of the Yankees for sure, and Bobby was the last person whom Nardi would suspect to be out playing around and breaking the law. He had a wonderful wife and a baby boy at home. Nardi was visibly upset at the circumstances that Ann had to face with Bobby, and was determined to find out exactly what was going on.

"Ann, let's move on to the reason why Leonard called me today," Nardi stated. "The exact situation, and don't leave anything out." Ann explained to Nardi that Bobby had mailed a package to himself from Queens.

"What do you mean, he mailed a package to himself?"

"There was a package in my hallway addressed to Mr. Robert Maseano. I noticed it when I came home. It was sitting right there in the hallway on the floor where the postman left it," Ann explained.

"How do you know he mailed it to himself?"

"I recognized his handwriting. There was no return address and the postmark was from Queens. He must have stopped off at a post office somewhere along his delivery route."   "That's assuming he was actually at work," Leonard said sarcastically.

"Well, Leonard, that's a good point."

Nardi turned back to Ann and asked, "Did you take the package in and open it?"

"No, I left it there in the hallway. If I would have taken that package in and opened it, Bobby would be furious. I'm sure he would have killed me for that," Ann exclaimed.

"Has Bobby ever been physical with you in the past?" Nardi asked.

"Yes, he has hit me a few times. Nothing too serious," Ann responded softly.

Leonard sat quietly until that moment, then violently erupted saying, "Why didn't you tell me he hit you? I'll kill that little fuck."

"That's why I didn't tell you, Dad. I knew you would blow up, and I was trying to hold my family together," Ann said, her head turned sharply toward her father. Leonard was furious and red-faced. He had to walk away and cool down for a minute, so he excused himself from the conversation. He walked down the steps from where he was sitting, opened the painted white wrought-iron gate, and headed up the block toward the church. He needed a break from this madness.

"Let's get back to the package, Ann," Nardi said.

"Bobby came home about a few hours after I first saw the package in the hallway. He breezed by me to stash the box in our bedroom. He had clearly been expecting the package and he wasn't going to share its contents with me. Whatever was in the box would remain a mystery until I had opportunity to sneak a peek. Finally, when the circumstances were right, I opened the bottom drawer of his men's chest and saw the package. It was wrapped in a brown paper bag. I looked inside the package and that's when I saw six brand new Rolex watches in their original boxes. Bobby only mentioned the package to me, but I never asked about the contents. There were much better hiding places he could have chosen. Maybe he wanted me to find them, so he'd have to kill me or something. I don't know."

"Where are the watches now?"

"Bobby took the package earlier today and left the apartment without even a goodbye. He left late morning or maybe it was early afternoon. No, no, it was definitely late morning. That was the last I saw of him. He could be anywhere," Ann cried.

"I'm going to open up an investigation first thing in the morning. Are you ready for things to go down bad, if I find out that Bobby is doing things he shouldn't be doing? This type of investigation could get ugly, and fast! In my experience, where there's smoke, there's usually fire."

Leonard returned and interjected, cutting Ann off before she could respond. "Nardi, whatever Bobby is up to, we have to know. We are ready and able to handle anything you find out about his actions. I can't have my daughter and grandson living with him if he is up to no good. Teresa and I will do all we can to help Ann and the baby through this. We need the truth."

"You'll have the truth one way or another."

"What about protection?," Leonard questioned.

"I think the best thing to do here and now is nothing," Nardi responded. "Bobby doesn't know we're going to be investigating him and quite honestly, we don't know the magnitude of this situation just yet. It looks bad, I'll admit, but we won't know for sure until it all comes out in the wash. Do you know what I mean? I would go about my daily business, as if nothing is wrong, at least until I can do some digging." Nardi turned his attention directly to Ann. "Ann, you have to act as if nothing is wrong. Make it like you never saw the watches and you're not concerned at all about his odd behavior. It shouldn't take too long to find out who is missing six Rolex watches. I'm going to start at REA Express Trucking in the morning, after all the drivers are gone for their morning deliveries. I'm confident they know about the missing package by now, if it came from there. Leonard, I'll call you as soon as I know something. Ann, can you do this?" Nardi questioned, looking for some positive signs that she was comfortable with the current plan.

"Nardi, I have no choice. But I would be lying if I didn't say I was scared of him."

"Remember, act as if you don't know anything. Nothing at all."

Chapter 12

Alba's Cafe was just as busy as Bobby Maseano had thought it would be on a late Saturday afternoon. Bobby knew that the chance of anything really horrible happening was decreased by the sheer number of customers who would be in or around Brooklyn's famous pastry shop. The line to enter was about four people deep from the door. That's not counting all the people in the shop and at the counter, which totaled somewhere around fifteen. "Not too bad," Bobby mumbled to himself. The pastry shop had six outdoor tables, each seating between two and four people. Every table was full. Bobby surveyed the occupants of the outdoor sitting area, wondering if any of them were wise guys on the lookout. There are always wise guys on the lookout for something around there. All the tables appeared to be full of happy and satisfied paying customers. There were four tables occupied by couples. One of the couples were elderly, probably in their early sixties. There appeared to be a husband and wife with two small sugared-up children. The table farthest away from him was occupied by three high school-aged giggling girls. Cute, but a little too young,

Bobby thought to himself. Bobby was convinced that there were no threats out there. The line to get into Alba's separated the six tables, three on each side. The sections were functionally separated by a three-foot decorative wrought iron divider, leaving only enough room for a single-file line in and a single-file line out. Bobby was sure there was a rear exit that Carmine used if and when he had to. Carmine Mancini was seen only when he wanted to be seen. And he wanted to be seen only when it benefited one of his businesses. Bobby was also sure that Carmine would be seated somewhere near that rear exit.

Bobby watched carefully as two of the patrons in the shop received their already boxed-up orders, paid, and began to exit. The first girl to exit carried two white boxes stacked one on top of the other. The bottom box was larger and appeared to be heavier than the top box. Bobby speculated that the bottom box must be a cake and the top box, either pastries or cookies. The powerful aroma wafting through the open door space of Alba's was undeniable. It assaulted the sense of smell, and there was no escaping it. When you first walk in it's the smell that overwhelms you. Bobby enjoyed the sweet, complex smells. He was here to pawn six Rolex watches, and all he could think about while standing there were the pastries. It's genius: funnel that aroma directly into the nostrils of anyone who walks in or even past Alba's, and their money just floats out of their wallet into the cash register. It's truly an amazing business plan. You could come here for a thirty-five cent cup of coffee and leave with twenty dollars' worth of pastries. That's real organized crime. Bobby admired the scene at Alba's, and knew there was a genius with money somewhere beyond the front door.

Bobby finally made it to the front counter after about twenty minutes in line and was about to be helped by a young girl in her late teens, maybe early twenties. The counter girls at Alba's wore uniforms, white tee shirts, probably a man-cut shirt under a chocolate brown French maid's-cut overall top with a pleated skirt bottom. Her skirt was hiked up with a few turns of the waistband, short and sweet. Bobby quickly fantasized about her firm young body. He had a vivid imagination when it came to the young ones. The young girl interrupted his day-dream with, "Welcome to Alba's. My name is Alicia. How can I help you?"

Bobby boldly responded, "I would like to see Carmine Mancini. Is he here and available?" He was shocked that the words came out of his mouth so abruptly and with such confidence. It actually scared the shit out of him. Alicia said nothing in response. She glanced to her left and quickly caught the attention of the resident linebacker-sized man with no neck, massive arms, and slicked-back, jet black hair. Bobby nearly shit himself right there and automatically began to second-guess his plan. "This is a huge fuck-up," he said to himself.

The neatly dressed giant confidently approached Bobby and asked, "Can I help you?" Fine beads of sweat droplets began to form on Bobby's forehead as panic began to set in. Standing as tall as he could while trembling and sweating, Bobby replied, "Is Carmine Mancini here and available?" The colossal man adjusted his dress shirt collar as he ignored Bobby's question and asked sternly, "What's in the bag?"

"I would rather discuss the contents of the bag with Mr. Mancini, if that's okay with you," Bobby said through chattering teeth. Cold sweat began to run down Bobby's back and became an added source of anxiety at that point. Clearly that request was not okay with him and this was made crystal clear to Bobby, as the mammoth well-dressed goon nearly crushed Bobby's elbow, aggressively escorting him to the back of Alba's and through a steel fire door marked, "Do Not Enter." Bobby was astonished as the man passed the "Do Not Enter" sign before he could ask in a shaking voice, "Why are we entering? It clearly says do not enter. Why are we entering?" Bobby said. Panic set in and Bobby's words would no longer form. That was a first for Bobby.

The unidentified elbow-crushing bodyguard for Carmine Mancini offered Bobby a seat by crunching down on his right shoulder from behind. Bobby quickly complied in apparent discomfort. The dimly lit space was a stark contrast to the comforting European decor in the pastry shop. Little attention had been given to what seemed to be a small office space. The conversation was minimal and the focus of the man shifted from Bobby to the mysterious brown paper bag package that now lay on the aluminum office table in front of Bobby Maseano. "What do we have here?" The man's English was broken, but Bobby fully understood the question.

The men employed by Carmine Mancini were always on high alert for anyone with a concealed device that could be used for looking or listening. Tape recorders, cameras, film, and Polaroids were constantly sought out in the cafe. It was no secret that Carmine Mancini owned Alba's, and the Brooklyn locals seemed to have an infatuation with him and his flashy ways. Pictures of Mr. Mancini were collected like souvenirs in the neighborhood. Tape recorders were especially frowned upon there. The boys knew that the NYPD and maybe even some federal agents had been trying to capture conversations that included Carmine Mancini directing the organization. Thus far the NYPD and the feds had failed miserably. They launched various undercover operations, all producing circumstantial material at best. Carmine Mancini played every hand close to the vest. No exceptions. Family business was conducted only with his inner circle, proven and made men. Even full confidants were searched and underwent a pat-down before any conversations concerning the actions or whereabouts of a family member were concerned.

Business went on as usual. The slight yet insightful modifications made by Carmine Mancini had kept him one step ahead of the police, enemies, and other families. Today would be no exception. The package with which Bobby Maseano had entered Alba's pastry shop just minutes before had landed him almost immediately into the clutches of a front man who would have no issue with blowing his head off if told to do so. Bobby was yanked from the aluminum chair, nearly out of his socks and shoes. He was placed on the wall just to the left of the aluminum table and frisked from head to toe. His shoes were inspected, as well as his belt and pockets. The man pressed his baseball glove sized hand against Bobby's throat and passed it downward to his belt line, repeating the search over and over until every square inch of Bobby's torso had yielded no recording devices. The man reached in from behind as Bobby stood, hands pressed against the wall with feet spread apart at shoulder width. His right hand laid on the back of Bobby's left leg just under his ass cheek. His left hand reached around front just under his sack, and the pat-down continued with his hands running down, then back up again over each leg. No wires were found. Bobby was squeaky clean and yet felt incredibly violated.

Once satisfied that Bobby did not have a tape recorder or camera of any sort on his body, the man was finally willing to listen to the matter of Bobby's business with Carmine Mancini. Bobby's hands slid from the wall and his feet came together as he felt the tension decline in the small confined space. Bobby looked straight ahead as he turned to face the man and stared directly into his buttonhole-stretching chest muscles and asked if he could take a seat. Bobby proceeded to reach for the brown paper package that had been placed stranded on the aluminum table just prior to the intense violation. He realized that he was never going to have a chance to meet with Carmine Mancini unless he appeased this gigantic asshole and revealed what the precious contents of the package were.

The man peered at Bobby with expectant eyes. Bobby took his lasered eyes as a threatening gesture and decided to tell the goon what his business consisted of. "In this bag I have six brand new genuine Rolex watches, which happened to come into my possession," Bobby said. "I want to sell this merchandise to Mr. Mancini at a steep discount. Times are a little rough for me right now so I need to sell them to help feed my family." Bobby played the sympathy card early in his quest to sell the watches. *All bullshit*, he said to himself almost as soon as the words left his mouth. Immediately after he finished his sentence he knew it had been a mistake. He thought he should have held on to the poor family story for leverage later on in the conversations if the negotiations didn't go as he had planned. The man became visibly interested, now showing a raised eyebrow and a hint of a smirk. His stone face was gone and Bobby knew this was the time to flash one of the fine timepieces.

Bobby reached for the package after gesturing for the man's approval, seeking his permission to move toward the package. The man gave a nod, signaling to Bobby that he had his permission to retrieve the package and show him the Rolex watches. Bobby reached for the package, noticing that his right hand and arm were still trembling when he stretched it out straight. With the package directly in front of him, Bobby began to unwrap the package from the top toward the bottom. Once it was completely open, he reached for the top of the bag to put his arm inside. He also noticed that the man now had a large firearm drawn and that it was held steadfast at his right side. The man did not point the pistol directly at Bobby, but its exposure was more than enough to get Bobby's heart pumping. The sweat droplets were back on his brow and he felt the first full drop form and race down his right cheek, then hide itself in his full mustache. Bobby withdrew one of the boxes, set it on the aluminum table, and with his left hand flipped the lid open and exposed the first of six precious timepieces. The Submariner was spectacular. It glistened even in the murky light of the cramped space. The man quickly reached for the box after holstering his firearm. Bobby wondered why he didn't see the gun prior to it being pulled out. The pistol was not holstered to his waist, so Bobby concluded that it must have been strapped to his ankle for concealment. Of course it was strapped to his ankle, Bobby thought. He can't just strap a piece on his hip. Not here in Brooklyn and definitely not in Alba's.

The man was elated at the sight of the Submariner. He wanted to see the rest of Bobby Maseano's supply and validate that they were all in the same pristine condition. Bobby extracted each watch one at a time from the bag and placed each one in front of the man for his inspection and approval. Six brilliant specimens of fine Rolex watches and they were stunning. The man couldn't help the grin that appeared on his face. He continued the inspection of each timepiece for what seemed to be an hour. Bobby sat there patiently waiting for a cue from the man, but he said nothing and gestured nothing. When he was satisfied that what he was looking at were in fact six perfectly new and real Rolex watches, he rose from his seat, walked to the wall directly behind Bobby and picked up the phone which was mounted near the corner. Bobby tried to hear the conversation but he wasn't fluent in Italian. Few words were spoken in English and it was even hard for Bobby to understand those words because they were broken.

Once that brief conversation ended, the man sat back down directly across from Bobby and stared intently at him. "Mr. Mancini is businessman, but he's not in the business of buying stolen watches," he continued in his worsening broken English.

"I never said these watches were stolen," Bobby replied. "I just happened to come across them." The look of disapproval was clear and apparent on the man's face. He knew Bobby was lying. Bobby could feel the man's anger. "Mr. Mancini can be sure that if he takes these watches off my hands we will both be happy with the purchase," Bobby said as if he were a professional salesman. "He's a man of impeccable taste. I have seen his taste in fine cars, fine clothing and fine women," Bobby added. "These watches need to be with such a man, to do with them whatever he wishes. Maybe he will give them away as gifts, for Christmas." The man's eye lit up like a Christmas tree. He was imagining one of those fine Rolex watches around his own wrist on December 25th. "Few men in this neighborhood will appreciate the value of these Rolex watches. Carmine Mancini is surely one of those men." The man agreed with a few silent nods of his head and smirky grin.

Chapter 13

Bobby sat at the aluminum table for an eternity, drenching himself in a cascade of his own nervous sweat. The walls were bare and uninhabited by color or decoration: no pictures, posters or even paint. Just walls, like the inside of a coffin without the white satin. This understandably added to the anxiety Bobby was feeling, and the giant man obviously could sense it. Bobby knew the man had been in this room before, and he was sure that his intentions were always to hurt or kill someone. The man definitely knew how Bobby was going to react to being trapped in the room with him. Bobby looked for bloodstains, but couldn't find any. He wished the lighting was better. Maybe that would help ease his nerves. Bobby could hear through the wall immediately to his right side as the pastry shop conducted its lucrative sweet business, and yet he felt a thousand miles away from safety. He tried to take solace in the fact that freedom from this cave was just through the door, but it was locked from inside the room, and the key wasn't in the deadbolt. He was paralyzed with fear and mobilized by greed. He longed for the cash, which was more important to him at this point than was his fear of the pain he might suffer if the pending deal went bad.

Bobby knew the destruction that these made men were capable of inflicting. Bobby had read the daily news stories of the organized crime syndicates, and those reports began to play in his head. He read about the beatings, murders, and brutality that was handed out as punishment for only minor infractions against the family's code of honor. He was stuck in a bad situation, which had the potential to get a lot worse from there.

Bobby was startled to hear the door to his left begin to open. He watched as the brass door handle turned to the right. Bobby assumed this was the outside door and that exiting that door would bring a person to an alleyway and a certain dead end. Bobby knew that the backs of these commercial buildings were gated off with chain link and that some even had razor wire atop. This was definitely not the way to exit. Bobby, if he was capable of mustering up the courage and if his leg muscles would cooperate, he could make a run for it out the front door, but he was locked in that cage. He was sure the back of the building was the wrong way to go. Bobby would have been a dead man if he had gone out the rear door. The alley way was in fact full of commercial garbage containers which obstructed a clear path to the fourteen-foot-high chain link fence. If someone had chased him out the back, he would have been an easy kill, especially if it looked like he was robbing the place. Carmine and company were efficient at staging crime scenes.

The steel door opened slowly without much sound. Bobby carefully calculated whether he should turn to his left to see what or who was coming his way, or wait to hear a voice and a command. He quickly decided to wait for a voice and kept his head straight forward, staring at his coffin wall. Bobby heard nothing except footsteps. As the shadow of Carmine Mancini made its way from the floor to the edge of the table and beyond, Bobby grew more anxious. Bobby knew that Carmine Mancini was the approaching figure, and that his life was in jeopardy.

FIRST VICTIM

Carmine Mancini pulled up an aluminum chair and sat in the space directly across from Bobby, who was terrified. Carmine was one of the most-feared men in all of Brooklyn, and his reputation was not that of a forgiving, God-fearing man. Carmine was silent. He picked up one of the Rolex boxes and examined the pristine Submariner. "Why have you come here with these watches? I am legitimate businessman. No stolen merchandise!" Carmine's broken words pierced through Bobby's ears. "Are you a pig?," he asked without reservation.

"Mr. Mancini, I came across these watches by pure luck," Bobby explained. "I work for a trucking company and this package was on my truck, but not on my manifest to deliver. I just never returned the package. I'm sure they're insured. I'm in a desperate spot here, I need the money to feed my wife and kid." The nervousness that Bobby portrayed was apparent to both of the other men in the room. The trembling voice, the sweaty brow, and the shaky hands were all telltale signs. Carmine was reading him like a best-selling novel. "Things are real hard for us right now and this would help me dig out of a hole. I swear to you, I am not a cop and my intentions here are only personal."

Carmine sat back in the aluminum chair and collected his thoughts for a moment. He flicked an ash from a nasty-smelling cigar onto the concrete floor and returned it to its rightful place in the right corner of his mouth. He quickly leaned in to further examine the collection. Smoke now consumed the cramped space, but Bobby did not dare to object. He sat far back in his chair to create as much distance as possible between himself and Carmine, which seemed to be the only thing he could do at that moment. And he was probably right, except for the fact that creating space between him and Carmine brought him that much closer to the mammoth man who stood behind him just to his left. As he went back as far as he could in his chair, he began to feel the breath of that man on his sweat-moistened neck. *This is too close,* Bobby thought, as he tried to shift his way out of the downward stream of used oxygen and carbon dioxide the man was releasing. There was no escape.

Mr. Mancini looked up past Bobby's head to the sky where the man's head was located and with a quick nod of his head, gave a silent but well-understood command. The man walked out of the cramped space through the door from which Carmine had entered. The steel door closed with a metallic thud. Bobby managed to see that the door did not lead to the outside as he had thought, but to what seemed to be an exquisitely decorated and well-lit private office. Bobby did not have a full view, but what he did see was impressive. Obviously an abundant amount of money had been spent on decorating the space, making it as comfortable as Carmine's own living room. There was a shiny dark wood wall inside, which stretched from floor to ceiling. The office desk was nearly the same color, and the floor was covered with light brown shag carpet. Not bad for a room that shouldn't even be there, Bobby marveled to himself. Not only was his heart ready to stop beating, but he almost stopped breathing as well.

The hulk of a man returned a short while later, slowly opening the steel door. Slow, with emphasis on the entry to creating an air of drama in Bobby's mind. Bobby had no idea where he had gone or what he was doing inside the office. He was hoping and praying that he was in the office accessing a safe and withdrawing Carmine's cash. He wanted out of that room more than he had wanted anything before in his entire life.

The beast entered with nothing in his hands, but someone trailed behind him. Almost fully eclipsed by the man was a young and very beautiful girl. The girl took one step to her left and said, "Ciao, Carmine." She approached Carmine and kissed him twice, once on his right cheek and once on his left. Carmine caressed her left hand inside his as he rose from the aluminum table. Bobby remained seated, waiting for some sort of introduction. Carmine glanced at Bobby and then back at the girl. "This is Luisa," Carmine said as if he were showing off a priceless work of fine art.

Bobby extended his right hand to shake her hand across the table and said, "It's a pleasure to meet you, Luisa."

"Luisa is a beautiful girl, no?" Carmine asked. Saying "No" at the end of that sentence, the way he did, was Carmine's invitation to Bobby to disagree with him. Like saying, "I dare you to say she's not beautiful."

"She is more than beautiful, she's gorgeous," Bobby affirmed, knowing that he gave the correct answer. Confusion quickly set in; he honestly did not know what was going on in that moment, and he certainly did not know how to react.

Luisa was stunning, and she had a perfect body. Bobby's assessment was made instantaneously. Not much was left to the imagination. Her blood-red dress hugged her hips tightly, leaving only slight ripples in the silky material as it rode up seductively. The dress was cut short. If not for constant downward adjustments, the hem would eventually climb directly to her waist. Her plunging neckline was confident, perfectly showcasing her vibrant young breasts. She had managed to accent perfection with a brilliant diamond cross necklace suspended from a white gold chain. Her wrists and hands were jewelry-free, nicely manicured, and soft to the touch. Her long, silky hair cascaded in waves down the sides of her face, framing it perfectly. The stunning red dress was made more fantastic by the fact that there was no back, something Bobby noticed when she greeted Carmine, swinging her hair from right to left, revealing the prize. Straps that began at her shoulder terminated to a point just above the small of her back.

Luisa was tall and statuesque and knew how to maximize the drama as she entered in four or five-inch black heels, something Bobby could not help noticing. There is something sexy about a girl who can work high heels with skill. He liked the sound they made on the bare concrete floor. Bobby loved the shape her calves took when they were flexed high above her heels. She click-clacked ever so gracefully and sexily upon her entrance. Being trapped in this room did not feel so bad anymore. Bobby comforted himself with the vision of beauty before him. The linebacker in the room seemed to disappear, if only for that moment.

"Luisa has a special function with my organization," Carmine said, snapping Bobby back to reality. "Her job is to make sure you are who you say you are. If you're a cop or a fed or anything else other than a man selling watches, you will die. It's her call. If she's not happy with your performance, you die. Do I make that clear?"

"Yes sir," Bobby meekly replied.

"Did I leave any gray area, or do you completely understand?" Carmine gave Bobby one last chance.

"I completely understand, Mr. Mancini."

Carmine offered Luisa to Bobby. Luisa extended her left hand to Bobby as if saying,

Take my hand and let's run away together. Bobby responded by rising from his seat and taking Luisa's hand in his right. Luisa guided Bobby around the table, then slowly and methodically closed the gap between them. Bobby was not sure what to say, but managed to execute, "Where are we going? Where are you taking me?" Bobby wanted to contest leaving his Rolex watches behind, but could not help being more interested in Luisa's open-back dress.

Luisa responded by turning toward him and gently pressing her right index finger to his lips and saying, "Do not say another word, just follow me." Bobby was not stupid, and he definitely did not trust Luisa. He was a willing participant in following her lead, yet as he exited the room he again reflected on the Rolex watches he was leaving behind and the reason he was there in the first place. For some reason the Rolex watches didn't seem as important to him as they had fifteen minutes prior.

Luisa led Bobby through the steel door into the office from where Carmine had entered just a short while ago. He followed her gait, stride for stride, not taking his eyes off her ass. Her ass was perfect, like a work of art chiseled from granite. They passed through the office he had been so curious about, not noticing a single additional item that he hadn't noticed the first time he gazed in. Luisa coaxed Bobby through another steel door at the far right side of the office. She opened the door, which led directly to a staircase, offering access to the second floor.

The staircase must have been original to the building. The wood was aged and scarred from traffic. It had what appeared to be the original weathered stain and finish. The treads and risers were worn down, and there were obvious depressions in the wood from many hard-soled shoes throughout years of heavy traffic. Luisa must have made this trip a thousand times for Carmine. Who knew how many girls had made the trip before her? There were pictures on either side of the darkened staircase. They were old and just as weathered as the stairs themselves. The pictures were of the old country, Italy, and they were labeled as such. There were many scenic photos of the country and some still lifes, all in deteriorating wood frames. Bobby's senses were on high alert by the time they reached the summit. At the top of the staircase were more decayed period snapshots. Bobby figured it to be a graveyard of old photos that someone felt horrible about discarding and instead retired them to this hallway for eternity.

The door at the end of a short hallway on the second floor was different from the rest.

It appeared to be the original door to the structure but with apparent recent refinishing. Luisa opened the unlocked door and proceeded to lead Bobby into the apartment. It was unclear to Bobby at first what he was doing up here, alone, with this beautiful young girl. Panic began to set in as he was sure he would never see the six Rolex watches again. He was also sure he would never see any cash from Carmine or anyone else for that matter. The apartment did not feel like a young girl's apartment. It had more of a business office-type atmosphere. Almost clinical. The living room was just off the front door, and was far too masculine to be Luisa's own apartment. An emerald green sofa was covered in plastic and perched upon thinly carved wooden legs. The coffee table was a dark hardwood with ornate carvings around the sides. Nice, but not very expensive-looking. The throw rug that lay under the coffee table was dark earth-toned with high-pile fibers, not quite shag but pretty close. It was clean and organized, but lacked the sensitivity of a female's touch.

Luisa, in an attempt to calm Bobby, turned to him, reached around him, pressed herself into his chest, then closed and locked the door behind him. She gently caressed his face saying, "Everything will be all right. Trust me, okay?" Luisa was definitely Italian, but spoke English very well. There was only a slight hint of an accent. Bobby loved the slight accent and was hoping to himself that it wasn't fake. "There is nothing to worry about if you haven't lied to Mr. Mancini. I'm just here to occupy your time and energy while your merchandise is gone through and inspected. My job is to make sure you are who you say you are, and we're going to have some fun while you wait. You're not a cop, are you Bobby? It will make me look bad if you turn out to be a cop."

Luisa did not wait for a response. "What do you drink? There's a full bar over there in the butler's pantry. I'll have Smirnoff and cranberry," assuming Bobby would tend bar. The butler's pantry was located off the left side of the living room, before the kitchen. Bobby assumed the role of bartender and left her behind to fix drinks without saying a word. He was clearly uncomfortable. Bobby poured Luisa her Smirnoff and cranberry with three cubes. He tendered himself a single smooth malt whiskey. He hoped that would calm his nerves.

When Bobby returned from the butler's pantry to the living room, Luisa was sitting on the left side of the sofa. She gestured for Bobby to join her on her right side, signaling to sit close by, tapping her open hand on the plastic of the emerald colored seat cushion. Bobby offered Luisa her beverage and sat where he was summoned. Luisa reached for a small glass-covered bowl which sat in the center of the coffee table. Bobby knew immediately what this bowl caine. "This will relax you in a way that whiskey can't," Luisa said. "Will you do some with me?"

Bobby had never tried cocaine before, but if Luisa had asked him to snort motor oil, he would have done it. He knew this was her test to see if he was who he said he was. Bobby allowed Luisa to take the first hit. After all, he was trying to be a perfect gentleman. "Ladies first," he said. Luisa hit the small spoon first. It was a tiny amount of pure white powder on the tip of the smallest spoon he had ever seen. Immediately after Bobby took his first hit, bells began to ring in his head. The ringing did not stop. He could feel the flood of adrenaline and an intense heightening of all his senses. Luisa calmed him and took another hit herself. If she had any inhibitions, she was surely trying to lose them.

Luisa leaned slightly to her right side, bringing her mouth close to Bobby's neck. She began to kiss it, softly at first, then slightly harder. Her tongue ran up his neck and hovered around his ear. Soft breaths followed and Bobby leaned in toward her, inviting her to continue. She ran the fingers of her right hand roughly through his hair as she pressed him closer and tighter. Luisa's left hand was seated on Bobby's left leg just above his knee, and it was making its way upward. She rubbed him hard through his pants until he paid attention to her advancements. She slithered to the floor and made her way between his legs, beginning to exhale her smoldering breath through his pants onto his rock hard penis. She breathed and rubbed, breathed and rubbed, deep inhalation followed by slow exhalation. When Luisa was satisfied that Bobby was at a point of no return, she unlinked his belt and with a violent motion pulled his belt clear from his pants. Bobby's pants and boxers were slid down by her delicate hands, and she stopped at his ankles. Bobby helped with a complying lift of his center mass off the sofa. She looked up at Bobby with seductive, devilish eyes as she descended and took him into her mouth. Bobby was rock hard and high as a kite. Feeling extreme sensation, but yet in full control, he leaned back into the plastic of the sofa for a flight he had never experienced before.

Luisa stood up in front of Bobby who was naked from the waist down. He was obviously still aroused by the sight of her. Luisa hiked up her blood-red dress past her waist. Her right leg raised, then rested it just to the side of Bobby's left leg. The other leg quickly followed to his other side. She straddled Bobby, placing him between her inner thighs at first. She kissed him hard on the mouth and he kissed her back just as hard.

He grabbed the back of her silky smooth hair and gave it a firm but gentle tug. Luisa moaned loudly, rolling her head back with the unexpected pull. He then lifted her dress completely off, over her head, exposing perfect young breasts. Luisa did not have any panties on, and this pleased Bobby even more. He caressed her breasts firmly and slowly. She let out another soft moan. He assaulted both nipples with the grinding motion of his thumbs and index fingers. Luisa was arched back with her hands resting on Bobby's knees, and she uttered, "I want you deep inside me. I want you deep, deep inside me." Bobby guided his right hand down between her legs. He felt the warm moistness of her body and slid himself into her. Luisa jolted forward, grabbing onto the back of Bobby's neck, and began to gyrate her hips front to back, taking him deeper inside. With each upward thrust, he was flirting with the right spot. He was sure of it. Bobby managed to hold off his climax until he was sure she climaxed first. Her body went slightly limp as her tense muscles began to relax. Moisture formed on her forehead. Her breaths were shallow and rapid. She held on tight to Bobby as he pounded her from below. Bobby was enthralled with her moans and the way she held on to him as if she were riding the Coney Island Cyclone. Suddenly and unexpectedly, Luisa collapsed into Bobby's chest, as he released inside her.

Chapter 14

Bobby enjoyed his newfound confidence. He felt more of a man in the previous hour then he had his entire life. No one could take that away from him. An intense euphoria galloped through his mind and body. At the moment of climax he didn't care whether the intense sensation was because of the whiskey, the cocaine, or this incredible vixen he had met just a short while before in a back office of a Brooklyn pastry shop. He had just had incredible sex with a talented young girl in an apartment he hadn't known existed an hour ago. Her body was imprinted in his mind, and that was all he could see. Luisa was maybe in her early twenties, and she was as tight as a drum. Bobby was enjoying his instant and rapidly recurring recall. He had experienced a satisfaction that had eluded him all his life. He didn't think it was only the unbridled sex with Luisa. It was much more complicated than that. There was some neurochemical satisfaction that superseded the physical satisfaction, and he knew he had to have more. A lot more.

Luisa appeared from the bathroom just off the living room. She seemed to be refreshed from the hot shower. However, she didn't offer

Bobby access to a shower of his own. She strode in naked, wet but not dripping with her hands up, collecting her water darkened hair into a ponytail. He took in the full magnificence of her body as if he were ingesting sweet candy. Bobby melted into the sofa as Luisa began to dress directly in front of him. She gracefully stepped into her dress, first the left leg, then the right. Bending over with her ass intentionally toward Bobby's face, she lifted her blood-red dress over her hips and rewrapped herself. After gathering her shoes and stepping up a few inches taller, she allowed Bobby to adjust her dress straps. She held her ponytail up in the air with her right hand, bent her neck down, which automatically arched her back, and had Bobby help her straighten the spaghetti straps that stretched the length of her back. He prayed that this would not be the last time he was with Luisa. With clearer thinking taking over, he realized that this was a fantasy created for him by Carmine Mancini. If Carmine Mancini was involved, the fantasy had to benefit him somehow. This was all smoke and mirrors for a higher purpose.

Luisa took Bobby's right hand with a gentle touch and escorted him toward the apartment door. She had one hand on the handle as she gazed back at Bobby and whispered, "Bobby, be careful when you're on this side of the tracks. Sometimes you have to run instead of walk."

"Luisa, what does that mean? I don't understand." There was some underlying message there that Bobby had missed.

She wasn't going to elaborate on her advice other than saying, "Carmine gave me that advice when he saved me from the streets. it took me a while to figure it out, but I finally did and when you figure it out it will make perfect sense to you also." She turned the old bronze handle and slowly opened the door. "You'll understand someday. Someday, when you have to run for your life."

Luisa led Bobby down the old rickety staircase, past the now-familiar pictures of old-world Italy. They entered the office of Mr. Mancini, and Luisa offered him one of the dark brown leather seats in front of Carmine's desk. "Wait here. Carmine will be right with you. Whatever you do, don't touch anything. Carmine knows where everything is and he will take it as a sign of disrespect if anything is tampered with," she added.

Bobby ignored her words of caution and questioned, "Will I see you again?" Luisa's sharp reply ripped through Bobby: "No, that was nice, but it was just business."

"That's it. Just an abrupt No, it was just business," he said to himself as she exited the office into the small dark interrogation room where Bobby had been confined thinking he was going to die. He figured Luisa was heading out through the shop. She must be done with her workday. He sat back in Carmine's office, looking around with his eyes but not his hands. He did not see the watches or the cash he was expecting. Carmine entered after a few brief minutes and once again did not have any words for Bobby. He came around Bobby's right side and took the comfortable executive leather seat behind his desk. Carmine leaned back on the reclining leather chair, propped his right arm onto the desk, and jammed a fat cigar in his mouth with his left hand. He twirled the tip of the eight inch cigar between his lips like it was a Blow Pop. He did not light it at first, but just licked and chewed on the end, maybe for effect, maybe for the flavor. He finally began, "So you're not a cop after all. I would have pegged you for a cop. Those pigs are trying to set me up, every fucking day. Ya know what I mean?" Bobby's response was just a weak head nod. "So did I have your time occupied to your liking while I had the watches checked out?"

"Luisa, holy shit, she was incredible."

Carmine snapped back, "Don't get no fucking ideas. She's a good girl when she's not working." Carmine gave Bobby a wink as to imply that he should know what he was talking about when he said she was a working girl. Bobby got his point, like a knife through the heart. Luisa was a high-class prostitute.

Bobby tried to change the subject. "Mr. Mancini, would you like to take those watches off my hands? I'm sure you'll be fair with me on the price, because you have been more than fair with me so far." The mafia boss and Bobby chuckled almost simultaneously. That was weird, Bobby acknowledged to himself.

"Bobby, right? What's your last name?"

He quickly replied, "Maseano."

"Are you from the neighborhood?"

"Yes, I'm from 24th Avenue and 83rd Street."

"So, you're Italian, and you're from Brooklyn. You grew up here in Brooklyn, right?" Carmine inquired.

"Yes sir."

"Good, so you know how all this works, right?"

"Well, not exactly," Bobby admitted.

"Okay, let me explain it to you. I'll be crystal clear, okay? I take these watches off your hands, because it's a good deal for me. I had them checked out by a friend of the family while you were upstairs socializing. The watches are mine now and so are you. I pay you a premium for the stuff. It makes no difference what the stuff is. If I buy it, I pay a premium. Why, you might be wondering, would I want to pay you more than you want for the stuff? Because you'll keep coming back with more and more stuff, that's why. You now only sell to me. If I find out your stuff goes to anyone else, then what happens, Bobby? You die," Carmine answered his own question.

Bobby seemed to be more relaxed now than he had been in hours, even though Carmine was basically threatening his life again. The ringing bells from the cocaine were finally gone from his head. Carmine explained the way he did business, and Bobby freely accepted his terms and conditions. "How much were you looking to take home after all is said and done here?" Carmine leaned back in his leather office chair and lit his cigar with his gold-colored Zippo. He took a few short quick puffs, drawing the flame into the eight-inch cigar to make sure he would not lose the light. Then he pulled a long, slow, and deep puff, quickly exhaling the thick vapor. The smoke quickly filled the office space, choking the life out of the room. Well, choking the life out of

Bobby anyway. Carmine didn't seem to mind the stench. He seemed immune to the polluted air.

Bobby tried to think of an inoffensive price while he gagged and coughed. Carmine seemed amused at the difficulty Bobby was having taking air into his lungs. Carmine thrived on offering pleasure, and pain as well.

Bobby, in fear of choking to death from the cigar smoke said, "I would like to get two thousand dollars for all six watches." Carmine did not respond right away. He sat back even farther in his office chair and watched Bobby squirm, sweat, and choke.

Carmine finally said, "I was going to give you five thousand for the whole lot. I gave you at least a thousand dollars in pussy, so I'm only going to give you four thousand. Let's be clear on what happened here today. Nothing happened here, you got that? You never stepped foot inside Alba's. You never met Bruno or Luisa. We never met. I never saw any watches. You know nothing about the apartment upstairs or the office you're sitting in right now. Nothing, you got it? If all that is good with you, then I won't have to shoot you." Carmine laughed sadistically. "Are we clear?" he asked.

"We're crystal clear. You have my word." Bobby just now realized he hadn't known the linebacker's name until that very moment. Bruno, the bruiser.

Carmine rose from his antique desk and pulled out a shit ton of cash, first from his right front pants pocket, then another shit ton from his left. He handed Bobby two piles of money, each secured with rubber bands. "Don't insult me by counting it. My business is built on trust and if you can't trust me, who can you trust?" he said jokingly. "When, not if, you happen, by chance of course, to come across more Rolex watches, gold or even diamonds you know where to come. Remember if I hear your name on the street because you're running your mouth, you'll turn up floating in the East River. Or maybe you'll turn up in a landfill on Staten Island. Bruno, show Bobby out through the front, like you're old friends. Get him a dozen pastries for his trouble, too." Bobby collected his bundles of cash and Bruno collected Bobby.

Bobby Maseano was not about to turn down a free dozen pastries, courtesy of Carmine Mancini and Alba's, even if he wanted to get out there as fast as humanly possible. The counter girl who took his order just happened to be the one who caught his roaming eye the least. It was a pure business transaction at the counter. There was no suggestive flirting, no checking out her ass or her tits, and no sly comments. Maybe it was because he had just had sex with Luisa. Maybe it was because he was flying high again with the four grand in his front pocket. Maybe it was because Bruno, the bone-crushing giant, was less than two feet away and he looked hungry. Bobby waited patiently at the counter for his pastries to be gathered. He once again marveled at the hustle and bustle in the shop, and he definitely did not make eye contact with Bruno. The young lady delivered the gold-imprinted white box with Bobby's requests. In the box were six sfogliatelle, three plain cannolis, and three huge almond biscotti. Bobby could not help smiling from ear to ear as he collected his box of confectioner's jewels. He turned from the counter and headed for the door, never again acknowledging Bruno. Bobby knew he was there but was not going to give Bruno the satisfaction of seeing any more fear in his face.

Bobby did not look back until he approached the corner of 18th Avenue and 75th Street. As he glanced back over his right shoulder, he saw no one and was confident that no one from Alba's had followed him. Bobby glanced up as he approached the Mustang and yelled, "What the fuck is that? A fucking parking ticket." He kicked the pole that held the parking meter. The cop who had written the summons had been there less than twenty minutes before. Bobby was able to read the carbon imprint of the time, but not the officer's name. "Motherfucker," he exploded. The ticket was left there on his windshield, tucked neatly under the driver's side windshield wiper to ruin his whole day. Bobby thought better of the situation once he was seated in the car and reflected on the piles of cash in his pockets. It was enough cash to make any man smile, even if he had just gotten a parking ticket. Bobby knew what he was going to do with the ticket. He was going to call his good buddy Detective Giovanni Nardi and have him take care of it. *Nardi will fix it*, he said to himself as he flipped the ticket over his right shoulder into the back seat.

Bobby fired up the Mustang and headed far away from Alba's, Bruno, and Carmine Mancini. There was no reason to take any chance out there on the streets with pockets full of cash and pastries that needed to be refrigerated. The drive home was a smooth, confident cruise. He drove 75th Street all the way to Stillwell Avenue, then headed for 83rd Street. Elvis played loudly on the radio. Bobby leaned back into the vinyl bucket seat, right hand on the top of the steering wheel, left hand flicking Marlboro ashes out the window, rocking along with is. When he pulled up onto the block and parked the car in front, there were a bunch of kids playing stickball in the street. He beeped the horn obnoxiously, as he always did.

"Hey Bobby, wanna hit a few?" One of them yelled out.

"He can't hit for shit," the little one said, trying to coax Bobby in.

"Sure, boys, I'll show you how it's done," Bobby replied. "Give me a minute. I'll be right back." Bobby parked the Mustang near where home plate was chalked in the street, then strode up the stoop and rapped on the bedroom window from the top step. "Hey Ann," Bobby yelled through the pane of glass. He rapped again and yelled for Ann to come to the window. When Ann did not respond, Bobby abandoned the pastries on the top step and headed for the street and the chance to hit a few ten or fifteen houses down the block. He played stickball between all the parked cars well into the night, until all the kids began to disperse. It wasn't until he was heading back to his apartment that he remembered the four grand that was still stuffed in his pockets and the pastry's he had forgotten on the stoop.

Bobby was good with all the kids on the block. His young son, however, would never have the chance to play stickball in the street with him like all the other kids did.

Chapter 15

Detective Giovanni Nardi was struggling to put the pieces together. Maybe he was having trouble accepting that all the pieces of the puzzle fit perfectly and that Bobby Maseano had gotten himself into deep trouble. He leaned back in the leather chair inside his cubicle, which was tucked away on the second floor of the 62nd Precinct. He assumed his usual contemplative position, leaning back deep into the heavily worn desk chair, propping his feet up on the desk, and staring blankly at the water stained ceiling. Nardi was struggling with the information given to him because of how close to home it had hit. He had never investigated someone in his own family. He folded his arms across his chest in an attempt to comfort himself. Nardi expected answers to his questions to come as easily as they usually did, but nothing came except a headache. Nardi was always reminded of how old and aged the decaying building had become. He had practically memorized every yellow water stain in the ceiling plaster. He had never really had any revelations while in this position, but he was usually able to at least come up with a starting point. He assumed this odd position whenever he was stressed. And he was really stressed at that moment.

He felt the blood rush out of his throbbing head when he tilted his head skyward. He lit up a smoke and blew the exhaled fog directly at the ceiling from which he was so desperately seeking answers. He wrestled with the mental blockades in his head. There were always clouded thoughts when he was investigating a crime, but it seemed more intense now, because he knew Bobby Maseano personally. Nardi was not troubled about the crime itself. Unfortunately, robberies had become extremely common and these types of crimes had been taking up much of his work days. Desperate economic times force even good, normally law-abiding citizens to commit criminal acts just to survive. Detective Nardi was seriously struggling with the most recent reports and with the implication that Bobby Maseano might have gotten himself in over his head. It didn't make any sense to him. He went over his notes from the meeting with Leonard and Ann. He knew Bobby, and he thought he had known him well. Nardi's initial thoughts were that maybe he should be looking for evidence to clear by. Maybe the whole thing was just a big mistake. Maybe Ann was imagining the whole thing and didn't know how to deal with her failing marriage. But even Leonard had considered the possibility that Bobby was in fact guilty of something. Leonard's opinions had always carried weight with Nardi. Robbery at this level was serious, and some charges would be felonies. Could Bobby really be involved? There had been no record of any wrongdoing on Bobby's part in the past. Nothing. Clean records everywhere Nardi looked. And he had been looking, albeit reluctantly.

"Hey Joe, can you come in here for a minute?" Nardi yelled over the seven-foot-high cubicle wall that separated their spaces.

"Yeah, give me a minute. I'll be right there," Joe yelled back. Detective Joseph Simmons had been on the job nearly twenty years and was a seasoned police officer and special crimes investigator. Joe was a big man, physically intimidating at just over six foot three inches tall and pushing three-hundred pounds. Joe was usually the bad cop, and Nardi always started off as the good cop. Joe was just better at playing the bad cop. He mastered the role, and Nardi was usually okay with playing the good cop. So it worked out well for the pair. Joe had enjoyed the cubicle right next to Nardi for a couple years, and they not only worked well together, but they had become good friends in the process. Nardi had a lot of friends there at the 62nd. He was fun to be around, he was well-respected, and he was a relentless detective.

Joe walked into Nardi's space a few minutes after he had bellowed over the wall. They often helped each other see past their nearsightedness. That's what they called it when you couldn't see the forest that existed beyond the trees, when you could only see what was right in front of you--like when you have a hard focus on your front sights and the target is locked in, but you can't see the family crossing the street right beyond where your bullet is about to travel. It was a tremendous help when you brought in a fresh pair of eyes. Joe quickly took a seat in front of Nardi's desk and kicked his feet up into a relaxed position, saying, "What's up, Nards?" Joe liked to call him "Nards" instead of Nardi; he didn't know why.

Nardi yanked his preliminary report out of the typewriter and passed it to Joe. He read the report quickly and said, "What's the problem here? It seems clear to me."

"Joe, would you like to take a ride to Queens with me? I could use you on this one," Nardi said. "We have to see what they know about some missing merchandise. We need to interview someone at this REA Company, and then we'll take it from there."

"What the fuck is wrong with you, man?" Joe exclaimed. "This seems like detective work 101 to me." Joe pulled his size-thirteens from the top of Nardi's desk and sat back in the chair, anticipating a response from Nardi.

"The problem I'm having is that this guy is like family and I'm just not seeing clear because he's related, albeit through marriage, but related nonetheless," Nardi explained. "My cousin Leonard reached out to me for help with a situation with his daughter and her husband. His name is Bobby Maseano. She told me about a package Bobby had mailed to himself from a Queens post office. Bobby works in Queens as a driver for this REA Express Trucking company. The package contained six brand new Rolex watches, which were positively identified by Ann. Bobby disappeared from their apartment with the watches and hasn't been seen since.

"So we gotta go to REA Trucking and see if they formally reported anything missing recently, right?" Joe said matter-of-factly.

"I know what we gotta do, I just don't want to do it," Nardi said. "I don't want to hurt Ann and Leonard with any real bad news. They are two of the sweetest people you'll ever meet. I hope this is just a mistake, but it doesn't seem like it."

"Come on, I'll drive. Let's go. This isn't the first trip to Queens we've taken together and I'm sure it's not going to be the last. So let's just go," Joe said briskly.

The drive into Queens from Brooklyn should take between twenty and twenty- five minutes. It rarely does. The roads were not originally built for the volume of traffic that pollutes the roads on a daily basis. The two detectives made confirming eye contact as if Joe was saying to Nardi, "Hey man, I got your back," though Joe never actually said the words. He didn't have to. Nardi just knew Joe would do whatever it took to get the job done, regardless of how unwelcome the outcome would be. Joe and Nardi grabbed their sport coats and headed out of their respective cubicles, down the hall to the stairs leading to the street. Joe's car was a classic unmarked Crown Victoria that everyone knew was a police car. *So why have a fleet of unmarked police cars that everyone in the neighborhood knows is a police car?* This was a thought he had nearly every time he left the precinct heading toward his parking space on Bath Avenue. It made no sense at all.

Initially, as Joe made his way from the 62nd heading toward the Belt Parkway, conversation was lacking. Nardi was obviously troubled by the trip to REA Express. Joe always knew how to get Nardi talking. "So Nardi, you know the Mets are in first place and I think they're going to win the whole thing this year."

"The Mets suck," Nardi replied. This was his standard reply to any conversation that had to do with the Mets or Red Sox. It didn't matter how well either team was doing in the standings. To Nardi, both those teams just sucked. They would always suck. Nardi glared over at Joe and proceeded to explain how Ryan and McGraw were worthless. Grote couldn't throw out a runner if he tried. Harrelson couldn't hit from either side of the plate and Seaver was seriously overpaid. Nardi did show a morsel of respect for Shamsky and Swoboda, though. "I wouldn't mind having those guys on the Yankees one day," Nardi said.

Nardi was a huge New York Yankees fan, just like Bobby Maseano, and they shared the same views, at least on their baseball team. "Thurman Munson, now that's a baseball player. He's going to be one of the great ones," Nardi said with conviction in his voice. "Joe, you can mark my words on that. He's going to make Grote look like a sandlot-league catcher." Nardi knew that this was a rebuilding year for the Yankees and that they would be lucky if they didn't wind up in last place. "We are going to build an empire around Munson, Murcer and Clarke. I would like to keep White also. I like Roy White," he added. Nardi knew the Mets did have a legitimate shot at the National League Championship in 1969 and maybe even the World ries. "Every team has to have rebuilding years," Nardi commented to himself, consolingly. Even the New York Yankees."

The Belt Parkway had the usual volume of traffic for 3:00 p.m., and neither of the detectives was surprised that it took nearly half an hour just to get to the Brooklyn Queens Expressway exit. Nardi didn't like to drive on the Brooklyn Queens Expressway. He knew it would take him directly alongside Shea Stadium, and he hated that building. Joe was actually looking forward to Nardi's reaction, which was the same every time they passed Shea. Nardi wouldn't even look at the stadium, and a feeling of disgust consumed him. This time, however, Joe just let it pass. The stadium came up on their right and Joe said nothing, probably because REA Express Trucking was coming up fast and he wanted Nardi in the right frame of mind when they arrived. Nardi needed to ask the right questions and more importantly, he needed to hear the answers. He had to be able to process the information as elements of fact, not adding a personal spin onto any of the statements that were made. Nardi was a veteran detective, and Joe had full confidence in his abilities. Joe knew Nardi was a professional, but he was actually glad he was being included on this one. He knew firsthand what it took to investigate someone you knew. There was usually an expectation of a bad outcome, and family and friends usually got hurt. "Hey Nardi, you all right?" Joe finally asked. "You know where there's smoke there's usually fire."

Nardi replied simply, "I know, Joe. I know. That's part of my problem with this whole thing. I can't get the smell of smoke out of my nose. It really stinks."

Joe pulled the Crown Vic in the front of the industrial building with the sign REA Express Trucking stenciled in white on the painted steel doors. Joe took the parking spot directly in front of the entrance, only because it was the first spot available in the small, yet fairly full parking lot. Both men exited the Crown Vic and proceeded to the double doors. Nardi pressed the buzzer, and the detectives were buzzed into the company's vestibule, where they were greeted by an attractive elderly woman with long silver hair maybe in her early sixties. "Good afternoon, gentlemen, and welcome to REA Express. How can I help you?" She did not initially offer her name to the two gentleman.

"I'm Detective Nardi and this is Detective Simmons, NYPD," Nardi began.

"Is there a problem, detectives?"

"You are--?" Joe politely asked the elderly lady.

"Oh for heaven's sake, I'm so sorry, detectives. My name is Helen, Mrs. Helen Carson. I work the front desk and the phones," she said, embarrassed. "Who are you here to see?" Helen asked.

"We need to speak to whomever is in charge of operations around here," Nardi replied.

"You want to talk with Harry Carson. He's my son. He's a good boy, ya know. Hard- working," she added as if that point were relevant or necessary. "He gave me the job here and I love it. Let me get him for you boys. Have a seat in there." Helen Carson pointed to a small office space just off the vestibule to the right. "And help yourselves to the coffee. I just made it. I'm baking cookies but they're not ready yet. They should be done in a few minutes."

"They smell wonderful," Joe said as the two detectives strode toward the small office.

Helen sat back behind the desk that consumed most of the vestibule, picked up the phone, and began to speak to someone on the other end. Nardi noticed the hand gestures she was making in response to the words being sent to her right ear. She appeared to be frustrated but stood her ground. Helen hung the phone up with a little more conviction than was probably necessary. She rose from her seat and walked slowly toward the office where the two detectives sat enjoying a delicious cup of freshly brewed coffee, French roast, Nardi thought. "Harry will see you now, gentlemen."

"Did that take some convincing on your part, Mrs. Carson?"

"Sometimes that boy forgets I'm his mother, ya know? I was just reminding him of that. Right this way," Helen said with a smile.

Helen Carson gingerly escorted the two NYPD detectives down the hall and through a door which led to the back warehouse. "This place is bigger than it looks from the outside," Nardi said.

"Wow," Joe added. Helen stopped at a set of steel stairs off to the left and out of the way of the hustle and bustle of the main warehouse.

"Gentleman, you'll have to go up to the top of the stairs. Harry's office is the second door on the right," Helen said. "I just can't make it up these stairs again today, ya know, with the arthritis and everything." Helen pointed to both of her knees.

"We understand, Mrs. Carson, and thank you for your help," Nardi said.

"And the coffee too," Joe concluded.

Joe and Nardi ascended the staircase and knocked on the second door on the right side of the hallway. "Come in," Harry said loudly as he too approached the door from the opposite side. Nardi reached for the handle and let himself in, followed by Joe. "How can I help you gentleman?" Harry said as he stood up tall behind his desk. Nardi and Joe were already presenting their credentials before Harry finished his question.

"I'm Detective Nardi and this is Detective Simmons," Nardi said bluntly. "Do you mind if we ask you some questions?"

"Please take a seat, gentleman," Harry said. Joe sat in the old wooden and half-broken office chair directly in front of Harry. Nardi sat just off Joe's right.

Nardi pulled out his pack of Marlboro from the worn plaid sport coat. "Do you mind if I have a smoke?"

"No, go right ahead, make yourself comfortable. Here's an ashtray." Harry slid a square green glass ashtray across the desk into Nardi's left hand. Harry joined him for a smoke while Joe just fanned the toxic cloud from his face. Joe stood abruptly from the chair, obviously annoyed at the smokers. He made his way toward the open window on the far side to catch a fresh breath, then lifted the window a few inches higher to let the cloud of cigarette smoke out.

"Have you had any recent trouble with any employee that you are aware of, Mr. Carson? You know, the kind that are always into some sort of crap?," Joe began. "Is there anyone who, off the top of your head, comes off as a bit of an asshole?"

"No, not really," Harry responded. "My drivers all check out and they have plenty of rules to follow around here. What's all this about?"

"Well, we got word that a valuable package was possibly stolen from the warehouse a few days ago," Joe said from across the room.

"The merchandise went missing somewhere in Brooklyn or Queens and as we understand, it hasn't been found or returned yet," Nardi interjected. Joe lifted the window up higher because the two assholes were choking him out.

"That's true," Harry responded. "There was a package that was supposed to be delivered to a jewelry store in Brooklyn and it's just gone. We have an internal investigation going on right now. All we know so far is that the package contained six Rolex watches and that it was insured for a lot of money. The insurance company is sending a claims adjuster down for an investigation as well. We have tight procedures here at REA, and nothing like this has ever happened before."

"What has your investigation turned up so far?" Joe asked.

"I personally went over every delivery manifest from that day and I can't find anything," Harry added. "The package was on the manifest of one of our drivers. As far as I can tell, the package was on his pallet ready to be loaded on his truck and just like that, poof, it was gone." Harry gestured with his hands as if he were a magician.

"What was that driver's name? I might have missed that point," Joe said, still hovering around the opened window.

"His name is Dennis Adams, but I don't think he had anything to do with that package going missing," Harry said. "He's a good family man with a good heart, ya know. But we are going to have to do something soon. Everyone knows about the missing package and if I don't fire someone for this, it will be anarchy here."

"NYPD has an active investigation underway right now," Nardi said. "We'll look into Dennis Adams. We've uncovered only circumstantial evidence right now, and need more time to look into some other significant matters."

Harry appeared perplexed at the whole situation. He did not fully understand the detectives' intentions. They were not offering up any information on who they were looking at for the robbery. But Detective Nardi made it seem as if they knew Dennis Adams had nothing to do with it. If the cops were saying that it wasn't Dennis, then they must have someone else in mind, Harry thought to himself.

Joe glanced at Nardi with a puzzled look on his face, not fully understanding where he was going with those odd statements. Why had he not said that we suspect Bobby Maseano of the robbery? Why did he not tell Harry that the contents of the package had been identified by Bobby's wife, Ann? But Joe was seasoned enough and sharp enough to roll with Nardi's story.

"Harry, I want you to give me some time on this issue," Nardi said. "There may be more here than meets the eye. I would like you to continue your internal investigation. If any new information comes to the surface, I want you to call me." Nardi slid a NYPD business card across the desk at Harry and stopped it in front of him. "Don't fire anyone just yet. Make sure everyone knows how aggressively you are investigating this matter," Nardi added. "Can you do that for me, Harry?"

"Sure," Harry replied. Harry didn't fully understand what the detectives were asking of him but was reluctant to inquire any further. The detectives thanked Harry for his time and understanding. Harry rose again from behind his desk and walked around to the front side. He extended his hand to shake hands with each detective: Joe first, then Nardi. Joe had a much tighter grip. Harry respected the firmness of the handshake. Detective Nardi only offered a weak, somewhat submissive handshake. Harry thought it was odd, considering his size and weight. Nardi brought his left hand up to Harry's right shoulder, and Harry assured Nardi that he would cooperate with the police investigation.

As the two NYPD detectives began to exit Harry's office, Nardi turned back to Harry and said, "I almost forgot. I'll need copies of all the personnel files before we leave." It came across to Harry as more of a demand then a request. Nardi did not wait for a reply. He turned away from Harry and headed for the stairs. "We'll wait downstairs with your mother. Her cookies must be done by now."

Chapter 16

Bobby Maseano was Superman. He was now associated with organized crime, even if it was just a glancing association. Bobby Maseano would never truly be on the inside of any real organized crime activity. Carmine knew from the minute he laid eyes on Bobby that he was a nervous wreck and that he could never be anything more than a petty thief. Carmine thought that if he had pressed him a little harder, he would have peed his pants right there in the back room. Carmine didn't want any more pee on the floor of the back room. Bobby was a small-time thief, and a punk thief at that. And that's all he was to Carmine.

Bobby bathed in the sensation of stepping on the other side of the tracks, and he felt every bit the criminal. He had taken the bull by the horns, wrestled with the alligators, and slain the dragon, metaphorically speaking, of course. He marveled at himself and how big his balls were, how he had mustered up the courage to approach Carmine Mancini, Brooklyn's mafia kingpin. Bobby admittedly had been extremely uncomfortable in that situation. Uncomfortable doesn't even come close to the sensation he had been experiencing. Like Russian roulette with one bullet chambered but with three mandatory pulls of the trigger. He truly did not expect to come out so high on top of the world. But he did.

Bobby thought that the deal he made with Carmine Mancini had the potential to change his life. Bobby was on the map now, or so he thought. Carmine would be looking for more valuable products, and Bobby was willing to acquire them. He had four thousand dollars in his pocket, but it felt like a million. Bobby had experienced the fiercest adrenalin rush ever. This was his bottom of the ninth, three balls, two strikes, bases loaded, and here comes the pitch, Boom! And the ball was on its way, on its way, and it was gone. The Yankees had just won another World Series Championship and the stadium was ing. There was pandemonium everywhere. The fans rushed the field, seats were being ripped from the concrete, and there goes the foul pole crashing down to the field. If you're a Yankee fan you can appreciate this adrenaline rush. It happened almost every October. That's how Bobby felt.

The cherry on top of the cake was the rampaging sex he had had with Luisa, heightened by single malt and cocaine. Bobby had never gotten mixed up with the hard drugs until now. He had smoked pot once in a while with the boys in the courtyard next to Cobblestones. The bar was pot-infested. Even if he didn't smoke, he would have a serious contact-high from the smoke just outside the side door. The high from cocaine was extraordinary, and he never wanted it to stop. Adrenaline, cocaine and sex was a brew that was unbeatable. *This is the stuff superheroes are made of,* Bobby gloated to himself. He was unstoppable for the first time in his life, truly Superman in his own mind. In that short period of time he had incredible clarity. He vividly saw his life, his early ambitions, all the highs and lows. It saddened him to realize that the lows greatly outnumbered the highs. He became emotional and fought back his tears. But he was sure Superman didn't cry.

Bobby's life as a young boy was rather unremarkable. He had gone through school with very few triumphs or failures. His grades at Seth

Low Junior High School and at Lafayette High School were run-of-the-mill at best. He didn't score any A's, but didn't receive any F's either. Initially, he had been extremely social, playing in a rock band after school and on weekends. Bobby played the bass guitar but didn't play it well. He was good enough to make the band, mostly because no one else had tried out for the bass. The band played gigs, but only in each other's garages and at an occasional party. They never played at Bobby's house, though. Mary Maseano, his mother, would not have it. Mary was not a sweet, caring, or loving woman; her glares were venomous. She valued her own social life more than she valued raising Bobby and his two sisters. Bobby became the *de facto* babysitter for the girls when Mary was off in Coney Island, playing cards and getting fired up. Bobby hated Mary for leaving them alone; it totally pissed him off, and he made sure Mary knew about it. He knew this was an enormous responsibility for a kid, but he had no choice. He loved and cared for his younger sisters. Mary, however, never took any of the kids with her; that would spoil all her fun.

Bobby wanted to play a better bass guitar, but Mary would have nothing to do with it. She wouldn't even allow a guitar in the house. She wouldn't allow him to take lessons, not even in school, where they were free. This became another source of animosity between Bobby and his mother. Most if not all of the arguments became superheated, and they always ended with Bobby conceding feat. Mary did support his love of baseball, however. She encouraged him to play ball every chance he could. Baseball got him out of the house for hours, and Mary liked that. Bobby had the potential to be an exceptional ballplayer. He had all the tools, as they say in the game. He could hit, throw, run, and field with the best of the kids in the neighborhood. Brooklyn was renowned for breeding excellent baseball players. Many of the neighborhood kids went to college on a free ride because of their baseball skills. Some even made it to the bigs. Bobby did not.

FIRST VICTIM

While at Lafayette High School, Bobby was approached many times by the head coach of the team as a freshmen to letter in baseball. He was almost guaranteed a starting position without even trying out. Coach Thompson was from the neighborhood and had firsthand knowledge of Bobby's skills. Thompson often watched the pick-up sandlot games in Shady Park, where during one game Bobby hit a ball clear out of the park and over the elevated B train platform. Coach Thompson watched the entire game and made notes on Bobby for later reference. That one game could have made Bobby a standout freshman baseball player for his high school. Bobby refused and refused and refused some more. Coach Thompson pulled out all the stops with Bobby. He tried everything short of bribing him to play ball, but Bobby could not be convinced to play ball for Lafayette. No one can be certain whether playing organized baseball would have changed the course of his life, but the speculation was that he had a surplus of stored-up energy that could have been put to good use on the ball field. High school baseball had changed the lives of many boys from the neighborhood, saving them from the streets and keeping them from becoming punks who were never up to any good. The team had a mandatory curfew because of the early morning practices. Grades had to be maintained to at least a C average, and if there was any trouble with the law, you were cut from the team immediately. No questions asked.

Bobby was not comfortable with the whole concept of playing on a team. He didn't want to be bothered with the practices, staying after school to run wind sprints, or doing calisthenics until he puked. Mostly, he steered away from organized sports because his mother wanted him to play. Anything was fair game if it meant he could spite that bitch. It might have been a different story if she had supported him in any other area of his life besides baseball. She drove him to despise the very idea of playing the game he loved so much. Bobby's agenda was to agitate his mother's ass as much as she agitated his. He and his mother got into some good old-fashioned Brooklyn brawls over the years. Most of the blowouts had something to do with the noise level in the house. The Beatles, The Beach Boys, Bob Dylan, The Who, The Doors, Elvis, and The Stones ripped through Mary's ear canals like a hot knife through butter. Mary had a violent streak in her and, when he ignored her cries for quiet, she often threw objects at Bobby; anything that crazy bitch was close to, like a glass vase, a knife, or an ashtray. She rarely had the accuracy in her pitch to hit him, but the fact that she was crazy enough to even try was enough for Bobby. He had imagined choking the life out of her many times.

Bobby would wait for her to drift into a deep slumber. When he was sure she was fast asleep he crept from his bed, barefoot, so as to not to make a sound. He stepped gingerly, avoiding the floorboards he knew to be squeaky. He had memorized each board's individual squeak. He grabbed the handle of her bedroom door and twisted it slowly to the right while pushing the door open, close to his body, to minimize the sound of the latch releasing from within the strike plate. He already had the hall light turned off, and he was sure to maintain the darkness in her room, even after he glided the bedroom door open. He stood there in the doorway for a few seconds to make sure she did not rustle. Bobby would slide along the wall until he was parallel to her torso. Then he would slither to her side and smash her head with his Louisville Slugger. Cause of death, solid ash to the cranium. "How's that for a home run swing?" he would ask her once the blood and brains began to flow from her head. Practice made perfect. She'd be dead just like that. Simple. Or maybe he would suffocate her with her own pillow and slow the whole process down a bit. Bobby could have choked her from behind with the moves he had learned from watching Bruno Sammartino wrestle. Bobby was plagued by these thoughts for much of his adolescent and young adult life, but he never had the balls to execute any of them. But he always wished he did.

Bobby did record these dark and deadly thoughts in a daily journal, which he regarded as his early therapy. The actual journal was a marbled black and white notebook, dog-eared and worn. The language that filled the pages of the journal started off with lucid thoughts and sentences. He vividly described everything Mary had been guilty of in his mind. He portrayed her courtroom trial as long and arduous. Bobby played the role of attorney, bailiff, judge, and jury in the increasingly rambling lines. He had an entry dated June 20th, in which the year was intentionally left out. No reason for the year to not be there. It just wasn't.

As the entry reads, "Came home from school today, 3:15 p.m., Mary left her bottle on the kitchen counter. It's half empty. I think it was full a few days ago. She must be messed up. Not worried about her kids. Fucking bitch is probably with Nancy, the other fucking whore. At least this time she's smart enough to fuck her bastard men in someone else's house." Written across this page in red ink, "Guilty, punishable by death."

Bobby's father had passed away a few years back, and Mary seemed to slip off the deep end when he passed. She had never been stable by any means, but when Nicola was hit by a car in downtown Brooklyn and didn't make it out of emergency surgery at Doctors' Hospital, she went certifiably insane. The ambulance was delayed arriving at the scène of the accident, because of roadway construction on DeKalb Avenue. Nicola was bleeding out on the street when the ambulance arrived. There were people trying to help him, but the bleeding was very severe. Nicola had open compound fractures to both lower legs and severe head lacerations. His left leg was severed almost completely off. Nicola was in surgery at Doctor's Hospital for six hours before the surgeon pronounced him dead. Bobby tried for days after the wake and funeral to console his mother, but Mary could not be consoled in any way. And he needed consoling, also. Bobby thought there was nothing in her heart except hatred for him and love for her bottle. Ever since that day, she had been a heavy drinker. Bobby was sure she was trying to kill herself, and he did not try to intervene in that quest. It could not come quick enough for Bobby. Free at last, free at last, thank God Almighty, he'd be free at last.

Mary passed away from a drug and alcohol overdose in November of the following year, eighteen months after Nicola had passed as a result of that fatal accident. Bobby remained the sole caretaker for his younger sisters. Screwed again by his mother! He did all he could for the girls, at least until they were old enough to fend for themselves around the house. Bobby allowed the girls to grow up pretty much as they saw fit. He never had any control over the girls or their actions. Bobby assumed legal guardianship shortly after his mother's death, which was the only thing that kept them from going into state custody. He hated every minute of those years, and he was not afraid to let the girls know about his contempt for them and their tion. Bobby expressed his hatred for Mary in his marbled notebook, but unfortunately it didn't stop with her.

Chapter 17

The 62nd Precinct is unusually quiet tonight, Nardi thought to himself as he studied the personnel files of the employees at REA Express Trucking from the comfort of his worn office chair. Nardi was going through the motions of examining every employee file from REA. He knew in his mind that there was really no reason to be so diligent, but he went through the motions anyway. Detective Nardi knew what was going on, and he knew the outcome would not be favorable for Ann and Leonard. Giovanni Nardi and Joe Simmons were the only two detectives left in the precinct headquarters at such a late hour. It was rapidly approaching midnight, and the two detectives had been at it since 6:30 a.m. Joe knew Nardi was dragging his ass on this investigation, and he was starting to get annoyed with him. "This case should have been done and turned over to the district attorney already," Joe complained. "We should have picked Bobby Maseano up weeks ago."

"There's something else going on here Joe, I'm just not one-hundred percent sure yet. Just call it an experienced detective's intuition," Nardi replied.

"Why don't you try and explain what the hell you're talking about?" Joe demanded.

"OK, let's go over it again," Nardi began. "We like Bobby for the six missing Rolex watches.

"Right?" Joe played along, waiting for the big problem to surface.

"The original package was missing from REA Express Trucking and that's where Bobby works as a delivery driver. We have Ann, who witnessed a package arrive at their apartment, and she says it was Bobby's handwriting on the package," Nardi said.

"So far I'm with you."

"Ann has identified the contents of the package and stated that there were six Rolex watches in Bobby's men's chest, which were put there by Bobby," Nardi continued.

"It's the same story we have been going over for weeks now. So, is there something else bothering you other than the fact that Bobby is related to you in a way?" Joe asked.

"Yes, Joe there is," Nardi concluded. "I just don't know what it is just yet. I have a feeling this whole thing is a lot worse than it appears."

Nardi had been in the detectives' break room earlier that day, somewhere around 11:30 a.m., when he was summoned from across the area by Detective Helen Pastore. She was adding cream and sugar to her coffee, trying to soften the shock of the horrible brew. Detective Pastore was a veteran officer and was now in the sex crimes unit. In addition, she had become the 62nd's sketch artist. She took her role in the NYPD very seriously and was all business. There was little small talk with Helen. If she had something to say, it was usually about a troubling case or something else related to work.

Helen informed the other detectives, beginning with Detective Nardi, that there had been a series of rapes throughout Brooklyn and Queens. The official composite would be released first thing in the morning, at roll call. "There are some differences among the cases, but there are a lot of similarities," she made a point of stating. She had interviewed and questioned four victims, two in Brooklyn and two in Queens. "We have a lot of confidence that these rapes were committed by the same man. The women were all attacked in their homes by someone posing as a deliveryman. The perp apparently states that there is a large package to be delivered and that he has to measure the doorway to see if the package will fit through or if it has to be taken out of the box to get it in. When the unsuspecting women open the door to let him do the measurement, he viciously attacks and rapes them. The man dresses in delivery attire, and he varies the colors and names of the company. In most cases, the girls were not expecting a package but opened the door anyway. The perp stays engaged in the attack for quite some time before vanishing out the same door he entered. All four victims so far have received medical attention. I have met with all four, and they were all shaken to the core," Helen added. "Details will be available shortly."

Roll call began promptly at 6:45 a.m. the following morning, as it had every day for the past three years. Lieutenant Jonathan Davis, a twenty-year veteran of the NYPD, usually conducted the morning briefing at roll call. Davis had a commanding presence and dominated over the fifty or so officers, demanding their attention. It didn't take much time for everyone to quiet down and give their full attention to the front of the room Usually there was the rundown of the latest events in the neighborhood. There was usually mention of the occurrences from within the precinct overnight. Roll call proceeded with a rapid succession of officers' names to ascertain their presence or absence.

Lieutenant Davis scanned the room for proper attire, and sometimes there would be a spot weapons check. Once he was satisfied that his officers were presentable enough to represent the
great city of New York, he would elaborate on specific assignments. Lieutenant Davis was in his element at the podium. He passed out knowledge that kept his men alive on the uncertain streets. But Lieutenant Davis began roll call in a highly unusual manner that morning.

He cut his sermon short, which was never a good thing. The officers became restless as Lieutenant Davis backed away from the podium and turned it over to the approaching detective, Helen Pastore.

Detective Helen Pastore entered the room and faced the nearly fifty NYPD officers and detectives in attendance. By the time she arrived at the podium, the officers were slightly unnerved. It didn't take much to unnerve a group of NYPD police officers in those days. A few homicides, a few robberies, or a few rapes, and they were all catapulted to high-alert status. Detective Pastore put an immediate stop to the restlessness as she promptly began speaking in an unusually bold manner. She introduced herself as a courtesy for those who didn't know her personally. "Good morning Officers," she began. "For those of you who don't know me, my name is Detective Helen Pastore, and for those of you that do know me personally, I am truly sorry." Most of the police officers in the room let out a chuckle and the tension eased. She had succeeded in breaking the ice with the attending officers and now had their complete attention. Most of the officers knew her, at least by name, and some of them knew of her mystique.

Most were especially aware of her ability to develop highly accurate composite drawings from a victim's sparse and sometimes-scattered description. She had a way of extracting the details which were normally overlooked by other sketch artists in the city. Detective Pastore was aware of the tricks the mind often played on a victim, although she was not a trained psychologist. She had been able to develop her abilities over many years and many cases. There was an element of psychology associated with sketching composite drawings for the NYPD; however, there was no formal recognition for this ability. Some of the details may inadvertently be erased from the memory while other details were amplified. How she was able to translate this scattered information into a strong likeness of a suspect was baffling to most.

Detective Pastore is an expert at building a rapport with victims, especially females. She knew how to get inside the victim's head and in effect relax them with her soft, calming voice, tender eyes, and caring soul. Her most important attribute probably was her ability to artisti-cally express in fine detail on paper, when the victim was only recalling very general characteristics. Detective Pastore was highly decorated and awarded for her abilities with a pad and pencil. Her craft had earned the NYPD nearly twenty arrests and convictions in recent years, a record which surpasses that of other sketch artists by a landslide.

Detective Pastore did not make it a habit of socializing with the of-ficers. Not because she was a detective and they were only uniformed police officers, but she just wasn't much into socializing with any-one. She did socialize with Detective Nardi, however. Her desire to isolate herself could be because of all the probing questions from eve-ryone who wanted insight into her abilities, but frankly she just couldn't explain it. Her life had become the NYPD and she loved that fact, but she also resented it in a way. It's was a twenty-four-hour-a-day job, and the pay was poor. The job didn't spare any time for rela-tionships, family or friends. There were times when she hadn't seen her apartment in three or four days straight. She always appreciated her neighbors, whom she could call on to help her out with Maggie, her four-year-old Doberman. Detective Pastore was an extremely dedicated police officer, and she was paying the price for that dedication by for-feiting every meaningful human relationship in her life. The situation made her a little bitter, but she would never give up her craft. And at least Maggie always forgave her for whatever length of time she would need to be away.

The overwhelming majority of the officers at roll call this morning were male and white. Joe Simmons was one of only about ten black officers in the room, and there were five other female officers besides Helen. She wondered to herself why she had performed that calcula-tion in the first place. She wasn't sure, but she did. The uniformed of-ficers sat directly in front of the podium in chairs with built-in writing desks. The detectives who attended sat off to the side on top of old wood desks or on the large window sills. Helen Pastore was not hard to look at, but she commanded respect nonetheless. Some of the guys loved the fact that she had a hard exterior and was basically unapproachable. The respect the men had for her clearly was based on her strong professional merits. Female police officers with good looks very often were harassed by the men in the department. This was not the case with Detective Helen Pastore. She had a hand in more collars than any other officer in the 62nd, and everyone knew it.

Helen quickly moved on to her pressing business. "Ladies and gentleman," she began "over the past few weeks there have been several attacks on young women in Brooklyn and Queens. The victims range in age from twenty-five to thirty-five. All are of slim build with an athletic appearance. There does not appear to be a connection to height, hair color, breast size or, occupation. What we know so far is that the assailant poses as a deliveryman. When he makes contact with the female, he says he needs to measure the door to make sure that a large box will fit through the opening. The victims I have spoken with so far have said they granted entry for the measurement even though they were not expecting a delivery. All of the attacks have been violent and sexual in nature. Three of the four women we've questioned gave statements and a description of the assailant. Another victim is in Queens Hospital Center on 164th in Jamaica. So far, she has refused to cooperate with police," she added. "We'll continue our efforts to try to have her cooperate with the investigation. We need her statement and description. I'm not confident that she will come around, however; at this point she is simply too distraught to speak with us and has refused every attempt I've made to talk to her in the hospital. We suspect that the assailant is a white male with average looks, in his late twenties to early thirties. He stands between five-foot-nine and five-foot-eleven. He has brown wavy hair, short on the sides and longer on top-- possibly a military cut. There has been nothing to suggest, however, that he has a military background. He is of a medium build, and he may be wearing a mustache, beard, and/or a wig. I've created a composite sketch from the descriptions of the three cooperating victims, which will be posted throughout the city's precincts on all bulletin

142

boards. There will be copies of the sketch on the table in the back and up here at the podium. Please take one on the way out and keep your eyes open for anyone resembling this sketch. All precincts in Brooklyn and Queens have been notified and all are on alert. The media will be notified, and hopefully the story will get out for tonight's evening news and tomorrow's early-edition paper. We are calling him "The Tape Measure Rapist," she concluded.

Detective Giovanni Nardi rose from his perch on the desk just to the right of the podium. He reached for a copy of the sketch and proceeded in somewhat of a hurry out of roll call and up the one flight of weathered oak stairs to the detective's unit, then navigated his way to his cubicle. He made it a point to be in such a hurry so that no one would have the chance to talk with him on the way out. When he sat at his desk he began a systematic dissection of the composite drawing. It was drawn in pencil, without any added color. Detective Nardi spent more time examining this composite than he had spent with any other composite in his entire career. He had developed strong opinions of the sketch, noting that the face was slightly narrow, the cheekbones were a little too high, the hair was too long on the top, and the eyebrows were too wide. Detective Nardi cleaned up the sketch in his mind's eye, anxiety growing within him. Nardi's eye clearly saw Robert Maseano. He reached for his desk phone with his right hand, knocking over a half-filled cup of police station brew, and began to dial. "Leonard," Nardi exclaimed, "We have to talk. I'm on my way over. I should be there in twenty." Nardi slammed the phone back to the cradle and bolted from the station like it was on fire.

Chapter 18

Leonard's nerves began to sizzle at the sound of Nardi's voice. He didn't sound too happy to be making the call, Leonard ed. Leonard returned from the kitchen after he hung the phone back on the wall. He sat down next to Ann, who had more or less moved into the four-room apartment in order to get away from her husband and to make sure he did not return and confront her in their apartment. Just by Leonard's posture, Ann sensed his tension rise dramatically. On edge and clearly agitated, he sat down with Ann and explained to her that Nardi was on his way over with some news and that it was probably bad.

"What did he say, Dad?" Ann questioned.

"It's not what he said, but how he said it that's bothering me. He did not elaborate, but I got a sick feeling in my stomach when he called," Leonard replied.

Teresa, trying to be the voice of reason said, "Don't worry until there is something to worry about. Right now you and the baby are as safe as you've been in a long while." Leonard followed up with a consoling stroke of the back of Ann's head and a gentle caress of his grandson's face.

The doorbell rang almost exactly twenty minutes after Nardi had called. Not taking any chances, Leonard said, "I'll go out front and make sure it's Nardi." The alternative would be to buzz the door and let whoever was there into the building, because Leonard could not clearly see the front door of the building from his apartment. As he left the apartment and strode down the hall toward the front door, he was relieved to see that it was in fact his cousin. Leonard opened the wood-and-frosted-glass door to let him in. There was the customary kiss on each cheek, the normal greeting for Italian men. Leonard invited him in, and his cousin followed as he turned to walk back to the apart-ment. Teresa was nervously waiting in the doorway. Nardi kissed Te-resa on the cheek as she stepped back to clear the entryway. Ann re-mained in the living room, seemingly melting into the plastic-covered couch. She did not move a muscle until Nardi entered behind Teresa. Tears began to form and flow down from her already-bloodshot eyes, followed by uncontrolled sobbing at the sight of Nardi, who sat down next to her. He wrapped his right arm around her and coached her on how to compose herself. Ann struggled with the request for about an-other ten minutes. Tears were still flowing down her face, but she was not sobbing any longer.

Nardi removed his arm from around Ann's shoulder, sensing that she was composed enough for him to begin. He removed the suit jacket he had been wearing, rolled up his sleeves, and loosened his tie. Although he was anxious himself, he wanted to try to portray himself as relaxed and at ease. Ann, Leonard, and Teresa were in the modest living room and all were paying close attention and anticipating his initial words. "Do you know where Bobby is now?" Nardi posed it as a gen-eral question which anyone in the room was permitted to answer.

"I haven't seen Bobby in days. He hasn't been home, at least not that I know of. The baby and I have been staying here with my mom and dad. I've only gone back to the apartment once with my father to pick up some things for the baby and me," Ann added. "Gracie, my upstairs neighbor, has been on the lookout for Bobby, but hasn't seen or heard him at all. The one thing I know for sure is that he will not come here to my parents' house. I'm thinking of taking the baby and heading upstate to my uncle's country house," Ann said.

"I think that's a good idea," Nardi replied. "You are going to want to get as far away from Bobby as you can."

"Why? What did you find out?" Leonard questioned.

The quiet in the room was deafening at that moment. Ann's face was drained of blood and she appeared pale and cold. Leonard moved in and sat as close as he could to show support for the upcoming news. Everyone braced and readied themselves. "Well, I'm pretty sure we got Bobby on the burglary charge," Nardi began. "My partner and I paid a visit to REA Express Trucking about a week ago. We met with the owner and discussed the missing package. He was forthcoming with the details and gave us copies of all the employees' files. That part of it is done. I still don't know where he got rid of the watches or who had the money to buy them. Leonard, do you have any idea where he would go to try and pawn those watches?"

"If it were me trying to fence stolen jewelry, I would try to contact someone who doesn't mind playing with dirty stuff," Leonard said. "I would start on 18th Avenue, in one of the cafes. Those guys have the money and everyone knows they deal in dirt. Even Bobby knows that."

"That's good," Nardi said. "We're building a case against a few of those pricks, and if we could pin fencing stolen jewelry on any one of them, that would be good. Real good. "It's just a matter of time before those guys hang themselves. They all make mistakes eventually."

"There have been more developments in connection to Bobby," Nardi cautiously continued. Teresa had gone to the kitchen to start a pot of espresso, when Nardi told Ann and Leonard about the recent assaults on women in Brooklyn and Queens. "The attacks have been relatively close together, averaging one attack every two or three days. We know

146

of four victims so far, but there could be more." The perplexed look on Ann's face told Nardi that she was not absorbing his words. That, or what he had been saying just hadn't registered yet.

"Are you saying that Bobby has been attacking women?" Ann asked.

"Yes, Ann, I believe that Bobby has been attacking defenseless women in various areas of Brooklyn and Queens." Ann's immediate thoughts defined an attack as an overpowering man, Bobby, roaming the streets of Brooklyn and Queens robbing weak and unsuspecting women. Maybe senior citizens. She couldn't imagine any other scenario. She was mortified at the idea that her husband was stealing from women. Ann had been robbed herself recently, and she related to how violated the women must have felt at that moment and for a long while after the incident.

Ann had been walking home from 81st Street where she was visiting her longtime friend Marilyn. They had spent the late afternoon and early evening together at Marilyn's house. Marilyn had a son who was close in age to her own son, and having little ones at the same time drove the two even closer than they had already been. They compared notes on breastfeeding, diaper changes, cereal feedings, and sleep cycles. On that day, as Ann turned the corner from 81st Street onto 24th Avenue, a young punk--maybe thirteen or fourteen--ran up from behind her and took her pocketbook, which was resting on the top of the baby carriage she was pushing. The boy just snatched it and ran down 24th Avenue, turning right up 82nd Street. There was nothing she could do. Her purse was gone. Just like that.

Ann did not grasp the magnitude of what Nardi was saying to her there in her parents' living room. She was stuck on the robbery concept and was not wavering from it. "Ann, this is much more complex than robbery," Nardi said abruptly. "There is so much more going on here in these attacks than you know. These attacks were not robbery-based," he added. "The victims have been brutally raped and sexually assaulted in their own homes. It appears that Bobby has been posing as a deliveryman, attempting to deliver a large package. When the female opens the door, he gains access and he attacks."

"Why, why do you think it's Bobby?" Ann asked, collapsing in disbelief. Ann's voice was shaky, her hands and feet moving spastically.

"We have interviewed three of the four victims and Detective Helen Pasture has come up with a composite drawing. Ann, it's not an exact match, but the likeness is remarkable and the more you look at the copy, the more it looks like Bobby," Nardi said.

"Do you have a copy we can see?" Leonard asked. Leonard held Ann's hand as Nardi removed a folded-up copy of the composite from his back pants pocket. Leonard took the paper, from Nardi, unfolded it, and glared at the image. Ann refused to turn her head toward the paper in a clear statement of defiance. Leonard studied the composite, citing the flaws at first before quickly citing the accuracy of at least some of the sketch's components. His stomach dropped to the floor in horror at the realization that Bobby Maseano could be a serial rapist. Ann summoned the courage to glance at the copy and in an instant recognized the features that were similar, if not identical, to Bobby's. The flood of conflicting emotions rushed through her like a tidal wave assaulting the shoreline. Ann knew in that instant that her marriage to Bobby was over. She knew that her little boy would never see his father again. She knew her sentence immediately--and it was life. Life without a husband. Life, as an inexperienced mother, forced into raising her son alone. Life, facing the truth that she had married a path. Life, trying to understand and make sense of what was incomprehensible to her in that moment. Ann received a life sentence long before Bobby Maseano would even be arrested.

Leonard and Teresa collected themselves for Ann's sake. The fury on Teresa's face was undeniable. "It will be all right, baby," Leonard uttered through his tears. "We will figure this out together, I promise."

"Leonard, take her keys and go with Nardi to her house and get some more things for Ann and the baby," Teresa demanded. "They're never going back there." There was no point in debating this with Teresa. If she said they were not going back to the apartment, then they were not going back to the apartment. "They are going to need the more essentials like clothes, diapers, baby food, stuff from the bathroom, and anything else you think they will need for two weeks. Whatever you don't get we will have to buy when we get to New Paltz," Teresa said. She instantly made a phone call to her brother Joey, who had the keys to the family cabin in upstate New York. The arrangements were made for the cabin to be available to Ann for as long as she needed it. Joey did not have any plans to be there right then, but he could be if he was needed in this emergency situation. Teresa declined Joey's offer to go there if needed, because she was planning for all four of them to be going up to the cabin in the morning, and the cabin was not that big.

New Paltz was the sleepy town where the country house was located. Access to the cabin's entry road was well-hidden, just off route 32. The cabin had three tiny bedrooms, a living area, kitchen, and bathroom. It was not the Hilton by any stretch of the imagination, but it would serve well as a safe house. The New Paltz home was in a rural area, nestled on ten acres of forested land, of which only about two acres had been cleared. The family had owned this property since the early 1900s. It had been a favorite weekend getaway destination for years, especially for the generations of kids in the family as they were growing up. Ann was very familiar and comfortable with the cabin and the land. She had spent many weekends and school vacations in the country while she was growing up. Ann was also well aware of the arsenal of weapons her Uncle Joey kept locked up in the cabin. Ann trusted the fact that Leonard still knew how to shoot a high- powered weapon. Leonard had served over four years in the United States Army during World War II, stationed in Germany for some of those years. He had seen his share of front-line combat. He was a marksman back then but hadn't shot a weapon with any intent since the end of the war. He wondered if he could shoot if he had to. He wasn't sure he would be able to do what had been unimaginable to him since May of 1945.

Leonard and Nardi agreed that they would go to Ann's apartment and collect some necessary items so she wouldn't have to go back there herself. They collected two large blue suitcases from Teresa's bedroom closet and headed off to the apartment. Nardi was not trying to be inconspicuous as he raced down 83rd Street and screeched to a stop directly in front of the apartment building. The Crown Vic was not disguisable in any way, so he figured they would be better off announcing their presence instead of trying to conceal it. The cherry light Nardi had slapped onto the roof was highly effective in attracting the attention of the neighbors. The screaming siren was equally effective. Neighbors materialized on their front porches, trying to gather intelligence and formulate a reason for the unmarked police car to have been pulled up on an otherwise-somber block.

Nardi left the car running, with lights flashing in front of the apartment as they entered the front door, carrying the two suitcases they had pulled from the trunk. Nardi had his pistol ready at his side. Leonard entered the baby's room first and collected all the clothes from the drawers. He grabbed everything that looked important from the top of the dresser: diapers, formula, hats, socks, and the baby's teddy bear. Ann's stuff was jammed into the other suitcase. By the time they were finished collecting what they needed from the apartment, it looked like it had been professionally ransacked. They did not touch Bobby's men's chest. Drawers were left open, unneeded clothes strewn around, and decorative items fell to the floor as if they were being discarded. Nardi and Leonard wanted to make sure that if Bobby was stupid enough to come back there, he would know that the NYPD was after him and that he would most likely never see his family again. On the way out, with two overstuffed and bulging suitcases, Nardi stopped, reached into his jacket pocket, pulled out his NYPD business card, and on the back wrote Bobby a message which said, "Bobby, run when you're on this side of the tracks." Leonard asked Nardi what he had written on the back of the card. "It was just a powerful quote from someone I know," he responded.

"Are you gonna tell me what you wrote?"

Nardi did not answer his cousin's probing question. He responded, "Some things are better left unsaid. Trust me on this one Leonard, you'll just have to trust me."

Chapter 19

Bobby had no intention of returning to his apartment or to his family. The Gateway Inn in Sheepshead Bay, Brooklyn provided the substandard living conditions he craved. They had cheap rooms available, and the Gateway Inn would be the last place anybody would ever look for him. This was a place that normal, decent people never saw anymore. For the most part, even the police ignored the drug use and prostitution that went on there. Everyone knew it was there, but most ignored its presence. It was a place that should have been condemned by the New York City Department of Health, and it probably will be when they get around to it. Not only was the Gateway an eyesore for the residents of Sheepshead Bay, with its corroding roof, peeling paint, broken windows, and awful stench, but it had become a squatting place for the discards of society. They were now the only clientele of the Gateway Inn. No one with any semblance of decency would be seen there. It would be the perfect place for Bobby to hide in plain sight.

Hippie free-love-type drug users had been renting these rooms for a couple of hours at a time, sometimes for a couple of days. The rooms became the runway where addicts could take flight and murder more brain cells. Other rooms were occupied by working girls, sucking and fucking for ten or fifteen dollars. It was the norm to hop from the bed to the drug dealers who were waiting close by to fix the prostitutes, once they had cash in hand. There were only a couple of hours of peace within their mind, body, and soul; then they began to crash back to earth, and the cycle repeated itself until the drugs were gone.

The dirty white one-story building was a mere shell of what it had been twenty-five years before. It had always been a motel, but back then it attracted elegant businessmen and families traveling to New York via John F. Kennedy Airport. The location was ideal, perched about halfway between the airport and Manhattan. It had been a much more appealing destination when the Gateway Inn catered to the upper class. Most of Brooklyn was also easily accessible from the Gateway Inn, being that it was literally located on the service road of the Belt Parkway. The gardens had been professionally manicured and the grounds well-kept. The fountain off the main entrance served as a majestic welcome for the patrons. Now it served as a bathtub for birds, rats, and the indigent. Back in the early to mid-1950's, the surrounding areas of Brooklyn were prosperous and family-oriented. The community as a whole was comprised of church-going, God-fearing people. Local businesses, especially the restaurants, flourished. There had been no shortage of Italian, Irish, or German establishments in that neighborhood at the time. Now it was a ghost town, except for the Gateway Inn.

Bobby rented his room one week at a time, always paying in cash. Cash meant no questions, and no questions meant no need to give any answers. Cash was king and Bobby knew it. Bobby was still sitting on thirty-five hundred dollars in cash. The no-name clown that was working behind the counter of the Gateway probably shot Bobby's first week's rent into his arm before he, Bobby, was settled in his room. Bobby was shocked when he didn't see a needle hanging from the guy's arm as they did their informal first cash transaction, because he was high as a kite.

The rooms at the Gateway were mostly rented by the hour to people who just wanted to mess around for a while, either with their drugs or their hooker. Maybe a few hours at most. It was rare that someone would want to rent this place for an extended period of time, like a week. Bobby blended into the waste that had collected at the Gateway Inn, becoming more invisible with each passing day.

Bobby was repulsed at the condition of the room. The mouse droppings on the doorsill were almost too much to handle. He turned the light on upon entering the ground-floor vacant room and slowly realized that this was home, at least until he checked into his eight-foot-by-ten-foot concrete cell. Bobby knew he didn't have much time left in the free world. Deep down in his gut he had to know. He felt the internal pressure building. Bobby stripped the bed down to the mattress and inspected it for bugs and body fluid stains. He found plenty of both. The few things Bobby had taken from his apartment included a tablecloth, sheets, two rolls of tape, Lysol, clothes, towels, soap, toothpaste, and bug spray. There were other incidentals in his large black canvas duffle bag, and he knew that those supplies were going to prove useful. The decontamination effort included unloading an entire can of Lysol spray onto the sad excuse for a bed. The tablecloth served as a physical barrier between Bobby's body and the cum and pussy stains that were festering just beneath him. The sheet was the only comfort from home and his former life.

Bobby traded his Mustang for a more utilitarian vehicle. The 1966 Ford Econoline appeared to have been driven in a demolition derby. It had been drastically aged beyond its three years off the production line. The right fender was pushed in, probably from a collision with another truck, based on the height of the red paint scrapes that were left behind as evidence. Both bumpers were smashed up pretty good. The hubcaps were mangled on both sides from someone who obviously couldn't parallel park on the city streets. The interior seats were not original to the van. The front seats were shit brown and the back seats were dark blue. Both sets of seats were stained, matted down, and smelled like dirty diapers. Mud stains on the floor mats indicated to Bobby that the van was used for work, maybe a group of construction workers or something like that. The two-tone tan-and-white paint was scratched and worn nearly down to the primer. It was perfect for Bobby and it would be unsuspected, almost invisible in the parking lot of the Gateway--if only the NYPD didn't run the tags on the car. Bobby had helped himself to license plates off a blue Chevrolet Impala which was parked in the Corvette's parking lot. He wondered to himself how long it would take for the owner of that Impala to realize the plates that were on his car weren't his. He might never realize it. *Who knows their license plate number anyway?* Bobby wondered as he switched the plates from the car to the van.

Bobby Maseano unpacked his black duffle bag, sorting out his clothes into the only dresser in the room. The dresser was in surprisingly good shape compared to the rest of the surroundings. *No one checks in here long enough to need a change of clothes,* he thought to himself. The dresser hardly got used in this motel room. Having a bed and dresser supplied by the Gateway qualified the room as being fully furnished. There was no refrigerator, stovetop, or television. There was no iron, ironing board or shower curtain, yet this was rented as a furnished motel room. Bullshit. Bobby Maseano violently shook each uniform piece to remove some of the superficial wrinkles. He then folded his uniforms with great care as to not create any more wrinkles than were already pressed into them. He hung the blue J and R delivery shirt in the closet first. Behind that one he placed Speedy's Delivery Corporation uniform top. This uniform top was green with white short sleeves. Next was a chocolate brown uniform, resembling a UPS shirt but with a different logo. The logo was printed on the left chest pocket, and read National Delivery Service under a cargo van with eagle wings attached to it. Several more uniforms followed in a wide assortment of colors and cuts. Bobby even unpacked a light brown uniform jacket. Each uniform top would be paired with one of four pairs of khaki or black work pants. He only had one pair of black work shoes, which he was fine with since black shoes went with everything.

Bobby lay wide awake on his plastic-covered bed, partially because he couldn't get past the fact that he was lying in a petri dish of dried human sex fluids and partially because his mind was racing at a thousand miles a minute. His thoughts changed extremely fast, approaching a psychotic pace, his visions becoming vivid and extreme. Bobby watched his dead mother straddling scores of men, one after another, then another, then a fourth, like trains pulling in and out of Grand Central Station. There was his father lying there in the street, mangled by the bastard who hit him. His wife Ann, trying to cut his neck as he lay asleep next to her. The shiny blade dulled only by his own coagulating blood. Then his band, beating him with their instruments. First the guitar, then the bass, then both drum sticks rammed deep into the place where the sun doesn't shine. He was a bloody mess and everybody he knew was trying to kill him.

Bugs eating at his flesh, then regurgitating it back into his open wounds. He was dying a deservedly slow and painful death. He was bleeding out from his cut throat and fading into an endless sleep. His heartrate was elevated, but unfortunately, not enough to kill him. Not yet, anyway. Beads of sweat formed on his brow and forehead. Anxious drops of sweat slid down the side of his head and collected in his ear canals. He was now also deaf. He couldn't hear a thing as his ear canals pooled and the voices turned silent. It might have been a minute or an hour that had passed, but Bobby, now listening through deaf ears, began to imagine sound. The soothing sounds of Atlantic, crashing on the shoreline. The water receding, then crashing again. And again. It never stopped. Visualizing this peaceful place, he began to feel the air leave his lungs. The peaceful place darkened, and the pressure of the accumulating water vaulted upwards. The sheer weight of the imploding seawater collapsed his chest.

Bobby found himself in a place he had never been before. Bedbugs were inching their way under his skin, burrowing their way toward his brain. He could not shake them off. He could not get them out from under his skin. He tried desperately to free his hands. If he could, he would peel back his skin and claw them out himself. Only his eyes were left untouched and remained intact. He could see everything as it happened, one potentially fatal event after the other, and yet he was not dead. He could not raise himself off the putrid mattress. He was trying to free himself, but his arms were locked in place. Was he tied down? If so, how and by whom? These nefarious thoughts that were ravaging his brain were launching explosions of adrenaline that he could not control. He felt his brain disintegrating within the confines of his own skull. The pressure was unbelievable. His temples were pulsating and blood vessels were rupturing in his head. He was flushed in the face and neck. He was leaking out, consuming the human stains that already existed on his deathbed. Exhaustion? Heart tack? Stroke? Death? Maybe worse?

Psychosis associated with a psychotic break is losing contact with reality, such as hearing, seeing, tasting, smelling, or feeling something that has no true external correlation, like someone suffering from hallucinations. There is a strong belief that something is true when it is false, fixed, fantastic, or delusional. There is an inability to sequence one's thoughts or control a flight of ideas that became increasingly disordered. Emotions are wildly inconsistent with external reality. This manifests itself in many ways, such as catatonia, manic episodes, or a complete absence of affect.

When someone is sliding into a psychotic episode, the people with whom they have contact pretty much know it. They can tell that something is going on, but they may not be able to pinpoint the exact point of the break from reality. People suffering from a psychotic slide tend to isolate themselves, so that it is often impossible to diagnose. This explanation may have provided some insight into the break from reality that Bobby Maseano had suffered before his rampage gathered full steam. The real question is, Why did Bobby's family, friends and co-workers not suspect or anticipate the psychotic break? Many lives could have been spared a lot of pain if someone, anyone, had stepped up and intervened before it became too late.

Chapter 20

Bobby Maseano woke the next morning swimming in a pool of his own sweat, which had collected in the folds and ripples of the plastic tablecloth used to separate him from the bed. His leg muscles didn't work right away. He was able to move them, but only in a spastic manner. Lactic acid had built up between the muscle fibers overnight caused by the intense contraction of these large muscles. He initially felt paralyzed. His limbs were stiff and sore as if he had walked many miles up a steep hill. His biceps were tender to the touch, as he noted when he grabbed his right arm with his left. His finger joints were also inflamed and burning. Bobby's temples were pounding and the base of his skull throbbed dully, but he quickly noticed that his neck was not split from ear to ear and he had not been bleeding to death. He wasn't sure that he was actually relieved by this. The psychotic torment was overwhelming. Death might have offered some relief.

Bobby realized he was naked only when his skeletal muscles started to cooperate with his central nervous system. It took a while for the synapses to align their firing and allow the signals to pass from his brain stem to the striated muscle fibers. The spastic movements slowly regressed and smoother fluid movements took over. He was confident that he would be coordinated enough to swing his legs over the side of the bed and reach the floor. His torso followed in a lever-and-fulcrum manner and he was sitting on the edge of the bed, steadying himself until the vertigo eased and the blur of the room came back into focus. His first two attempts to raise himself upright off the bed failed. The third attempt was successful, as he steeled himself into an upright and locked position, yet still hovering near the bed. Forward motion was unsteady, causing him to drift right into the dresser, then back left into a wall. He made it to the bathroom and managed to stumble to the sink.

Looking up at the man in the mirror, he began to panic. The image in the mirror was unrecognizable. He rolled his right-hand index finger over the open wounds around his eyes and mouth. Bobby frantically began to swipe at the bugs that were leaching out of the newly-formed cavities. His fingers traveled the topography of the wounds, elevating at the peaks and descending into the valleys. He rinsed the blood and pus from his fingers in order to keep the view clear. His distraught face was a twisted image of wrinkles, pus, blood, black teeth, and wounds seeping unidentifiable crawling bugs. Bobby twisted the faucet handles in the shower on the left side of the white pedestal sink. He waited for the scorching water to fog the mirror. The images faded away as the mirror fogged. He filled both hands with hot water and buried his face in his palms. Bobby enjoyed a brief moment of relief as the hot water suffocated the bugs and sped up the coagulation of the blood seeping from his facial wounds. He felt the wounds mending, just as he had felt them lacerate. Bobby was convinced that it was the water rushing out of the faucet in the slum motel off the Belt Parkway that would save him. His wounds were closing and his muscles were firing in harmony with his brain's command signals. He wiped a viewing path in the mirror by removing the condensed water droplets with the palm of his left hand, and his face was whole again. His beard had now landscaped his face. Other than that, he recognized himself again. What he couldn't explain was the blood droplets running down the side of the porcelain sink. He had no dripping wounds of his own anymore.

Bobby stood in the shower, hands stacked one on top of the other just above the showerhead, allowing the hot water to massage his pressurized head and neck. He felt tall in the shower, with no motion other than shallow respirations, until the hot water had run out, going from comfortably hot to stingingly cold in a matter of seconds. The trance-like state was abruptly interrupted, and he was forced back into his own body and mind. Bobby was still confused by the seemingly real events of the previous night and early morning and he tried to convince himself that what had happened to him didn't really happen at all. He worked on explanations while he dressed himself in the J and R uniform. He finally settled on the conclusion that it had all been a nightmare, which would have been believable if it weren't for the blood drops in the sink and the puddle of sweat still pooled on the plastic tablecloth. *Those were real enough,* he thought to himself; then he slapped the pool of sweat with his index finger just to make sure. The splash was proof that at least that puddle was real.

Bobby Maseano departed room seventeen of the Gateway Inn at 11:35 a.m. on Monday morning. He was neatly dressed in the J and R Delivery uniform shirt, a matching company ball-cap, khaki work pants, and black work shoes. Bobby wanted to appear official and thought he had pulled it off. He was as crisp as he could be without an iron or ironing board. The Econoline was parked directly in front of room seventeen, facing the street, not the Gateway. Bobby opened the driver's side door and hopped inside. The ignition would not turn over when he turned the key toward the front of the vehicle. He tried two more times while pumping the gas with his right foot. The air inside the van now smelled of gasoline, and he knew he had flooded the engine. "You can't do this, Bobby," he yelled out-loud in the empty van. "You can't fucking do this, not today. Don't you know how to start a fucking car, asshole?" he added out-loud. "Of course I know how to start a fucking car, asshole," he responded to himself. He pushed the gas pedal all the way down to the floor. He knew this would open up the carburetor, releasing the excess gas and hopefully normalizing the air-to-gas ratio. He had taken an auto mechanics class in high school, but had only received a C because of his lack of effort. But he must have been paying attention the day they discussed flooded carburetors. Bobby cranked the engine again. It struggled slightly, then started with a large plume of black smoke from the tailpipe. It lingered while he raced the engine, trying to make sure it didn't stall. Bobby thought about but quickly dismissed the idea that there were bugs in the carburetor. *There weren't any bugs,* he assured himself.

Bobby Maseano was finally off to work. He pulled the Econoline from the parking spot directly in front of room seventeen, then left the parking lot and headed west on Sheepshead Bay Road. The entrance to the Belt Parkway was two blocks up on the left. Paranoid that he was being followed, Bobby made six unnecessary turns, two right turns, followed by four consecutive left turns; and fifteen minutes later he found himself exactly where he started. From Sheepshead Bay Road through the residential area on East 23rd Street, Avenue X, East 24th Street, Avenue Y, East 25Th Street, back to Avenue X, then right back to Sheepshead Bay Road. The entrance to the Belt Parkway was in the same place it had been fifteen minutes ago, right in front of him.

The marbled-black notebook Bobby had been so careful to protect for so long was finally going to make itself useful. Bobby merged into afternoon traffic on Brooklyn's Belt Parkway, heading toward the Brooklyn Queens Expressway. Bobby would have protected the information in that book with his life if he had to. He was sure of that. Bobby wrote everything in the notebook. The rubber band that contained the first fifty or so pages sealed the thoughts he was having when his mother was alive. Now the same book served a different and higher purpose. Traffic was slow-moving on the Belt, but Bobby was driving exceptionally well today. He wasn't changing lanes unnecessarily. He wasn't speeding. He was doing a perfect fifty-five, because that's what the speed limit was, and he wanted to obey every traffic law on the books, especially today. The worst offense he committed on the way to Flushing Avenue was flicking a few dead Marlboro butts out the driver's-side window. That's not cool, but it's not illegal either. Bobby was cruising in the slow lane as he approached his exit and flipped his right blinker on, signaling his intention to get off at Exit 30, Flushing Avenue. Bobby was very familiar and comfortable with this area of Northern Brooklyn, bordering on Western Queens. This area had been in his delivery territory when he was on the job at REA Express Trucking. He had made countless deliveries in the neighborhood, and he knew the area as well as he knew his own part of Brooklyn.

Bobby Maseano pulled his van over on the corner of Flushing and Throop Avenues, directly in front of All Saints Church. Bobby admired the church's exterior structures, as he had done every time he passed it. The architecture of the old church rivaled some of the most-respected churches in New York City. To Bobby, the enormous peaks of the castle-like church signified reaching up toward the heavens. The church was solid brick and had aged, developing a wonderful patina. The stained glass windows depicted all the Stations of the Cross, which were a representation of the passion and death of Jesus Christ. Bobby always sat under the Twelfth Station, which symbolizes the time when Jesus died on the cross. He wasn't sure why he was drawn to this station, but he was. Bobby wasn't sure what the symbolism was or whether it meant anything to his own life. He just related to the death of Jesus.

The massive arched, solid oak doors embellished with wrought iron crosses were always open to the parishioners during business hours. Bobby wandered into the church through the magnificent front doors. His intention was to say a few prayers and ask God Almighty to have mercy on his soul for what he was about to do. He had one last hope. Bobby prayed that God would grant him the power to stop the pain. Bobby wanted to stop the pain he was experiencing and the pain he was inflicting. Bobby also knew he would have to answer for his actions. He didn't know if it would be worse to answer to man or God, but he was sure he would eventually have to answer to both.

He sat quietly in the back row of the church toward the right side wall with the intention of being as inconspicuous as possible. He glanced toward the outside wall to make sure he was properly seated near Station Twelve. There were four women in the church, scattered throughout. Everyone wanted or needed time to reflect on their lives and their deeds. Bobby reflected on his life and crimes--those in the past, the present, and the future. He did not ask God for forgiveness, just for understanding. He admitted to himself and to God that he knew what he was doing was wrong; however, the drive to inflict pain and torment was unstoppable and undeniable. Bobby kneeled down there in the back row, folded his hands in front of him, and lay his head on top of his clasped hands. "Father, forgive me, for I have sinned," he whispered to himself and God. "Give me the strength to stop what I have been doing. I just want to stop. Please understand that I can't control my actions. I'm evil, and the worst thing is that I know it. Please, Father, help me," Bobby begged. He began, "Our Father, who art in heaven, hallowed be thy name..." The prayer turned silent as he internalized his interpretation, and he continued repeatedly for nearly twenty minutes. Once satisfied that he had said his piece and that God's ear had heard his voice, he stood up, walked toward the center of the church, peered at the altar, genuflected toward the brass cross bearing Jesus' limp body, and made one last sign of the cross. As he turned to face the back of the church and began to head toward the exit, he felt an undeniable wisp of air blow over his face. He felt it, but attributed it to the slow-moving ceiling fans twelve to fourteen feet above the rows of wooden pews. Bobby walked toward the exit and dipped his hand in holy water which had been blessed by the Cardinals and sent from the Vatican. The holy water was surprisingly cool to the touch. Bobby made one last sign of the cross, touching his forehead first, then his chest, then each shoulder. The spot on on his forehead where his right index finger touched felt warm. With every step toward the church's main doors, the spot became warmer and warmer, almost to the point of becoming uncomfortable. The sensation on Bobby's forehead carried with it, in his mind, an unfamiliar, divine meaning. He chose to ignore its meaning, and that may have been the closest to salvation he would ever come.

Chapter 21

Bobby departed All Saint's Church with a disturbed feeling in the pit of his stomach and a burning sensation on his forehead. He struggled, trying to rationalize an explanation for both of the morning's events. He had come for quiet prayer here many times and had never before left with an uneasy feeling. He had offered, in silent prayer, his innermost thoughts, desires, and confessions. He was not looking for absolution, but everything going on in his mind seemed less disturbing if he whispered his confession in church. His desires had been darkening lately, and he knew he was struggling with intense sexual compulsions. Upon reflection, his abnormal ideations began in what he considered a normal circumstance. It was the kind of thoughts that make you aroused while you are having vivid daydreams or while you're gawking at the pictorials in *Playboy*. Bobby had all but memorized the measurements of the flawless playmates. Some of them were so fine that he had recorded notations in the marble notebook out of fear that the actual magazines would be lost.

Elizabeth Jordan was five-foot two inches with a thirty-three-inch chest, twenty-one-inch waist, and a weight of just under one hundred pounds. Elizabeth dominated the May issue in 1968. Bobby was a huge fan of Elizabeth.

June brought a Norwegian beauty to Bobby's fingertips: Britt Fredriksen, who was five-foot-four, with a thirty-four inch chest and thirty-four inch hips. She made a spectacular centerfold. The February issue had not been out of Bobby's possession since it first hit newsstands in late January.

Nancy Harwood was the featured playmate for the month of February, and her images were quickly seared into Bobby's brain. He periodically viewed the magazine to see if she was really as spectacular as she was in his recall. She was fabulous at five-foot-seven inches. Her chest was a bulging thirty-six inches with a lean twenty-two-inch waist. The inside information on Nancy Harwood was that she was a virgin at the time of her *Playboy* spread. Bobby liked the unspoiled nature of the blossoming virgin. He described graphically in his notebook how he would deflower the beautiful young virgin. Let's just say that if he ever had the chance to act out his entry, Nancy Harwood would have been stripped of her clothes, beaten, repeatedly raped, and left for dead in the Playboy Mansion.

All that aside, Bobby Maseano held the August issue of *Playboy* in the highest regard. Gale Olson had an adorable cuteness about her and it came through in her hot August spread. Gale was one of those playmates who had the ability to keep her photos erotic without being considered pornographic. She had that special something that made men appreciate the beauty and innocence of the female form. Bobby appreciated Gale Olson as a strikingly seductive playmate. Bobby never jerked himself off to the Gale Olson spread. He did, however, always keep a few *Playboy* issues tucked neatly under the driver's seat of his vehicle. The spectacular August issue, featuring Gale Olson, was never kept under Bobby's seat and he never used it for masturbation. Gale was too good for that.

The uneasy feeling Bobby experienced at All Saint's had not yet left him. Turmoil and anxiety were beginning to peak. Bobby had not even descended the rough and chipped granite steps that would lead him to the street. He made it back to his van but was feeling lightheaded. Panic and mild hyperventilation were taking over, and his elevated respiration rate was disturbing. Bobby occupied the driver's seat of the Econoline van for a while without even turning the engine on. He concentrated on his breathing. In through the nose and out through the mouth. In through the nose, out through the mouth. After a while, Bobby felt his heartbeat slow, and then slow down some more. "Relax," he repeated to himself. "Relax. Relax."

An eerie calm began to consume Bobby Maseano as he sat there in the driver's seat with his eyes closed, listening to the hum of the traffic passing by. With that calm also came increased confidence. He was never confident in his behavior when he was in an acute manic state. He knew his actions were based more on impulse than on rational thought. Bobby was able to focus himself on his notebook, opening to the sixth page after the bound pages which contained descriptions of his mother's indiscretions. He hadn't looked back over those pages in years, but he kept them anyway.

Bobby pondered his fate, as well as the fate of entry number six. The words were jumbled in a sort of adolescent secret code. The jumbled words and descriptions, comprised of mixed-up numbers and letters, graphically described ten women whom Bobby had been following for months. Only Bobby knew the meaning of the jumbled letters, and if the book had ever been found by law enforcement, Bobby was confident that they would never be able to break his code. He had even forgotten some of the sequences in his scientific code. Bobby often wasted precious time making sense of his own incoherent groups of alphanumeric sequences. Each of the descriptions that followed the mixed-up letters read like its own *Playboy* article. There were measurements, likes, dislikes, hair color, breast size, and Bobby's personal critique: a manifesto, as if he were Hefner himself. He must have encountered these women before, maybe not on a personal or intimate level, but he must have encountered them. The descriptions that were written down could not be random, because there was explicit detail noted. The jumbled text in Bobby's notebook read in interview form, as if he asked a question and they provided the information. He painted the pornographic picture for himself through their conjured-up responses.

Bobby started the Econoline on the first try this time and let out a sigh of relief as he dropped it into drive and headed away from All Saint's Church, straight through the green light directly in front of him. He drove cautiously to his destination. He planned to park around back near the rear service entrance. The commercial vehicle curb markings were painted red, signifying a No Parking zone within the confines of the red paint. Bobby nosed the van in behind a Pontiac Catalina that was attempting to pull out into traffic just as he was making his way around the corner. Bobby sat patiently, surveying the area, and waited for the cycled street light to turn off, which darkened the area just above the van. Bobby had known he was going to park on this street for some time. He had been to this building with deliveries many times. But he wasn't expecting this parking spot to be available as quickly as it was. It was perfect. The street light was about twenty or so feet behind his parked Econoline, and when it cycled off, that would be his signal to jump out of the van and benefit from the cover of darkness. The red painted curb made him confident that there would be no one parking in front of him. Leaving the block after he did her would be easier than he thought.

Bobby was as patient as he had ever been with the street light. He was calm and not agitated anymore. He sat low in the van, watching the commercial delivery dock of the high-rise apartment building, The Chesterton. There were eighteen floors, not including the commercial office and retail space which took up nearly the entire ground floor. The exception was the residential vestibule, which residents had access to from the front and side entrances. He observed the commercial traffic as well as the residential traffic of the building. When activity was slow and while the street light remained illuminated, he thumbed his way through his June issue of *Playboy*. He needed to ready himself. He counted three commercial vehicles in total. One truck was from a local florist. The guy pulled up to the loading dock and parked his vehicle in a designated spot. He got out of the truck, walked around to the back of it, removed his floral delivery, and walked up to the loading dock door. He rang the bell and waited thirty-seven seconds by Bobby's count, pulled on the handle, opened the door, and walked in, carrying his bouquet. The second delivery Bobby Maseano recorded was twenty-one minutes after the flower delivery. The car was a pizza delivery vehicle. The young man who was making the delivery approached the door, rang the bell, and waited thirty-three seconds, by Bobby's watch. He was in and back out of the building in seven minutes and twenty-six seconds. Ground-floor delivery, Bobby thought to himself. The last delivery Bobby had recorded was a furniture delivery truck. It appeared to be a bedroom set being delivered. Bobby decided to adjust his own plan when the seventy-something-year-old security guard propped the double-wide delivery door open to allow the men to bring in the new bedroom set.

The streetlight had just cycled off, and for some reason, at that moment Bobby was not expecting it to go dark. He mistimed the light's cycle. Bobby opened the driver's door of the Econoline, turned toward the back of the vehicle, opened the double cargo doors, and removed a fairly large brown box, which appeared to be awfully heavy but in actuality was not. The parcel was addressed to Ms. Joann Molinari, Apartment 3B. Bobby walked the length of the driveway carrying the package, making it seem to be extraordinarily cumbersome. Although he was in a completely different-colored uniform, he was able to blend in with the actions of the four tremendously large furniture delivery men carrying the bulky items into the building. Once through the exterior door, he navigated the first right turn almost immediately. The old man whose job it was to watch the delivery door never saw Bobby en-

ter, or if he did, he was too flustered with the furniture delivery to notice or care very much. Bobby entered the stairway marked Number
One and climbed up to the third floor. Confident that the stairway was
not used very frequently, he lowered the box to the floor and donned
his J and R Delivery hat. For some reason, he felt fully disguised and
undetectable with his newly grown full beard and his J and R Delivery
uniform. He placed wide black-framed glasses onto his face to further
alter his appearance to Joann.

Bobby watched from the third-floor staircase through a six-by-nine-
inch viewing window in the upper half of the steel door. The door was
heavy-gauge steel and probably fire-rated for at least two hours. The
stairway was hot and humid. Lurking behind the steel door became
uncomfortable, but he was determined to wait it out and stick to the
plan, regardless of his level of discomfort. Bobby was concerned about
other residents coming home from work for the evening. He wanted as
little activity as possible in the hallway of the third floor. Bobby could
not exactly see apartment 3B from his vantage point. The apartment
door was, by his estimation, about six feet out of view and located on
the far wall, just beyond the fire extinguisher alcove. Bobby heard the
elevator bell ring, and almost instantly heard two men talking about
Sunday's baseball games. They approached the stairwell door, but continued on down the hall without a break in the conversation or even a
glance toward Bobby's position. He suffered through three more ding-
dongs of the elevator bell and three more idiotic, mundane conversations as unknown people strode within inches of him. Other than the
heat and humidity, Bobby could have staked out the third floor all
night. The thrill so far was remaining undetected, first in the street
parked in the van, then entering through the loading dock, and now
perched in the third-floor stairwell.

At exactly 7:05 p.m. Bobby decided that he was satisfied with the
lack of activity on the third floor. It had been nearly twenty minutes
since the last elevator had stopped at that floor. He had not heard any
conversations or rustling of any kind in that length of time either. He

pulled the steel door open with his left hand, then braced it with his right foot. The large box was awkward, even though it wasn't heavy. He walked the hallway carrying the large load and stopped at apartment 3B. The name on the apartment door bell read J. Molinari. "Bingo!" Bobby exclaimed to himself as he read the name. He laid the box on the floor just to his right, making sure it would still be visible when Joann answered the door. Bobby rang the bell and waited for a response. It took a minute but there was a voice on the opposite side of the steel hallway door. Her voice sounded like it was an inch away. It probably was a lot more than an inch away, but to Bobby, the closer he imagined Joann to be, then the closer she would be. As she approached the door from the safety of her apartment, her voice, calling out, became louder. "Who is it?" Joann questioned.

"Delivery for Ashley Thompson," Bobby replied.

"Delivery?" she asked. "I didn't know Ashley was expecting a delivery today." Ashley Thompson was Joann's roommate and best friend. She was a working nurse during the day and attended classes at Queens Community College at night. Bobby had her information detailed in his marbled book. He had her license plate number, parking space number, and class schedule at Queens Community College. He knew what time her classes ended and what time she arrived back home on average. He had watched her for twenty straight weekdays. He wasn't interested in Ashley, though. The key to enjoying his time with Joann was knowing Ashley's whereabouts.

Bobby had chosen Joann when he made a legitimate delivery to Ashley over two months ago. Joann had accepted Ashley's delivery back then, which was a small fifteen-inch television for Ashley's bedroom, and Bobby was nice enough to set up the rabbit ears for her when he made the delivery. Joann was extremely grateful and furnished Bobby with a five-dollar tip and an ice-cold glass of lemonade for his efforts. "Ashley is going to be so happy when she gets home. It was really sweet of you to set it up for her," Joann said to Bobby.

"It was my pleasure, Ms....?" Bobby questioned in anticipation of finding out her full name.

"Joann, Joann Molinari," she responded.

"I'll make a note of that right here in my notebook, and if I ever have to come back here I will definitely remember your name."

"That's so sweet," Joann responded.

On that initial encounter the clean-shaven and well-groomed deliveryman was engaging, easy to talk to, and kept his distance, careful not to set off any alarms in Joann's mind. He was able to initiate a conversation with Joann regarding a framed picture in the living room of herself and another, less-attractive young female. Joann was forthcoming with the story of how she and Ashley had been friends since childhood and how when they moved out on their own, they decided it would be more economical and convenient to share an apartment, at least while they were still in school. "After all, we weren't making that much money yet," Ashley mentioned to Bobby. "Once we're both out of school we should be doing much better."

Joann peered at the delivery man through the peephole in the steel door. She could not see what he was attempting to deliver. She did notice the black-rimmed glasses and the full, straggly beard, though. "Do you know who the delivery is from?" she said from behind the closed door.

"Yes, Ma'am," Bobby replied. "It's for Ashley Thompson from P.C. Richard & Sons." Although Ashley had not mentioned a delivery of electronics, Joann couldn't help wonder what state-of-the-art equipment she was going to be able to share with Ashley. Maybe it was a new record player or a new console she had hoped to get for herself.

"All I know is that this box is big and heavy," Bobby said while Joann pondered what to do next. "Listen, if you want to refuse the delivery, that's fine. I'll just take it back to the warehouse and she can make arrangements to pick it up tomorrow."

"No, no, just hold on a minute." Bobby began to feel butterflies in his stomach, the kind you get on a first date with that special someone. Then he heard the chain unlatch and the sweet sound of the dead-bolt retracting into the steel of the door itself. Then the killer sound: the throw of a third lock. The door began to inch open and with its opening began the amplified squeal of the stressed hinges. Bobby was furious at the hinges for making that noise. He was also mad at himself for not anticipating that echoing noise. The concrete hallway amplified the sound at a bloodcurdling pitch. He was furious, until he saw her through the wide-open door.

Chapter 22

As the door opened Joann looked even more stunning than Bobby had remembered. He had anticipated this moment for over two months straight. Every day the burning image of this woman consumed his thoughts. Just like Gale Olson did. Every day, except the day he had spent with Luisa. That day he didn't think about Gale, Joann, or any of the other masterful entries in his marbled book. The other women, for that one day, were insignificant to Bobby. He couldn't help but express a somewhat suppressed smile, which was nicely concealed by his full beard.

"Can you bring that box in and leave it here in the hallway?" Joann asked. Joann had no intention of having this deliveryman come any farther into her apartment than necessary. Bobby picked up the box as if it weighed two hundred pounds. His struggles did not go unnoticed by Joann, but there was no offer on her part to help. Bobby bumped the large box into the doorframe two or three times, trying to work it into the apartment.

"I don't think it's going to fit through the door," Bobby announced. "Let me measure it before I kill myself here." He reached into his khaki work pants pocket for his tape measure. He carefully measured the width of the door opening to be thirty-six inches. Then he took the tape measure to the box and measured it at thirty-seven and a quarter inches wide. This was no surprise to Bobby. He knew the box would not fit from the minute he chose it. "Ma'am," Bobby said. "This box is not going to fit through the door."

"Well, let's open it here in the hallway and see if it fits when it's out of the box," Joann replied.

"That would work, but, I can't open any packages. Company policy, ya know," Bobby said. "Can I use your phone to call my boss and ask him if it's OK for me to open the box in the hallway and just carry the contents in?" Bobby continued to slowly inch himself in.

Joann had a skeptical look on the face as she said, "Ya, I guess so. Come in."

Bobby leaped clear over the box and followed Joann as she escorted him to the phone in the kitchen. He closed the door behind him with more loud squeaks and squeals. He was able to suppress his reaction to the amplified noise this time. Bobby followed Joann to the kitchen, taking inventory of her casual, yet flattering apartment and the way she presented it. In a matter of less than ten steps, Bobby had mentally recorded her great-looking ass, which was nicely filling out tight-fitting faded and frayed bell-bottom jeans. Her white nearly-see-through blouse was a nice complement. Her breasts were bare, covered only by a tan-colored buckskin vest. Joann's hair was dark blonde with a part straight down the middle; it was pulled back in a ponytail and tied with a pink-and-white printed headband toward the middle of her back. She was shoeless, but there were a pair of white sandals parked near the apartment entrance. Joann reminded Bobby of Brigitte Bardot, just smaller in breast size.

The blow to the side of Joann's head immediately knocked her down to the kitchen floor. Bobby calmly put the phone on the counter instead of hanging it up on the wall, knowing that any callers would get frustrated by the busy signal. Joann was disorientated and bleeding from gaping wounds on her head and right ear. The roundhouse came with great force, catching her in the ear and temple area. She appeared drunk to Bobby as she lay there, flapping like a fish out of water. At that moment she was unable to form sentences or even words. Sounds came out, but they were muffled and somber. The ringing in her ears and head must have been intense, because all she could do was hold the right side of her head as the tears began to flow.

"Do not scream," Bobby commanded only two or three inches from her left ear. "I'll fucking kill you right here if you make a sound." Bobby allowed Joann to hold her right ear, her hands between her ear and the floor. Bobby ripped at her sheer blouse and vest with one, maybe two swipes. Joann's left breast was fully exposed, but her right one was still covered by the torn material. Bobby turned her over on her back, removing the rest of the material, fully exposing her breasts, then violently flipped her back over. He wasn't going to miss this opportunity. Bobby had patiently waited months to see her breasts, and he deserved to see them both. Bobby handled her breasts with surprising restraint. He caressed and kissed them as if they belonged to a willing participant. Her breasts were milky white and slightly freckled. There were faint tan lines, which Bobby objected to, seeing the tan lines as faults on otherwise perfect breasts. He ran his fingers around her nipples, then pulled at them, only to let her know where he was. He ran his tongue lightly around her nipple before he sucked down hard on the right breast, then the left one. He was reluctant to move away from her breasts but knew he had too. He quickly contemplated where to spend most of his time, sucking on her tits or fucking her. Tough decision.

Joann wasn't completely knocked out and within a few minutes began to regain her faculties. She slowly began to protest the attack as her consciousness increased. Her moans and groans became louder and more frequent; then words began to form. "Why, why are you doing this? Please don't. Please, please." Her voice gained higher pitch with each newly-formed word. Tears welled in her eyes as she began to understand the magnitude of what was happening to her. Bobby brushed her streaming tears away as he pressed his pelvis into hers. He lowered his face to hers, fully mounted face to face, chest to bare breast, and pelvis to pelvis. Bobby produced a small but highly effective Buck knife from his right pants pocket. He opened the blade and held it above her still-glazed-over eyes, making sure she had a good look at the shiny steel blade. Bobby braced himself with the hand that held the knife. Joann had the sense that the knife was somewhere near the right side of her head between her temple and her carotid. She felt the blade graze but not cut her face and neck. A bead of liquid scattered its way around her ear and down the back of her neck. She was not sure if it was blood, sweat, or tears.

Bobby's intention was to have her conscious. He didn't want her to be limp and unengaged. He didn't want to fuck dead fish. After all, she had waited over two months to have him. Didn't she? He hoped that she wasn't cooperative and submissive. He didn't have to knock her out, but he sure he would if he had to. He wanted a little fight. He hoped for her sake that she had it in her to survive. Bobby pressed his body weight down hard, pinning her further to the floor. He reached under his groin, feeling for her waistband button. With the button popped and the zipper pulled down, he reached into her pants and simultaneously pulled the jeans away from her body and down toward her feet. First the right side, then the left side. Then the right side again, then the left, knife still lingering by her side. Once the jeans and panties were past her hips they almost flew from her body. Joann kicked and squirmed under Bobby in a futile attempt to get free from the pressure of his body weight. He was crushing her into the floor. Bobby kicked her pants and panties away once they were clear of her ankles. Joann's legs were free from the restraint of her own confining jeans, and the squirming movements became more convincing and deliberate. She wrestled with Bobby's body weight, trying to get at least a leg free. She was unable to completely disengage from his grips and mount. Next Bobby reached for the button on his pants. He had purposely worn oversized pants, which easily slid down to his ankles with the downward pressure from his left hand. Basically with no effort at all. Bobby was set deep in his mount between Joann's legs, holding them up and in place with his upper thighs. He leaned in close, bringing his face close to her left ear, and let out a sigh of relief. Bobby breathed softly into her neck and gave a few gentle strokes up her neck with his tongue, followed by one soft kiss, then three hard kisses on her mouth. Joann shriveled up like a raisin in an attempt to distance herself from this monster. She could not free herself from him. The floor was unforgiving in its strength to hold her in position. She would rather have died in that moment than have that animal inside her.

Joanne Molinari lay on her kitchen floor, struck in the side of the head, regaining consciousness, bleeding and wanting to die. She was too afraid to scream. Joann did not want that knife thrust into her. She didn't want his penis thrust into her either. Joann did not want to be cut, nor did she did want to bleed out in a slow death. Joann kicked with her legs and thrust her pelvis away from Bobby when she felt his nakedness between her legs. Bobby reached down between his legs, grabbing his hard penis and attempted to thrust it into her. Joann's body resisted valiantly at first as the smooth muscles of her vagina kept him out, clenching together and closing off the canal. Bobby was relentless in his efforts to get inside her. His thrusts would eventually overcome the resistance Joann's body had manufactured. There was no stopping him now. Bobby had penetrated her, and the slow and steady back and forth movements of his hips violated her over and over with each thrust. Joann sobbed and whimpered on the floor with each entry into her body. Her body began to decompress as she realized she had no fight left in her. She had succumbed to the reality that she was being raped.

Bobby continued to thrust himself deep into Joann for what seemed to be an hour. He delayed his climax until he could not breathe anymore. His muscles tensed as sweat dripped off his head onto Joann's still-exposed breasts. Bobby's eyes rolled back into his head as his eyelids fluttered fighting off the rush of adrenaline and oxytocin flooding his brain. His heart was pounding hard and fast. Joann lay beneath him in anguish and disgust. Looking up at him, she prayed for the strength to survive this ordeal. Her moans quieted. Her sobs were faint, only audible on the inward stroke. Bobby tensed deep inside her. The thrusting halted on his final inward stroke, filling her with the venom of a monster. Bobby collapsed momentarily onto Joann's body as if this were a session of unrelenting love making and not the vicious sex crime. Bobby's focus was on Joann's face as his hips began to plunge his softening penis into her again. Once again, pressing his weight into her body to keep her pinned, he whispered, "I love you, Joann. But you're disgusting. If you make a sound I'll kill you."

Bobby wielded the Buck knife blade once again. Joann was sure Bobby would kill her if she did anything she wasn't supposed to do. Joann chose life over death at that moment. She did not say a word when he was finished. Bobby dismounted the beauty and she folded her lower half upward into a complete fetal position. The compression of her midsection forced a rush of evil semen from her body. Bobby kneeled down beside her and stroked her sweaty wet hair back from her face. Bobby, considering his escape, contemplated cutting Joann across the face so he would be the last one to please the beauty. Instead he clenched his right fist and raised it above the side of her face and smashed her squarely in the cheek. Joann never saw the second punch coming. She could not bring herself to look at the monster in the face anymore. Bobby heard the crunch of her zygomatic and maxillary bones. She did not move a muscle. She lay there still in the fetal position, semen oozing from her vagina, and now bleeding from her nose and mouth. Not a sound. Not a single movement. Nothing.

Bobby pulled up his work pants, zipped up his fly, and latched the button. He opened up Joann's refrigerator and helped himself to an ice cold Tab. He was parched, to say the least. He stared down at Joann, who lay motionless, and took in all the beauty of his accomplishments that evening. He took a few deep breaths while collecting his tape measure and making his way toward the front door. Bobby listened with his ear pressed into the steel door for any activity that might be occurring in the hallway. When he heard nothing he slowly opened the door and peeked out to make sure the hall was empty. He then opened the door, moved the large box to the side, and headed for the staircase. Entering the staircase and beginning his descent to the main level, he removed the J and R uniform shirt and discarded it with the hat into a trash receptacle on the second-floor landing. Bobby would never use that uniform again anyway. He continued to the first floor, which had much more activity now. He waited briefly, less than ten seconds until the coast was clear for a clean exit directly out the front doors. The doorman greeted him with a "Have a good evening, sir," as Bobby walked by as casually as his rushing adrenaline would allow him too. "Thank you, my friend, you do the same," Bobby replied, struggling to maintain his composure.

Bobby strolled back around toward the back of the building and toward the Econoline with the gait of an innocent man. He was not in an extraordinary hurry to get out of Queens. He didn't appear to be concerned with the possibility that Joann might have recovered and called the police. He just strolled to the van, opened the door, and hopped inside. He pulled the keys from the glove box, which was where he had left them. The van started on the first try. *Thank God*, he thought to himself. He put on his left blinker and pulled out of the parking space and headed back toward the Brooklyn Queens Expressway. He fired up a Marlboro at the first traffic light and popped in Elvis' "Jailhouse Rock" in the eight-track. He loved Elvis and "Jailhouse Rock."

Chapter 23

Detective Giovanni Nardi had been directly or indirectly involved in five sex crimes so far in the past month and a half. Bobby Maseano had not been seen recently in Bensonhurst or any of the other surrounding areas. Detective Helen Pastore had attempted to interview all five victims, but there was the usual and expected resistance on the part of a few of the women. Detective Pastore had developed a solid composite of the NYPD's main suspect, Robert L. Maseano, and it had been circulated throughout all five boroughs of New York City. A BOLO was broadcast citywide, and the NYPD was considering Bobby Maseano armed and dangerous. The Tape Measure Rapist was a hunted man, and Nardi knew it was just a matter of time before his former friend made a mistake. The only recent activity was a parking ticket issued to Ann's Mustang for an expired parking meter while his vehicle was parked near the corner of 75th Street and 18th Avenue. To date, there had been no correlation between the date and time on the ticket and any crime being reported in that area on that particular day.

Ann, her parents, and the baby had been escorted from their Brooklyn dwelling to the family country home in the Catskill Mountains in upstate New York. The Ulster County Police Department, in cooperation with the NYPD, agreed to provide twenty-four-hour surveillance for the family and the property. Bobby was well aware of the country house and could possibly reason that they would temporarily relocate there. But for now, the family was safe, secured, and protected.

Leonard, Ann's father, had retained an attorney on Ann's behalf for the purpose of starting the divorce proceedings. Ann reluctantly agreed to start the process after little debate and many tears. The initial filing for divorce was explained by Andrew Ficarra, Esq., which set grounds as described in the Domestic Relations Law 170 in New York State. The proposed grounds included the irretrievable breakdown in the relationship for a period of at least six months, and cruel and inhuman treatment of the spouse. Additional filings included abandonment and adultery. Mr. Ficarra explained each of the grounds, advised her in the meaning of each, and offered answers to any questions she or the family had. Andrew Ficarra, Esq. was confident that by the end of their phone conversation Ann, Leonard, and Teresa would all understand the grounds under which he would file her divorce application.

"First, we should discuss the meaning of cruel and inhuman treatment of one spouse to another," Mr. Ficara said to the family on the other end of the phone line. "If the treatment of the plaintiff, that's you Ann, by the defendant, that's Robert, has risen to the level that the physical or mental well-being of the plaintiff is endangered or it has become unsafe or improper for the plaintiff to continue living with the defendant, then that ground is satisfied. "Does that make sense to you, Ann?"

"Yes, Mr. Ficarra, it does," Ann replied. Leonard and Teresa nodded, signifying that they understood the explanation as well. They all huddled around the earpiece of the only phone in the house.

"It is not a ground for divorce simply because a couple has been arguing," Mr. Ficarra explained. "When you speak of the acts of cruelty, you must be clear and to the point. If you have dates, times, and places, that's always a plus. If you can't recall exact dates and places, you can use the words "on or about" when describing the incident. Are we clear on this ground?" Ann, Leonard and Teresa all responded in the affirmative into the one speaker.

Mr. Ficarra moved on to the explanation of abandonment under DRL 170. "Abandonment is an action for a divorce when the defendant, Robert, abandons the plaintiff, you, for an extended period of time," Mr. Ficarra began. "The catch here is that the law usually requires the time period to be one year. Based on what you've told me, this one may be thrown out, unless they allow our extenuating circumstances. We're going to file it anyway. It can't hurt anything in our case."

"So, if I'm understanding you right, the victim, I mean the plaintiff, has to be abandoned for a full year?" Leonard asked. "How's a woman supposed to survive for a full year if her husband decides to leave?"

"I don't like it either, but there is not much I can do about this one," the attorney replied. "Moving on to the adultery," Mr Ficarra said. "We have action for a divorce based on the sexual or deviant sexual intercourse performed by the defendant with persons other than his or her spouse during the course of their marriage," he explained. "This ground is usually difficult and expensive to prove, but in this case, Robert is being sought after by the police for multiple sex crimes. We have a case just based on the police statements, and I don't think they even have to arrest him for the judge to rule in our favor. If we are all satisfied with the explanations of the grounds and there are no questions, I will file the application for divorce first thing in the morning," he concluded.

"Mr. Ficarra, I want to thank you for your time and effort in helping me get as far away from my husband, soon-to-be ex-husband, as possible," Ann said. "You are saving my life here."

"Ann, I will be in contact with you as soon as I hear anything from the courts," Mr. Ficarra said. "Oh, and you're very welcome." The call was ended as Ann hung up the receiver. This was the first time in months Ann enjoyed a small feeling of hope and solace, even if was just for that moment. It was a huge change from the fear and hopelessness she had become so accustomed to.

Nardi had been dialing the phone in New Paltz for over an hour. Constant frustration was taking over, because he was burning his candle at both ends. His days became nights and his nights became mornings. He was becoming red-faced, hypertensive, and short-fused. The whole department had been working overtime trying to uncover some leads that would bring Bobby Maseano into custody. At half past nine, the phone rang in the country home. Leonard answered it on the sixth ring, thinking that if someone was ringing the phone six times without hanging up it must be important.

"Hello," Leonard said.

"Leonard, it's me, Nardi. How's everything going there? Is everyone safe?" Nardi asked.

"We're fine up here," Leonard said. "There's a New Paltz police car in the driveway twenty-four hours a day."

"Good, they were more than willing to place a car there. All I had to do was make a phone call and ask," Nardi said.

"How is the investigation going there for you? Any news?" Leonard asked.

"Things are bad right now, Leonard. There was another assault a few nights ago in Queens. The girl was at home alone when a delivery man rang the doorbell to her apartment. The package was supposedly for her roommate. When she opened the door to allow the delivery, the box wouldn't fit through the door. He asked her to use the phone to ask his boss permission to open the package in the hallway and take the merchandise out of the box in order to get it in the apartment. When she allowed him access to use the phone, he attacked her, punching her in the face near her temple, which rendered her unconscious. He proceeded to sodomize and rape her for an extended period of time. Bobby busted this one up pretty good. He seems to be getting more violent as time goes on. The numbers are climbing, and this one was the worst one yet." Leonard remained silent and in disbelief on the other end. "Detective Pastore, Simmons, and I went to Queens County Hospital where the victim was being treated. The rape was confirmed by the E.R. doc. She was more than willing to give us a description, except she couldn't talk much because of the head trauma, the broken jaw, and the amount of morphine she was given. She'll be in surgery tonight to wire her jaw back together, and we're planning to see her tomorrow sometime in the afternoon," he added. "The vic, I mean the girl, did manage to tell us that she didn't really resist. Well, she resisted a little, but Bobby had a knife to her throat and threatened to kill her if she made a sound." Nardi could only imagine what Bobby would have done to her if she had really resisted. He quickly dismissed those thoughts. "She said the sadistic look in his eyes told her that if she really fought him, she would wind up dead," Nardi concluded.

"Nardi, you have to get him. He is not going to stop until he kills someone or he gets killed himself," Leonard said.

"Do you want me to talk to Ann?" Nardi asked.

"No, I'll talk to her and Teresa. I'll have to go slow with that kind of news. Both of them are on the verge of cracking over this whole thing. Next time you call I hope you have some good news for us, Nardi," Leonard said.

"Me too, Leonard, me too," Nardi responded.

Leonard hung up the phone. He began to explain to Teresa and Ann how the NYPD were turning up blanks in the manhunt for by. "They have six sexual assault cases that they are attributing to Bobby so far, and they are no closer to an arrest than they were after the first rape," Leonard began. "The police have widened their search area to include the Bronx and Staten Island. Detectives from all over the city are working the cases. NYPD detectives think that he may be holed up in another borough other than Brooklyn and Queens. He may be distancing himself from the boroughs where he has been attacking. Nardi thinks it's a weak theory, but it's a theory less. Nardi thinks Bobby is still somewhere in Brooklyn." Neither

Ann nor Teresa said a word in response to Leonard's commentary. But the tears and gasps were plentiful. "Detective Helen Pastore, the detective who sketched the first drawings of Bobby, is releasing an updated composite, because the last two victims have reported the assailant with facial hair, wearing a ball cap containing a logo on the front, and wearing black-framed glasses. Nardi told me that both composites will be circulated throughout the city in the morning. Oh, and the Mustang was traded for a blue and white Ford Econoline van."

"He traded the Mustang for a van?" Ann questioned as if she hadn't heard her father correctly.

"That's right. He traded the Mustang for a van. He probably needed something big to carry all his stuff and he couldn't fit everything in the Mustang," Leonard replied. "Nardi went to visit the man. I can't remember his name right now, but he already registered the Mustang." Leonard continued, trying to recall the man's name. "Nardi obtained his name and address with the cooperation of the DMV. He told Nardi that he was more than willing to trade the van for the Mustang. The van is not even worth a thousand dollars. The Mustang was probably worth close to three thousand," he added in frustration.

"That fucking Mustang was mine, not his," Ann finally screamed out loud. "That mother fucker!"

"Watch your mouth young lady, I'm not gonna tell you again," Teresa scolded.

"Bobby obviously never went to the DMV to register the van," Leonard said. "Nardi has the NYPD looking carefully for any and all white and blue Econoline vans on the road. Nardi has Detective Joe Simmons working the bars and strip clubs."

Nardi did have firsthand knowledge of Bobby's history in the topless bars. He may have frequented one or two with Bobby after a few of the Yankees games they had watched together. Nardi was a cop, not a saint. "Nardi thinks he may be spending his time in the dark corners of the clubs, submerging himself in boobs and butts. Of course, when he's not busy busting women up and violating them," Leonard added.

Nardi had also given Leonard a list of the problems he had encountered in compiling a pattern in these cases. "None of the girls, so far, has any connection to the strip bar scene or the sex industry. None of the women were huge party girls. None worked in bars or clubs. None were prostitutes. None had any drug charges. There are a lot of inconsistencies in body type, height, weight, hair color, hair length, complexion, breast size, race, and socioeconomic status," Leonard continued to explain Nardi's recent comments. "There is no consistency in their location either. There were girls living in large buildings in industrial areas of Queens and there were some living in one-family walk-in apartments in Brooklyn. All were sexually active, but none appear to be overly promiscuous. All were single, either living alone or with a female roommate. Nardi said that there was not much to go on except the solid composites, the consistently false pretense of having to make a delivery of an oversized package or box and needing to measure the doorway to see if the box would fit through the opening. Bobby produces credentials with his picture, but with different names at each place. He is always in a delivery uniform, none of which appear to have been used twice. The color of the shirt and the logos didn't match on description comparison. They think he must have picked them up in bulk at a uniform supply store and is using the different-colored uniforms to throw authorities off. Detective Joe Simmons is checking out the uniform shops in Brooklyn to see if anyone fitting Bobby's description has been in shopping for clothes. Joe has already been to Ideal Uniform, Meyer's Uniforms, and Primo Uniforms. None of the employees at those shops are making a connection to the composite," Leonard concluded.

Both Ann and Teresa looked exhausted from the effort it took to at least try to follow all the details Nardi had discussed with ard. Both women had the same thought at almost exactly the same time. Grab and hug the baby. Leonard also thought it to be a great idea, and he joined in as well. Comforting each other was all they could do to hold onto their sanity.

Chapter 24

Bobby Maseano navigated his way over discarded trash and broken beer bottles in the shadow of flames and billowing black smoke which now engulfed the Ford Econoline van on the eastbound side of the Belt Parkway. The van was unrecognizable in a matter of seconds and fully consumed within minutes. The syphoned gasoline Bobby used as the accelerant and the subsequent explosion would make the Econoline almost unidentifiable by the time the FDNY and NYPD responded to the remote area.

Bobby had parked the van on the eastbound side of the highway in a turnoff between Sheepshead Bay and Ozone Park. The turnoff was a favorite spot for teens who needed a dark, secluded area for some private time to make out. The spot was near the ocean, where there was a small beach area which made for a perfect spot for kids to practice and hopefully someday master the act of sex. There were always a few cars parked there, especially from dusk on. It was not really considered a romantic spot, but it did a good job of servicing adolescent hormone surges. Romance was the furthest thing from the minds of those horny kids.

Bobby parked the van in the far right corner between the sand dunes and a small path which had been cut into the overgrown weeds by the pathfinders seeking the privacy of the small isolated beach. This notorious beach had become known for its accumulation of Coney Island whitefish, especially after a good Saturday night. If you're from Brooklyn, you surely know about Coney Island whitefish, which were spent condoms that polluted the small shoreline, only visible with the morning light. There were two cars already there when Bobby pulled in, but he decided to set the blaze anyway. After all, he did have to walk back home to the Gateway Inn. The windows on the parked cars were condensed with droplets of vapor from the deep heavy breathing. When the heat generated from the groping youngsters met with the chill from the outside ocean air, there was instant condensation and immediate privacy. Bobby was sure that dresses were up around their waists, bras and blouses were either unbuttoned or off, pants were down around the ankles, and dicks were erect and at attention. Bobby was betting that not a single person would see a thing, at least until the van was blazing—and maybe not even then. He was right on both points. The cars didn't move from their spots until Bobby was across the highway, heading west, and the van was in a full and unpredictable blaze. He had felt bad about breaking up the leftovers of a good blow job or a good pussy fingering, but it had to be done. The Econoline had to go, and this just worked out to be the perfect spot.

Bobby opened the gas tank, which was on the beach side of the vehicle, away from the intruders who were parked just a few yards away. The length of garden hose Bobby had cut from the hose reel he found on the north side of the Gateway Inn made an excellent syphon. He cut, then helped himself to about eight feet of hose, which he assumed would be enough. Bobby did not know how far down the gas was or how far down it was to the bottom of the tank. He figured that eight feet should be long enough to hit the gas in the tank on one end

190

and hit the bottom of the Rossi glass wine jug he had with him, to catch the gas as it syphoned out. It would have been an easier calculation if the gas gauge had been in working order, but of course it wasn't. Nothing worked right in that heap of shit for a van, Bobby thought to himself. He helped himself to the glass jug from the shed when he cut the hose. *It was nice of them to leave it open for me*, he commented to himself as he went shopping for the supplies. Bobby introduced the garden hose about four feet into the gas tank when he heard the gas splashing around in response to the movement of the hose. He sucked hard on the other end until he got a harsh mouthful of gasoline. The speed at which the gasoline rushed into his mouth nearly choked him. He was careful to protect his airway by pressing his tongue as far back in the mouth as possible, effectively cutting off the gasoline's travel into his lungs or stomach. He drove the end of the hose he was sucking on into the jug and collected nearly a full gallon of gas. He spit out nearly another gallon. Bobby allowed the syphoning to continue even after he removed the jug. The gasoline was now pooling under the vehicle, and soon all four tires were immersed in the volatile liquid. Bobby opened the passenger side door and began to violently yet effectively soak the seats and dashboard with the flammable liquid. He did the same to the back seats, rear carpet, and the makeshift bed area behind the rear seats. Bobby could see the volatile liquid vapors escaping through the open doors. He took a few steps back toward the beach and pulled out a pack of Marlboro from his shirt pocket. The gasoline followed him, navigating a path that might have been created by cascading rain water as it flowed back toward the ocean from where it had evaporated. The trail of gas headed directly for his right foot. With a flick of his stainless steel Zippo, he lit a cigarette. He took a long pull of his brand and flicked it into the puddle that had collected just two or three feet from his body. The flames were instantaneous, and quickly became intense and all-consuming. Bobby turned from the burning van and headed home to the Gateway Inn. He had left some of his used delivery uniform shirts, ball caps, one pair of black-rimmed glasses, three pairs of worn and fragrant panties, and two D-cup bras, one blue and one black, both with lace trim, sitting on the passenger front seat. He also had the *New York Post* and the *New York Daily News* opened to his published composite, sitting on the center console, waiting to be incinerated with that effective flick of his cigarette.

Bobby was about a hundred or so yards west of the flaming van when the rear of the van jumped nearly ten feet off the ground from the explosion. There was nothing left except molten metal and jet-black smoke which was erupting from the mile-high fireball. The occupants of the other vehicles were not aware of the burning van until the explosion shattered nearly all their windows. *Put your dicks and pussies away. It's time to go*, Bobby said to himself, smiling with sadistic satisfaction. Even at that distance he felt the heat from the blast on the back of his neck. Bobby was shocked at how fast the FDNY and NYPD were responding. In the distance, just in front of him and dead west, he saw the first flickering lights of the emergency vehicles. While focused on the unfamiliar ground he was navigating, he heard the roar of the sirens racing past him, heading east on the Belt Parkway toward Long Island. The Gateway was looking good to Bobby right about now. It was looking like home, sweet home. He could hide in plain sight, and at that moment that was just fine with him.

It wasn't so bad living with the discarded members of society, the people whom everyone wanted to forget about, and probably for good reason. They would never forget Bobby Maseano by the time he was done with them. People here were so fucked up most of the time they didn't react to the explosion or the flames which were less than a mile away. The night sky over Sheepshead Bay broke its silence with a thunderous boom. The sky illuminated with a turbulent orange glow, but at the Gateway there was nothing: not a move from anyone. Not one of the drugged-up zombies even twitched a muscle fiber, blinked an eye, or perked up an ear at the sound or sight of the police cars, firetrucks, and ambulances blasting by them to extinguish the blaze he had set not more than twenty minutes ago. He worked his way up the embankment from the westbound side of the Belt Parkway and toward the Gateway Inn. Once he had stepped over the guardrail, Bobby happened upon three junkies with glazed eyes and shallow breathing and assessed the scene as he approached them from behind. The group was not coherent and was definitely not interested in him or his movements. He decided to just leave them alone. They would never recognize him. They wouldn't even recognize themselves in a mirror. He had nothing to worry about with these three. Bobby continued on down the street to his final destination, room seventeen.

The girl who was sitting in front of Bobby's room, just to the left of the door, was propped up on a large designer pocketbook with her back resting on the air conditioner which was mounted just under the room's only window. She couldn't have been more than seventeen, maybe eighteen at most. Her complexion was mostly clear, with soft pinkish white features. She was a little soiled, but overall not disgusting. He could not formulate a visual of her body, because it was masked by a long, heel-length flowing floral print strappy dress. Bobby could tell at first glance that she was not a regular here at the Gateway Inn. Like him, she just wound up here at the end of her ride. Bobby had been renting a room here for nearly two weeks, and he had never seen her here before. No one even remotely resembling her in any way. She was soiled, but cleaner than the rest of the pseudo-residents out there. She had long strawberry blonde hair, parted off to the side; it didn't appear to have been unkempt for very long. Her hair was not matted down and did not look greasy. She only had a few visible injection marks, and her fingertips were not overly discolored. Her fingernails were manicured and polished in a pink rose color, most likely professionally done. The girl wasn't fully unconscious, and Bobby thought to himself that she must have been strung out here for only a short while. He turned the key in the lock of the door to his room and kicked it open with his left foot. He bent over to assist the girl to her feet by hooking his forearms under the her arms off to the sides of her small breasts, locking his left hand around his right wrist, centered over her thoracic and lumbar spine. The girl looked heavier than she was, mostly because of the loose-fitting dress that did nothing for her body.

Bobby could have taken anything or anyone he wanted to from outside the Gateway Inn that night, but the girl with the strawberry blonde hair would be the lucky one. Most of the activity--or what was left of the activity for the night--seemed to be between rooms twelve and seventeen, all of which were on the ground floor. They were in the front of the building but not directly facing the street. These rooms provided the best vantage point to see the Belt Parkway and the approaching street, East 23rd street. There had been some semblance of a commotion inside room fifteen when Bobby passed it on his way to his room, just two doors down. The intense cloud of smoke coming from the open window was not from a Marlboro or two, but rather from a pound or so of pot. He could not make out the conversations as he hurried by, not because of the superior quality of the outer wall construction, but rather because of the incoherence of the improperly formed words. The level of inebriation was bordering on stupor, comatose, and flat-line. Bobby was sure that this girl melted in with those zombies when her night had started, then broke away in a small moment of clarity. The drugs would not allow her to escape, weighing down her legs and ramping up her heartbeat to the point of collapse. Luckily for Bobby, she had collapsed directly in front of his room. Her faint, rapid pulse failed to supply enough oxygen to her brain until sleep became all she was capable of, even if it was on the cold, hard ground .

Bobby was able to carry the girl without struggle or incident. She was dead weight in his arms, but the prospect of feeling that young girl's naked body was incentive enough for him to deadlift her from the ground and parade her into his room. Bobby sat her in the chair that he had been sleeping in since the night the bed and its microscopic inhabitants attacked him. Bobby was gentle with the young girl as he caressed the side of her head, pulling back her strawberry hair in order to have a full frontal view of her face. She was cute, and Bobby was now becoming interested in his capture. Her profile was not in his book, though, and that fact was a source of anxiety. He frantically opened his book and began to write. He convinced himself that everything would be fine if he just wrote about her in his book. He wrote for nearly twenty minutes, but his rushed entry was not as descriptive as he would have liked. He longed for more, for her true story. He wanted to know how she had wound up on the streets of Brooklyn, taking up residence outside the Gateway Inn. Upon examination of the contents of her bag that doubled as her body support, he first discovered her student identification card from Kingsborough Community College.

"Jennifer Wilson," Bobby read the name on the card. Jennifer was a senior at Kingsborough Community College, majoring in political science, with a minor in English. Her student identification, PS 13724, contained a much more flattering picture than the one that was slumped before him at the Gateway Inn. She had a nice smile. He quickly embedded the new visual into his mind as he rummaged through her pocketbook without regard for its owner. The strawberry in her strawberry blonde hair was not at all her natural color. Her school identification card revealed a much blonder Jennifer. Bobby liked the strawberry choice. He appreciated the grownup cut and color. Jennifer had a small amount of pot in her bag, along with a marble-size amount of a brownish tarry blob, which Bobby assumed was heroin. He had never seen heroin up close and personal like this. He became sure that his find was heroin when he came across three insulin syringes at the bottom of the bag. The syringes were not in a package and did not present to Bobby as new and unused. Remnants of the brownish substance stained the inside of the syringe as well as the plastic wrap. Bobby also found a Bic lighter and two stainless steel kitchen spoons, slightly bent at the junction where the handle meets the spoon. Her driver's license told Bobby she was from the east side of Brooklyn, toward Mill Basin, which Bobby knew to be a very nice upper-middle class area. The question he couldn't answer was what she was doing out there, strung out at the Gateway Inn.

Bobby confiscated the drugs and drug-related paraphernalia from Jennifer's bag and hid it in the ceiling tile just above the chair in which she was passed out. He knew that the drugs would come into play later on in the evening or at the latest in the morning. He began to methodically disassemble her attire from the bottom up. He slid off the pink-and-turquoise paisley printed Emilio Pucci slingbacks from her feet and tossed them to the side as if they were a pair of worn-out Keds. Bobby massaged her soft, pedicured feet, hoping Jennifer would awake from her stupor. One hand on each ankle, he rubbed his way up her firm, smooth legs that must have been shaved clean less than a day ago. The blonde stubble was almost invisible to the naked eye, especially in the dim and dirty lighting in room seventeen. Her legs were smooth enough for Bobby, and the friction of his hands rubbing on her legs became sensuously arousing. Her panties were soft and silky with wide lace at the waist. Bobby imagined the panties to be powder blue, but he wasn't ready to open his eyes and fully unwrap his gift yet.

The one-piece dress, which did not flatter her at all, was an easy victory. It was above her ass and over her shoulders and head before Bobby realized he had taken it off. He was even more pleased to find the panties and bra were black. Black was definitely becoming his favorite color for panties. Bobby reached behind her upper back and unclasped the two fasteners that held her small breasts in place. He brought the elastic strap with the fasteners around front, causing the bra to cascade down, falling away from her breasts. He allowed the bra slide slowly off her breasts down her flat midsection, only stopping because of the fold of her body, caused by her seated position. Using one middle finger on each side of her panties, he worked them down over her slender hips until they fell to the floor. Bobby marveled at the gratification he was experiencing, gawking at the non-combative beauty. He usually enjoyed the fight. Jennifer Wilson didn't fight, claw, scream, cry, or whimper. She was not rejecting him and he felt her consent, as she breathed in deep when he first spread her legs apart. She might be the best one yet.

Chapter 25

Bobby had business to take care of in Room Seventeen at the Gateway Inn. Jennifer Wilson now lay naked in the bathtub, which was full of comfortably hot, soapy water. Bobby knew she was returning back to planet earth. The massive hits of heroin and God only knew what else was beginning to release her central nervous system from its near-fatal grip. Her brain would be foggy at first when she came around, and if Bobby was right, all she would care about would be getting more drugs into her veins. Her moans began, softly at first, which was the first sign that the heroin's grip was releasing. The bubbles all but disappeared as the water slowly drained from the bathtub. Bobby released some of the towel he had jammed in the drain hole to prevent the soapy water from leaving her body. She was clean--not like a pampered newborn, but clean enough. Jennifer hadn't awakened as Bobby scrubbed her body from head to toe, inside and out. He shampooed her hair and washed her body, partly because he wanted to experience every nook and cranny of her, but also because he wanted to get a sense of how she would present when she did not look like a gutter rat. Bobby ran a cold shower as the last of the warm bath water drained from beneath her heels. Ice cold water was just as good as a slap in the face or a kick in the ass when you're on the verge of joining the living again. Jennifer Wilson was starkly and suddenly back from the dead. Her eyes opened and she attempted to wipe the cobwebs from her eyes and regain focus. Her first thought was to wipe the foamy drool from her mouth. There was no drool. She might have been drooling a little while ago, but if she was, Bobby had washed it away. She was wiping at nothing but water on her face.

"Who the fuck are you?" Jennifer slurred. She thought she yelled, but her volume was no more than a whisper. "What the hell am I doing here? Where am I? And if I didn't ask already, who the fuck are you?" Bobby stood at the sink in his boxers, never once looking at Jennifer as she fired off questions. Jennifer attempted to raise her naked body out of the grimy, grayish porcelain tub, but her legs were not capable yet.

Bobby explained the events slowly. "When I came back to my room last night, here at the palatial Gateway Inn, you were in my room slumped over in the chair, barely alive," Bobby explained to the confused, naked, and wet girl. Bobby took a lot of credit for reviving her and nursing her back to life. "You overdosed. Your friends were scattered outside and you were in here. You must have broken in and passed out in that chair. You were foaming at the mouth and barely breathing," Bobby added.

"Why am I fucking naked?" Jennifer inquired. She tried again to lift herself from the soap-scummed tub.

"That was your idea, baby. I couldn't get you to keep your clothes on. You grabbed me and sucked my dick half the night," Bobby said.

"Bullshit," Jennifer said. "I don't ever suck dick!"

"You did last night, a few times," Bobby said with a smirk.

Jennifer used all her strength to raise herself from the bathtub. She passed up Bobby and two towels which he had laid out for her as she frantically searched the room for her pocketbook and drugs. She ignored her clothes which were folded and placed on the edge of the nightstand. Jennifer wasn't concerned with covering up her naked body, just getting her drugs. Her bag was there on the floor next to the chair, empty of all drugs and supplies. She attacked the bag as if there was a morsel of food in there and she hadn't eaten for days. As panic set in, her body began to shake as if she was shivering in the snow.

Jennifer knew the room wasn't cold, but she couldn't fight the shakes. "What are you looking for, Jennifer Wilson?" Bobby questioned.

"How do you know my fucking name? I need my medicine," Jennifer managed.

"Medicine? I have your drugs," he said, in order to stop her frantic search. "Don't worry, you'll get them back when I'm done with you."

"What do you want from me?" Jennifer asked.

"I want to take you for real this time. None of this bullshit of laying there like a dead wet fish. I want to feel your fight. I want you to fight for your life while I'm taking you. If you don't fight, you may lose your life," Bobby sadistically told her. He stepped on the arm of the chair and braced himself against the wall. He moved a ceiling tile from the white aluminum frame and took the stash down into his cradling hands. Jennifer stared up at Bobby with incredible anticipation, like she had been stranded for days in the Mojave Desert without any thirst-quenching liquid, as if every involuntary swallow of airborne sand were grinding down the layers of her esophagus. It was like he was dangling the lifeblood of ice cold, thirst-quenching, God-given water in front of her dehydrated and decomposing body. Bobby knew she would do anything for the drugs. Anything.

"Here's how this is going to work," Bobby said.

"Please, mister, I don't even know your name. Why are you doing this to me?" She began to violently twitch.

"That's really not that important Jennifer, now is it?" Bobby asked. "We both chose to run on this side of the tracks, now didn't we?" Bobby jumped down from the chair and spread Jennifer's drugs and supplies on the dresser top. He worked the plastic wrap from the tarry substance and picked off an unknown dose, then dropped it in the center of her stainless steel kitchen spoon. Jennifer stared with intense anticipation, still convulsing. Bobby added a few drops of tap water from a filled glass and began to cook the substance up to a small fierce boil. The heroin melted quickly into the pool of heated water, and just that quick, the dirty-looking suspension was hot and ready. Bobby filled three insulin syringes all the way up to fifty units, about half of the syringe's capacity. "Jennifer, get dressed," Bobby demanded. Jennifer gave her captor a puzzled look: didn't he expect her to have to have sex with him for the drugs? Bobby demanded, "Just get dressed, bitch, just get dressed. It's not fun if you're already naked. I told you I was going to take you. I never said you had to give it."

Bobby capped two of the insulin syringes and left them on top of the dresser next to the heroin-laden spoon and cigarette lighter. Jennifer was being a good girl for Bobby and he'd definitely be a good boy for her. She knew Bobby's game at this point, but could not bring herself to run, scream, fight, or even respect her body more than she craved the heroin high. She sat silently in the chair Bobby had demanded she sit in. Her leg muscles were rapidly firing, causing them to bounce from built-up nervous energy. Jennifer had already tied a makeshift tourniquet around the bicep area of her left arm. Bobby commented on her resourcefulness in this heightened situation. He dropped to his knees, reached for her left arm, and palpated the cephalic vein, then patiently waited for the blue tone of the vein to become apparent from under her pinkish white skin. The vein was a perfect highway to Jennifer's brain, where the heroin would drown her in her own neurotransmitters. The cephalic vein bulged out and became an easy target for the thin-gauge needle. Bobby pierced the skin that was stretched thin over the target vein. The needle disappeared into her arm with the ease of a hot knife through butter. Bobby pulled back gently on the plunger to draw in her red lifeline. The blood that appeared in the barrel of the syringe became one with the toxic, possibly lethal, mixture. He released the tourniquet's python grip from Jennifer's arm and watched for the magic. Bobby depressed the plunger, sending the heroin into her body at warp speed. Jennifer's eyes rolled back and she let out a sigh, as if she had just had a tremendously gratifying orgasm. Her head flopped to her left shoulder as she temporarily lost muscle control of her upper extremities and neck. She gazed through transfixed, glazed-over eyes, staring out the translucent window glass.

Bobby leaned into Jennifer's only exposed ear and warned her to fight for her life. "You will die here if you don't fight for your life. Do you understand that, bitch?" Bobby said. He had the other two syringes ready for the lethal punch if Jennifer did not hold up her end of the deal. Bobby grabbed, then massaged her breasts. Jennifer began to struggle, pushing his hands off her breasts. "Good girl, Jennifer," Bobby whispered. "You just might make it out of here alive. Keep fighting, keep fighting." He pulled her dress straps down off her shoulders, exposing the lace of her black bra. Jennifer jolted up her right shoulder, then her left in protest. Jennifer Wilson had not formed or attempted to form any words toward her defense, just defiant body gestures. Bobby pulled back violently on the straps so that the top was now at her waist. Her bra came down with Bobby's thrust of the straps. He leaned in slowly to kiss her supple breasts, but Jennifer sank herself deeper into the chair. Bobby went in hard this time, and her minor resistance was no match for his upper-body strength. He took her right breast into his mouth and sucked hard. Jennifer tried to react to protect herself, but the attempt failed. He moved to her left breast, exerting even more pressure on that nipple. She moaned in pain, which Bobby interpreted as moans of pleasure. Bobby assisted her to her feet and steeled her up as he managed her dress, bra, and panties off with only a couple of strategically placed downward tugs. She fell back into position almost on command as Bobby released the upward bracing of her body. Jennifer objected with more conviction as she felt her legs being tossed over her attacker's shoulders. She could not defend the move, because she was unable to put any pressure on her leg muscles and could not react to her brain's defense commands. Bobby launched his tongue around her vagina, then deep inside, taking in her essence as if tasting a glass of fine wine. "No!" was all that Jennifer could muster from her cloud-nine high. "No!" she said again. "No!" for a third time.

Bobby felt her body tense as her muscles became rigid on the inside but flaccid in their defensive abilities. He wrapped his forearms around her outer thighs and shuffled her ass toward the edge of the chair. Then he removed her legs from his shoulders, holding them vertically, one leg in each hand. Jennifer managed to lunge her right leg toward Bobby's head. She caught him on the left side and rang his bell for a few seconds, but the impact had little lasting effect.

"Son of a bitch! That was excellent, Jennifer. I need more of that. Come on baby, fight me. If you don't, you'll die. I know you can hear me, whore." All he had to do to gain control was to increase the firmness of his hands' grip on her ankles. Jennifer's head was contorted, depressed into the small of the back part of the chair. Her ass was hanging off the edge of the chair, gravity slightly depressing her breasts to her sides. Bobby resided in the middle of her legs, pressing himself closer and closer. He slid into her with little effort. She was still moist in the vaginal area from the workout he had given her with his tongue. Jennifer was kicking from above, trying to knock Bobby out with a swift shot from her heel. Right, then left, then right again. She might have hit Bobby once or twice, but the impact was not severe enough to make him stop his repeated penetrations. Bobby finished with a final inward thrust and an animalistic roar. He dropped Jennifer's legs to his sides as he raised himself from his dominant position. The rest of Jennifer's body slid from the chair, culminating in a pile on the floor. She just lay there, discarded like yesterday's garbage. Jennifer was naked, wet, and sticky from semen and saliva on her neck, breasts, vagina and inner thighs. Tears rolled down her expressionless face as her high began to wear off. Bobby retrieved the tourniquet from the floor beside the chair. He wrapped it tight around Jennifer's other arm and with the skill of an experienced phlebotomist, found the right cephalic vein, and plunged half of the second syringe into her arm. Bobby had injected another dose of heroin without knowing the strength, concentration, or what the lethal dose would be. Jennifer melted into the fibers of the carpet, where she lay stagnant and unresponsive.

Chapter 26

The separate composites that were released by the NYPD depicted the suspect with and without a full beard, and with and without a ball cap and black-rimmed glasses. The composite drawings were plastered in every newspaper in the city. CBS Evening News anchor Walter Cronkite alerted the New York public by showing the various faces of the man whom the police believed to be the serial rapist who had been terrorizing the city. Mr. Cronkite sat behind his wooden desk with official news documents strewn about. The television cameraman had him positioned on the left-hand side of the viewing screen. The offset image of Cronkite would allow room in the frame for images of the composite drawings to appear. They materialized on cue, in murky black and white, to his right in the same screenshot.

Cronkite verbally warned women of every age to be aware of delivery men trying to furnish unexpected packages. He stressed the word "unexpected." He pleaded for every woman to study the composites and be aware of her surroundings. "Even in your own house," Cronkite warned. "The Tape Measure Rapist is terrorizing women in Brooklyn and Queens, and he probably won't stop until he is caught. The police are confident that they will stop this man, but they have little to go on right now." Walter Cronkite concluded with a phone number for anyone to call if they had information on the crimes or the suspect. Bobby watched Cronkite's news broadcast from the lobby desk area where the one and only vending machine was located. He rushed back to Room 17.

The double-edge Wilkinson blades and scissors he had acquired from black book entry number three's apartment would prove to be effective grooming instruments for modifying his appearance. Bobby had allowed enough time to pass from the adrenaline rush of being inside Jennifer Wilson and was now calm enough to take a straight razor to his own throat. The police were doing their part to catch him, and he was committed to doing everything he could not to get caught. He was enjoying the cat-and-mouse games. Who's the cat and who's the mouse? Bobby trimmed his long brown beard down to a few centimeters of length with paper-cutting scissors. He proceeded to lather up his face, simultaneously rinsing the taste of Jennifer Wilson out of his mouth. He worked the razor carefully around vital parts such as his ears and mouth, creating a convincing goatee. It was not the easiest shave he had ever done, but he was confident with the results. Bobby was comfortable with his face shaved, but was visibly shaken at the prospect of shaving his head bald. He enjoyed the new look of his face, and thought that the next one he did might enjoy it also. He finished hacking at his face and began chopping at his head. Two straight-edge Wilkinson's made easy work of removing his hair down to the scalp. Coupling the newly bald head with a well-groomed goatee, Bobby admired his new disguised appearance.

He couldn't refrain from staring at himself in the cracked mirror over the pink pedestal sink. The mirrored glass was cracked and scratched in many places, but he could still see the new version of himself as it emerged. He splashed cold water over his head and face, trying to calm down the burn from the straight-edge razor. Aftershave would have proven valuable, but he was stuck with the short-lived effects of cold water. Bobby exited the bathroom and started to gather his belongings. He picked out one of the remaining uniforms and proceeded to dress for what he referred to as "work." Bobby packed his duffle bag along with the final syringe filled with the heroin mixture. He unrolled two one-hundred-dollar bills and placed them on the dresser next to the remaining drug paraphernalia belonging to Jennifer Wilson. She remained on the floor in front of the chair where Bobby had raped her. She had not moved an inch in the last hour. He felt for a distal pulse and found one that was faint, but steady. Respirations were shallow and becoming slightly rapid. Bobby reached for her arm, where the needle and syringe was hanging, and plunged the remainder of the heroin into her vein, saying, "Thank you for fighting. I hope you make it. You were delicious. Definitely the highlight of my time here at the Gateway Inn."

Bobby doubled back to Jennifer's pocketbook, looking for her keys. He wasn't sure how she got here, but hoped that she had driven herself. The keys were mostly unmarked except for the Chevrolet keys. He recognized the familiar Chevrolet bowtie. Bobby removed the car keys from the keyring and put the others back in her bag. He spotted the car almost immediately upon leaving his room at the Gateway Inn. There were five or six cars scattered around the parking lot, but there was only one Chevrolet, which from a short distance appeared to be a hunk of junk. "She must have been fucking stoned every time she drove this thing," he said out-loud to himself. The car was in extremely poor cosmetic condition. There were dents, dings and scratches all over it; every quarter panel, door, and fender was scuffed or scratched. "Thank God it's not pink," he muttered as he approached the vehicle. The Corvair fired up on the first turn of the key, and Bobby hoped to himself that it would be a more reliable ride than the Econoline. He put the car in reverse, backed out of the parking spot, and headed for the Brooklyn streets.

Bobby was confident that he had a few days with the jalopy of a car. "If Jennifer woke up and found her car gone, what would she do?" he asked himself. "Would she call the police? How would she explain her being at the Gateway Inn? How would she explain the needle holes and the bruises in her arms? How would she explain the heroin in her system? Would she report the rape? How could she? She was a college-age junkie. How will she explain it to her parents?" The more questions Bobby threw out at himself, the more confident he was that Jennifer would not and could not go to the police. What if she saw his composite in the newspapers or on television? Was she coherent enough to even remember his facial features? Bobby decided he had two solid days before he had to ditch the Corvair and find another vehicle. He turned the car around with a legal K turn and headed in the opposite direction of his original plan.

Bobby decided he was leaving Brooklyn. He was beginning to feel the increasing heat and was losing some of the confidence he originally had in his new appearance. Neither the police nor the newspapers had mentioned anything about Bobby and his connections on Staten Island. He thought he would be safe on Staten Island, and he really needed to sleep. Bobby knew the island well. From experience, he knew that the Cosmopolitan Motel on Hylan Boulevard was only a few miles into Staten Island and that they would rent him a room for cash, no questions asked, just like the Gateway Inn. And he wanted to be out of Brooklyn, at least for a little while. *The element at the Cosmopolitan should be slightly higher-class,* Bobby hoped to himself as he made his way over the Verrazano. The Corvair barely made it up the incline from the exit off the Belt Parkway to the top deck of the massive bridge. There was no chance of getting pulled over for speeding in this piece of shit. Bobby wondered if he could get pulled over for going too slow up the ramp. He did not need to be pulled over. Even with the deception of his altered appearance, he didn't want to take that chance. He floored the Corvair, but it only responded on the downward side of the bridge, because of gravity's help. Bobby was grateful for gravity and promised himself that the next car he helped himself to would have a capable engine, with at least enough horses to make it up and over the fucking bridge. Bobby welcomed the upcoming retreat. "Clothes," he shouted inside the Corvair. "I need food and clothes," He entered Staten Island and paid the fifty-cent fare to the toll collector. Obtaining food and clothes would be his immediate priority.

The Cosmopolitan Motel is definitely a step up from the Gateway Inn, Bobby mentioned to himself as he pulled into the vacant parking space directly in front of the office. He left the Corvair running as he disembarked the little shitbox. The fucking piece of shit didn't have heat or air conditioning. The girl behind the counter was nice enough. She welcomed him in when he arrived. "Good afternoon, sir. Welcome to the Cosmopolitan Motel, my name is Ashley. What can I get for you this evening?" Bobby felt nothing toward this girl. He didn't feel a tingle in his crotch. He didn't even survey her ass or her breasts. Ashley was not repulsive in anyway, but she just didn't do it for Bobby. There were no disturbing images forming that would keep him up that night, and there was no reason to stroke himself. He had taken more sex in the past few weeks than had been given to him during his entire previous life. He needed a break.

Bobby appeared to be melancholy, somber, dehydrated, gaunt and, he thought to himself, possibly anemic. He wished he had some vitamins to replace everything he was using up. Ashley's short-cropped hair was pumpkin orange; or at least that's how it appeared in the dirty yellowish light of the office. That was the most attractive thing about her. He didn't like the color of her hair. But he did like the bold statement it made about wanting to be different. He didn't see her as anything more than a clerk helping him get his much-needed slumber. "I need a room for a week or so. Can I rent a room for that long? I need to be in a quiet section, preferably on the ground floor," Bobby said to Pumpkin Head.

"Don't worry, mister, I have the perfect room for you, and believe me, no one will bother you," Ashley said, waiting for a quick response.

Bobby did not respond to her conjecture. He rushed the conversation, offering, "I'll give you cash and you give me the key to a ground-floor room. That's it. No other questions. I don't care what you do with the money. Put it in your pocket for all I care. I just need to sleep. Can you do that for me, Ashley?"

"Yes sir, just give me a minute and let me pick the best room for you," Ashley said. She fumbled to her card index of rooms to see which ground-floor room at the far end of the building would be best for the cash-paying man. "Have you ever stayed here with us before?" Ashley asked.

"No, why?"

"You look kind of familiar. I thought maybe I'd seen you here before," Ashley replied.

"All us bald guys look alike," Bobby said jokingly. His insides began to churn. Ashley had manufactured fear in him with that last statement, and he instantly wished he had a sexual interest in her. She was lucky he didn't. But even if he had had an interest in her, he knew his tanks were bone dry. There was just nothing left.

Ashley handed Bobby the key to Room 123, which on the ground level toward the south end of the cream-colored one-story U-shaped motel. The front door to his room faced Hylan vard. Bobby handed Ashley $150 to cover the $105 invoice for the next seven days. He demanded that she keep the change. She had never been offered a $45 tip before, and she was elated. If it were more acceptable she would have hugged and kissed Bobby right there in the office. But it wasn't and she didn't. She was still beside herself, though. The forty-five dollars Bobby parted with more than doubled her wages for her whole shift. Bobby leaned in close before turning to leave the office and whispered, "Ashley, you never saw me here tonight. I'll have a crisp one-hundred-dollar bill for you when I check out next week, but only if no one bothers me for the entire week. Not even the maids."

"Got it Mr....?," Ashley responded inquiringly.

"Now Ashley, didn't I say no questions? You want that hundred-dollar tip, don"t you?"

"You're right, sir. I know, I never saw you. I got it now." Ashley said nervously. She could just about feel that crisp hundred dollar bill in the palm of her hand. "I never saw you. I Promise."

Bobby turned the key in the lock on the door of Room 123. Immediately he was smacked in the face by the sweet aromas of apples and cinnamon, like the way a warm, fresh-baked apple pie consumes your olfactory sense. The wicker basket on the nightstand was full of scented dried fruits, flowers, and twigs. The room was furnished with two well-tailored queen-sized fluffy-looking beds. The duffel was tossed on the floor, and Bobby was naked before he had taken five steps into the room. The bed revealed, as he yanked back the bedspread, the cleanest, whitest, softest sheets he had seen in a while. He sat himself on the edge of the bed on the side closest to the bathroom. The longer he sat on the edge, the more his body began to melt deeper into the cotton cloud. He leaned his body to the right and collapsed deep into the feathered pillow. He tried to rest his eyes for just a few minutes. Just a few minutes turned into thirteen hours.

Chapter 27

Detectives Nardi, Simmons, and Pastore arrived at Coney Island Hospital at 10:07 p.m. on Saturday night. Nardi took the liberty of parking the silver Crown Victoria in the lane next to the ER, which was clearly marked with a "No Parking - For Emergency Vehicles Only" sign. Out of frustration for the amount of road trips that he and his fellow detectives had made to hospital emergency rooms in the past few weeks, he felt he had earned a reserved parking space. The three detectives climbed up the five concrete steps from the ambulance bay and entered the hospital entrance dedicated for paramedics only. The emergency room at Coney Island Hospital was one of the city's busiest. The teaching hospital was a level one trauma center and attracted some of the most horrific cases in Brooklyn.

The silver-haired security guard, who couldn't stop a teenage girl from offending the hospital, was very helpful to the three detectives. Nardi spoke while simultaneously flashing his credentials. "I'm Detective Giovanni Nardi. These are Detectives Simmons and Pastore," Nardi addressed the guard. "We need to get into the emergency room and talk to a patient who was brought in by ambulance about an hour ago.

"Follow me, detectives. I'll take you in," the guard responded.

It's always the same shit, Nardi said to himself. *We're always two steps behind this son-of-a-bitch".* The thought continued as the three detectives followed the uniformed older gentleman past reception, then past triage. The double-locking alarmed emergency room doors opened as the security guard inserted his key in the receptacle in the wall and turned it to the right. "Here you go, detectives," the security guard said. "Do you see that nurse over there?"

"Which one?" Detective Pastore inquired.

"The big black one in the blue scrubs and lab coat," the guard pointed out. "That's the nurse who's in charge of the ER, and she'll be the one to help you-- if she feels like it."

"What does that mean?" Joe Simmons asked.

"She's big, and mean as a snake," the security guard chuckled.

"Thanks for the heads-up," Nardi said. "We got it from here."

The three NYPD detectives promptly approached the ER supervisor. All three of New York's finest had their credentials ready and did not appear to want to play any games with the beefy nurse. Nardi approached first, tilting his head to the side to read her name off her official hospital identification tag, Jasmine Jackson, R.N. "Mrs. Jackson, I'm Detective Giovanni Nardi. These are Detectives Simmons and Pastore," Nardi began. "We are here to see and interview a Jennifer Wilson. She was brought in by ambulance about an hour ago. Can you point us toward her room?"

"You're gonna have to wait, detectives. Ms. Wilson isn't going anywhere anytime soon. I'm in the middle of an emergency behind curtain three." The nurse in charge of the ER appeared to be completely in charge of everyone, including the detectives. She just hushed three of the NYPD's finest detectives and didn't even wait for a response. She vanished behind curtain number three, and the detectives were left breathing in the trail of her dust.

The detectives waited patiently; well, not so patiently, for about ten minutes. Detective Nardi began to walk the ER floor with his badge detached from his hip and held out in front of him so as to explain to any curious patients or employees why he was peeking around behind numerous curtains. Nardi, with Simmons and Pastore following close behind, inspected 12 of the 26 curtained-off rooms. Behind the thirteenth curtain, in the dark, was Jennifer Wilson. Detective Nardi didn't know how he knew it was her; he just knew it at first glance. Nardi put out an open hand as if he was inviting Detective Pastore to take the lead, the usual and customary procedure for this trio. Detective Pastore placed her right hand on the left shoulder of the woman with the bruises on her arms. She gave a gentle nudge and said, "Ms. Wilson. Are you Jennifer Wilson?"

The girl didn't answer right away. She opened her eyes, maintaining eye contact with Detective Pastore then said, "Yes. Where am I, and why can't I move my legs?" The detective wisely ignored Jennifer's question about the restraints around her ankles.

"You're in the Coney Island Hospital. I'm Detective Pastore with the NYPD. These are Detectives Simmons and Nardi. Is it alright if I ask you some questions? Would you be good with that? I promise it won't take long," the detective said. "Jennifer, we think the man that attacked you has done this to other women. We have to stop him and we need your help. The whole city is on high alert, and what you remember and are willing to tell us will bring us that much closer to getting him off the streets." Jennifer's eyes closed as the detective popped off the first barrage of questions that needed answering.

The curtain flew open. "Detectives, Ms. Wilson is obviously not fully coherent yet; however, the effects of the overdose are wearing off and she should be more cooperative when she is fully drug-free," the man said as he pulled the curtain back into place behind him. Detective Nardi noticed the doctor's name tag and marveled at the physician's way of taking over before anyone had said anything. Dr. Libo was about as young an emergency room intern as the detectives had ever seen. He appeared to be no more than sixteen, maybe seventeen. They weren't sure he even shaved his face yet. The doctor was not taken aback by the three detectives who were crowded into the small area. He had seen many detectives show up in his emergency room in the past few months, and he was getting used to their lines of questioning. They were all surprised at how well-composed Dr. Libo was, for such a young doctor.

"It may never be known what spared her life. The toxicology reports showed a massive overdose of heroin. It's amazing she's still alive," Dr. LIbo said. "I can't tell for sure if she would have made it without the help she received. She was knocking on death's door for sure. There had to be some sort of divine intervention. She could have died from cardiac arrest, respiratory failure, or complete nervous system shutdown," the doctor explained. "She might have had a couple of hours at best, if she hadn't been found when she was. Detectives, I assume you want to hang around for when she completely wakes up?"

"We need her story, Doctor," Helen stated. "Doctor, can you tell us what you know as of now?" Simmons asked.

"Her name is Jennifer Wilson. Her address is in Mill Basin, based on her driver's license. She is a student at Kingsborough Community College, and she injected or was injected multiple times with an unknown amount of heroin. We counted a total of six recent needle marks in her arms--three in each arm. The toxicology screen was positive for a few other controlled substances, but in much smaller amounts. Alprazolam, tetrahydrocannabinol, and a trace of cocaine. The heroin levels alone could have been lethal. I personally have never seen anyone survive that severe of an overdose. She had multiple contusions on her torso and back, and bilateral bruising on her areolas and vagina. There is also bilateral bruising on her inner thighs and ankles," the doctor continued.

"The areola?" Nardi asked.

"The area that surrounds the breast's nipples," the doctor explained. "The nipple of her left breast had what appears to be teeth marks, which broke the skin. Her vaginal area was bruised, and three small labial tears were noted on examination. We sampled her vaginal fluid for semen and sperm. Both were confirmed under microscopy. Detectives, this young lady is lucky to be alive. Let her sleep for now. There is coffee in the cafeteria. You may be here for a while. I'll check back with her in an hour or so," Dr. Libo concluded.

The detectives agreed with the young doctor, who preferred that she sleep for a while longer. He explained that it was psychologically safer for Jennifer to fully wake up on her own. "Her brain will function better when it is free from the stress of surging neurotransmitters," he explained. The detectives needed her account of the attack and her description of the attacker, who they believed would be confirmed to be Bobby Maseano.

The monitors above and to the side of the bed that Jennifer Wilson was resting in were a haze of green, red, and yellow flashing lights, up-and-down bleeps with varying high-pitched dings, buzzes, and alarms. It was sensory overload for the detectives. They observed the screens reporting digital imagery and relaying continuously changing information to the nursing and medical staff. The audible and visual stimuli agitated the senses of everyone except Jennifer Wilson, who had reverted back to a comfortable rest. She remained in a sleep bordering on comatose. Nurses would never be able to keep up with the physical demands and requirements of the ER patients if they had to monitor all her vital signs manually. Pastore marveled at the superhuman abilities of the nursing staff. Jennifer's body temperature was 98.4 degrees Fahrenheit, blood pressure 110 / 72 mm Hg, heart rate tachycardic at 107 beats per minute, pulse weak, EKG in normal sinus rhythm, oxygen saturation approaching 92%. The gravity-assisted Baxter intravenous bottle and tubing controlled the flow of lactated Ringer's Solution into her arm at 125 ml per hour. Oleandomycin and tetracycline flowed from separate intravenous bottles into the same arm.

After a while, Jennifer opened her heavily bagged and bloodshot eyes to the bright white light that was trying to awaken her brain. Dr. Libo was evaluating a small facial laceration just above her right eyebrow. She began to come around when he trained the task light just above her eyes. "Ms. Wilson, I am Dr. Libo. I'm the attending physician here at Coney Island Hospital. You were brought here by ambulance a couple of hours ago. Can you hear me? Ms. Wilson, Ms. Wilson." He raised his voice. "You're in the emergency room. Do you understand me? If you understand me, squeeze my hand." The doctor waited for a response as he held Jennifer hand gently in his. There was only a flicker of a response, a minor squeezing motion of three of Jennifer's fingers around the doctor's hand. Her hand went limp before the doctor was able to ascertain whether the movement was voluntary or involuntary. "Ms. Wilson!" the doctor exclaimed out loud.

Jennifer's eyes jumped open as if she was confronting death directly. The screams she bellowed in that moment were gut-wrenching and blood-curdling. "No, no, get off of me. Get off of me! Help! Help me!, I don't want to die! Please!" Jennifer screamed at the top of her lungs. The pleas for her life and for the man to stop resonated throughout the emergency room. Doctors and nurses ran to her bedside and the commands began to fly. It looked as if Jennifer was going to hurt herself trying to get out of the bed, pulling at the intravenous lines, removing the wires of the EKG machine, and grabbing for anything she could use as a weapon. Her legs were still fully restrained to the hospital bed, but she was trying desperately to reach the syringes and needles. In her struggles, she knocked over the entire tray which was just to her side. She was straining to kick at anyone who approached from the foot of the bed. Jennifer tried to free herself from the blood pressure cuff by biting at it. Dr. Libo called out medication orders. "Let's push 3 mg haloperidol and 1 mg alprazolam," he ordered.

"Yes, doctor," one of the four nurses responded. The syringes, full of the ordered medications, were attached one by one to Jennifer's intravenous catheter and slowly pushed through the line into her vein. The sedation that ensued sank Jennifer back into the adjustable hospital bed. Her arms began to calm, resting back to her sides, and her anxious legs were only kicking weakly now.

Detective Nardi, followed by Simmons and Pastore, saw this opportunity as their best chance to sneak an interview with Jennifer. They told Dr. Libo, more than asked him, that they were going to attempt to talk with Jennifer before she fell back into a deep sleep or got super-agitated again. The detectives did not wait for a response from the doctor. Detective Pastore slid back the curtain that surrounded Jennifer's bed and approached her cautiously. Helen Pastore thought it best if the two male detectives steered clear of her, so they left the room. She needed to assess Jennifer's recollection without increasing her anxiety level. Detective Pastore pulled her long blonde highlighted hair back into a ponytail and settled into a chair next to Jennifer's bed. "Jennifer, it's Detective Pastore. Can I talk to you for a few minutes?"

"Yes," Jennifer replied in a compliant, sedated voice.

"Can you tell me what happened to you in the past few days?"

"How much time do you have, detective?" Jennifer said as her eyes began to well up with tears.

"I need you to start at the beginning, from when you left your house," Detective Pastore said. "Take your time, but try and be as complete as possible," she added.

"I'll do my best," Jennifer said to the detective. Detective Pastore was mentally prepared for a long and gut-wrenching emergency room interview with Bobby Maseano's latest victim. Jennifer Wilson only managed to get out a few words before the chemical sedation overtook her. She melted back into the hospital bed and became unresponsive to Detective Pastore's questions within a few minutes; then she relapsed back into her pain-free place.

Chapter 28

Rain was pounding on the roof of the Cosmopolitan Motel when the dreary morning rolled around. Bobby had half a mind to take another day off. But he thought too much rest and relaxation would make him dysfunctional in ways he didn't want to be anymore. He threw back the stark white sheets along with the white blanket and floral printed bedspread. Bobby had the air conditioning on with the fan on high, and he was now freezing in the small room. It was really coming down now, you know, like if it was raining cats and dogs. It was the pounding of the water crashing against the motel windowpane that finally woke him after nearly thirteen hours of solid restful sleep. Taking this room at the Cosmopolitan Motel recharged Bobby in ways he couldn't understand. He was refreshed and fully erect. It was nice to use a bathroom that didn't have rat shit on the floor. The mirror was crystal clear, clean, and had no cracks in it, unlike the shithole bathroom at the Gateway Inn. Bobby turned the hot valve on, almost full strength, then the cold, to soften the blow of the scalding water propelling itself out of the industrial-sized shower head.

FIRST VICTIM

Bobby pondered long and hard about the next entry in his black book. He read some of his descriptive words about her and enjoyed his recall, as his notes were just as vivid as his waking mind. He thought about kissing her neck, working his tongue around her navel and fondling her breasts. He wanted her now, more than he had since he first saw her wearing her tight, black, satiny workout clothes. Bobby was not particularly attracted to brunettes, but this one was exceptional. He could only imagine the striations of her toned and sleek muscles pumping up under her flawless olive-colored, sun-kissed skin. He would bury his face in-between her thighs, just so he could feel her impulse to crush his head between her knees. Bobby visualized her fight. She would have a lot of fight in her, much more than any of the others. She might even mount him if he allowed her the chance. Bobby stroked himself slowly as the hot and steamy water rushed off his body. He punished himself in the shower. He started and stopped, then started and stopped again, getting himself close to a climax, but not allowing himself the release. He tortured himself with the slow stroke of his own soapy right hand. Pure torture. Bobby repeated this insane game until the motel water ran cold. The blast of instant cold helped shut his mind down, denying his erection for the moment. But he was fully expecting to have it back soon enough.

Shaving his head and face with cold water was not as pleasing to him as it was when the water was hot, soapy and steamy. His pores felt closed, and his coarse hair seemed hard and stiff. Bobby shaved the stubble from his face and head, once again taking it down to the scalp. The sensation of shaving his face and head excited him all over again. It wasn't just shaving to him. It was the creation of a new and unrecognizable person. Black Clairol hair dye would also add to his new character. Bobby liked the new look. The black goatee made him not only look sexy, but it also made him look mean. This new look was a far cry from his otherwise-common good looks. He was stunning, and he liked the look so much he thought he might keep it permanently.

219

"The girls are really going to love me now," he said out-loud to the new image in the mirror.

Traffic always sucked heading back into Brooklyn from Staten Island. It was never an easy trip. Paying the fifty cents toll to cross the bridge twisted Bobby's nuts every time he made the trip. He wanted to smash into the car in front of him in the worst way. He wanted to smash the car in front of him and the one to the side of him, and he wanted to throw it in reverse and smash the guy behind him, too. Bobby contemplated it seriously for a good while, until Elvis came on the radio. Elvis always calmed Bobby down. Elvis was going to be the king of rock and roll one day, he thought to himself.

Bobby usually avoided Staten Island because of the traffic and all the asshole drivers on the road and at the toll plaza. But it couldn't be avoided today. He finally made it to the toll plaza and held his arm out of the Corvair's window to supply the toll collector with a crisp one-dollar bill. Oh, how that pissed him off! Something terrible. Bobby hadn't thought to get any change for the dollar bill before he got onto the highway at the Hylan Boulevard entrance. The exact change lanes always moved quicker. You just pull your car up to the collection basket, toss your coins in, and off you go. The dickheads at the toll booth were in no hurry. They got paid by the hour. The black man in the carbon monoxide death chamber appeared to be ten feet tall from Bobby's vantage point, way down in the Corvair. Their eyes met as Bobby gazed up toward the heavens and the black man looked down toward hell. Bobby had a bad feeling about the way the black man was eye-balling him. Had he seen his mug in the papers? Had he heard Cronkite's reports? Had he seen the composite drawings stapled to the telephone poles? *What the fuck is taking this asshole so long?* he said under his breath. *It's only two fucking quarters, Buddy, you can do it. Come on, you can do it.* He was the slowest motherfucker Bobby had ever witnessed. It took about a full minute for the black man's arm to reach from the tollbooth all the way down to Bobby's extended hand in the shallows of the Corvair. Maybe it was the paranoia that was creeping into his thoughts which made it seem that slow. Either way, Bobby got his change and headed away from Staten Island and from the peeping black man.

"Hey boss, you there?" Dante said over the CB radio. The enclosed radio resided in a clear plastic coffin-looking box mounted to a four-inch-wide aluminum post inside the toll booth. "On your next trip out to the row, bring the Xerox copy that's hanging in the break room," Dante said.

"Which one?" Lieutenant Jacobs said.

"The one of that white boy the police are looking for," Dante responded.

"There's a few white boys on the wall. Can you be a little more specific, or would you like me to bring the whole fucking wall outside?" Jacobs snapped.

"The one who they like for attacking those white girls," Dante replied. "I think I saw the asshole in a Corvette."

"Really? Don't make me close your lane for nothing," Jacobs bellowed. "How sure are you? 5%, 10%, 50%? How sure?"

"I don't know how sure I am, but I think it was him in a Corvette."

"All right, all right, I'll send someone out to relieve you and we'll go over it in my office," Jacobs said. "I fucking hate paperwork, you know," he added as he slammed the phone back down on his desk. Dante returned the handset back to the holder. He collected tolls for about ten more minutes, until he was relieved of his duty. Dante made his way across the five active lanes to the office. Jacobs and Dante discussed the probability or possibility that the man in the Corvette was Bobby Maseano.

The man on the other end of the connected phone line answered, "Port Authority Police Department. This is Sergeant Spinella. What's your emergency?"

"This is Lieutenant Jacobs from the Port Authority Building at the Verrazano Bridge. I have one of my guys here who possibly identified Bobby Maseano."

"Bobby, who?" Spinella asked.

"Bobby Maseano. The guy who is all over the news, in the papers and probably on the fucking poster right behind your head," Jacobs replied.

"Oh, *that* Bobby Maseano," Spinella replied with a fuck-you attitude. "Where did he spot him?" Spinella asked.

"In toll lane six heading into Brooklyn," Jacobs replied.

"OK, Mack, I'll send a uniform out there and take his statement," Spinella said. "We'll forward the statement to NYPD." Spinella hung up the phone abruptly.

"Let's hit the control room and watch the tape recording of lane six," Jacobs said. "Let's see what we got on tape. I'm curious to see if all that money the city spent on those camera things is going to be worth it," Jacobs added.

The state-of-the-art security cameras that the city had installed produced a grainy, dark, and somewhat out-of-focus image. The license plate number could not be seen clearly. "That's not a Corvette, you asshole," Lieutenant Jacobs said to Dante. "Are you sure that's the car you spotted him in? That car looks like a Corvair, not a Corvette, Dante."

"Well, that was definitely the car," Dante replied. "Corvette or a Corvair, what the fuck's the difference. I can't afford either one, but that was the car."

"Asshole," the lieutenant exclaimed. "Dante, let's head back to my office, so you can start to write out your statement for the Port Authority Police shithead they're sending. I really don't have time for this bullshit." The two men climbed the three flights of stairs up to the administrative office of Lieutenant Jacobs. Dante sat at a small black office table loaded with papers and four half-empty cans of Coca Cola. He cleared a one-foot-by-one-foot space through the garbage-laden table and began to write his account of the alleged first sighting of Bobby Maseano in nearly a month. "Hey lieutenant, it really smells like shit in here," Dante said before he began to write.

"Thanks, I'm going for the I-don't-really-give-a-fuck decor. How am I doing so far?" Jacobs asked.

"Perfect. You'll be there in no time," Dante replied. Both men shared a slight laugh.

Bobby parked the Corvair across from Maple Grove Cemetery on Kew Gardens Road. Bridget Jenkins lived one and a half blocks up Kew Gardens Road on the left-hand side of the street. Her apartment building was desirable to renters partially because of its proximity to the Kew Gardens train station and partially for the affordable rent, due to its proximity to the cemetery. Bobby had been here many times before. He took advantage of the apparent fear people had of the cemetery. Most pedestrians seemed to avoid the street and sidewalks that were parallel to the cemetery. *They must be afraid of the ghosts and goblins, Bobby chuckled to himself.* Most passengers that exited the train station walked in the opposite direction, away from the cemetery, even if the most direct route was down the street where Bobby was parked. Bobby noted the average time that Bridget exited the train station at Kew Gardens in his marbled notebook. He had watched her from four or five different parking spaces, and she had proven to be very punctual. Bobby wouldn't like to wait for Bridget. She was a good girl, and Bobby was going to be sure to thank her for being punctual and never disappointing him.

Bobby had fantasized about Bridget Jenkins on many occasions. He always thought she would make a great centerfold. He could only imagine, for now, how spectacular her breasts were going to be. He imagined her long tight legs, exceptionally heightened by red heels which would only be visible from under her black, boot-cut pants, as her legs strode confidently forward. Bobby could hear the cadence of her walk as her heels click-clacked on concrete. Rhythmic sounds relaxed Bobby's anxiety. It was hard to describe the movements of her hips. Her strides made a statement, and Bobby had heard her calling to him many times. He had followed her nine times from the train station to the massive luxury apartment building. He was always sure to follow without being seen or heard. He longed to see her naked body. Bobby needed to feel the softness of her skin, to drink her in and have her fall in love with him.

The rhythm of her gait took over Bobby's thoughts. He could hear only her click-clack, click-clack even before she had arrived. He heard it everywhere. His own heartbeat became the click-clack of her heels against the stone cold cement. The anticipation of her ascending from the subway was too much for him. He knew he had about thirty minutes before she arrived. Just to pass the time he watched other women arriving home from work, walking down the street, avoiding the cemetery. None of them walked the way Bridget did. None of them had the confidence she possessed. None of them walked with much confidence. None of them made him hard. Bobby tried to pick someone else. He wanted to spare Bridget. He loved the girl with the long legs and free-flowing darkly colored hair. Why had he not taken her yet? He had had plenty of opportunities--nine previous opportunities to be exact. But why had he not done it? Bobby wondered to himself, sitting in the Corvair.

Bridget Jenkins exited the Kew Gardens train station at 7:35 p.m. and raised an umbrella to fend off what was left of a full day of soaking rain. Bobby immediately noticed the disappointing outfit Bridget was wearing because of the rainy weather. She didn't have on her heels. She was wearing sneakers. Bridget appeared shorter than Bobby had remembered. Her legs were not majestic, and her walk was sort of common. That infuriated Bobby. He slammed his right fist into the steering wheel out of frustration and fury. She was still exceptional in his mind, but he did not like the way she presented herself to him that night. It was just that the heels did something to her walk, and he really loved that. He would have to try to forgive her so their night together would be special.

Bobby left the Corvair in its parking spot alongside the cemetery and quickly closed the gap between himself and Bridget for the tenth time. Bridget took her usual route home and Bobby loved the chase, even minus the missing click-clack, click-clack. She entered the building's main entrance and vanished, as she always did, into one of the building's four elevators.

Bobby entered the building at 7:47 p.m. There was nonexistent security at the front desk. Maybe the security guard was taking a leak when Bobby entered; he really didn't know. There was literally no one from security anywhere to be found. Not that anyone had ever stopped him before, but there was always a chance. Tonight it was clear sailing. One of the elevators was already on the ground floor with the arrow facing upwards when Bobby pushed the button. All the stars seemed to be aligning for Bobby. The elevator was as fast as it had always been, and he was on the fifth floor in a matter of seconds. Bobby was still in a foul mood because of the whole shoe situation and was honestly not happy with Bridget at all. He walked firmly down the hall from the elevator and stopped directly in front of apartment 5N. Before he had a second to square himself up in front of the door and either knock or push the doorbell, he smelled something strange, yet familiar, pot, marijuana. Bobby felt further disappointed in Bridget at that ment. Bobby dropped to his knees and put his nose to the space between the bottom of the door and the door sill and inhaled deeply. Definitely marijuana.

Chapter 29

Bridget Jenkins had been smoking pot recreationally for five years, on and off. The first time she tried pot was during her 1964 company holiday party at Tavern on the Green. After the big bosses left the party shortly after 11:00 p.m., the fun really started. The outdoor deck was a perfect location for her to unwind. Bridget lost all her inhibitions that night. They're still talking about her striptease act. She would have gone totally crazy if it weren't for Steve Johnson. Steve was one of the few AT&T employees who was still at the party, and he had all his faculties intact. He didn't even have one drink in him. Bridget was sure that Steve would make a huge deal about her wanting to be friendly with some of the boys. She was single and wanted to mingle. It was one thing if everyone was having a good time together, but it was a whole different story when there was one nerd who was just sitting there, observing and making mental notes. Steve creeped her out anyway. He was always looking at her all weird like he wanted to talk to her but didn't have the balls too. She didn't trust anyone who wouldn't even have one drink. Bridget just thought he was square. She loved an occasional pot party and it didn't matter if she was alone or with her stoner group of friends. She was fine taking the edge off or just partying all by herself.

She picked up a nickel bag or two a few times a week when she left her office on Avenue of the Americas or, as it's better known in Manhattan, Sixth Avenue. Bridget only bought from one dealer, a young yet refined Spanish gentleman she had met through a co-worker, Julie McDaniel. Julie was a recent NYU graduate, worked at AT&T Monday through Friday and happened to go-go dance at a few local strip clubs on weekends for extra money. She had the face and the body for go-go dancing, and smoking a little pot gave her the confidence she needed. Sometimes she made more money in one night as a dancer than she did working all week for AT&T. The dealer, whose name remained confidential, serviced the whole office building. There were nearly one thousand potential customers in one building. Bridget was a regular, and Carlos Rivera knew where to be and when. She had been a regular for some time, and they had become comfortable with each other, developing a mutually beneficial relationship.

Bobby Maseano rang the doorbell with an authoritative push. Dingdong. "Who is it?" Bridget called out.

"Maintenance man." Bobby yanked at the delivery company patch on his shirt and it came off in his hand with one good pull.

"Maintenance?" she questioned.

"Yes ma'am, I need to measure your doorways to see if the new washer and dryer will fit in the closet," Bobby replied. He already knew where the washer and dryer were located inside her apartment. Bobby had looked at a few apartments in this building already, and had plans to move in once his relationship with Bridget skyrocketed. He especially liked a one-bedroom apartment on the second floor. It had really nice views of the cemetery.

"What new washer and dryer?" Bridget asked.

"I have a new washer and dryer in the loading bay for a Ms. Bridget Jenkins, in 5N," Bobby replied. "From what I understand you are to get a new washer and dryer every two years, so there is less of chance of a major leak in the building. That should be spelled out in your lease. It's like preventative maintenance on your car, ya know," Bobby added.

"OK, just a minute," Bridget responded. Bobby waited patiently, but he was still a little disappointed about the marijuana smell. Bridget Jenkins opened the door to apartment 5N without even looking through the peephole. "Come on in, baldie," she said playfully to Bobby. Bridget was high as a kite, and Bobby wondered how in God's name she had gotten so high so fast. Outside had he closed the gap between them relatively fast, so she could not have been up in the apartment for more than a few minutes by herself.

Bridget blessed the inside of a large, oversized men's white crew neck tee-shirt with her naked breasts. Bobby could see her erect nipples through the lightweight cotton fabric. She didn't seem to mind him staring at her, almost putting them out there as a welcoming invitation. Her bottom was barely covered with cutoff jean shorts fringed with white threads instead of a hem. Her cheeks were peeking out where the white pockets protruded past the fringe line. Her legs were fully exposed, and Bobby could not ignore the view. He barely noticed her face through the sensory overload.

Burning marijuana smoke hovered in the air about a foot from the ceiling, slowly making its way to the four open fifth-floor windows in the living room. The blinds were open and the sheer curtains were pulled back, allowing fresh air to flow in and marijuana smoke-polluted air to escape. The Dansk cookie tin was open on the kitchen table, but there were no cookies to be found. The supply of pot and rolling papers was plentiful inside the tin. Her bare feet made no sound as she turned her back to Bobby and headed toward her supply. "You caught me at a bad time, Mr. Maintenance man," Bridget said. "Just a minute ago I was dancing around here naked and now I'm not. Isn't that a bummer," Bridget flirted. "Do you smoke?"

"Only Marlboro, ma'am," Bobby replied.

"Want some real good stuff? My guy grows it himself in an apartment in the city." Bobby did not respond.

"I think it gets better every week," she rambled on. "How long have you been shaving your head? Can I rub your head? If you let me rub yours, I'll let you rub mine. Bobby again did not respond. "I think bald is beautiful," Bridget went on.

Bobby stood there in complete shock, allowing Bridget to rub his head with both hands. Bridget wanted Bobby to relax and smoke a joint with her. "This is a party in the making," Bridget whispered to Bobby as she continued to rub his baby-bottom-smooth head. Bobby was tense and at a loss for a response to Bridget's advances. He stepped backward, away from Bridget, placing himself deeper into the kitchen. She began to rub Bobby's chest and work him back into the corner. He was like a caged cat looking for an escape. Bobby had nowhere to go. Bridget turned toward the kitchen table to light another joint. Bobby was frozen in place with no reaction, positive or negative. He allowed her to burn through half the joint, seemingly with one or maybe two long pulls, and again she offered the joint to him. This time he took the joint and began to smoke it gingerly. He knew he looked like a novice and really wanted to keep his wits about him. As he inhaled for the last time on the joint, Bridget crossed her arms across her chest and in one sweeping motion had her man-sized tee shirt off and thrown on a kitchen chair. Bobby squirmed to the side in an escape attempt. She cut him off and simultaneously unbuttoned the only button on her barely visible jean shorts. Bobby cut back in the other direction, his head now ringing from the pot smoke that consumed the small one-bedroom apartment. Bobby did not plan on getting high with Bridget, and he definitely did not like her aggression.

Bridget had Bobby a little high and pinned in the corner of her kitchen next to the sink. He eased her back as she leaned in to kiss him. Bridget liked Bobby and wanted him to take her right there, in that moment. He turned his face away from her as she persisted forward. Bobby had waited for this moment for so long. He had imagined her naked body in all its spectacular glory and there it was. His for the taking. Bridget was offering herself to him and he could have her, consensually.

Bridget was not playing the game fairly, and Bobby didn't like the way she was acting. Why was this gorgeous creature asking him to take her? Why was she mostly naked in his presence? He hadn't had the chance to instill fear into her. That was no fun! Bobby was actually the one who was afraid right now. He was not aroused. Even when Bridget slithered out of her shorts to bare herself as fully naked, Bobby was as soft as a marshmallow. His body would not respond to her. He was not heating up, nor was he sweating. His heartrate was not explosive and fast. He had no tingling sensations anywhere. She was destroying this for him, and he was angry at himself for choosing the wrong girl. This bitch was not the girl he had thought her to be. He was furious and disappointed with her again for the second time that night. Bobby was cowering down to her drug-induced aggressiveness. He did not like her this way. He had followed her ten times and never had he imagined that she was like that. Bobby had to gain control of the situation and gain it fast. Bridget was fully naked and Bobby did not know what to do or how to handle her. "Come on baby, let's just party for a little while," Bridget crooned. Bobby's eyes turned red and watery as the cannabinoids rushed through his bloodstream and settled into his brain. Her red lips were pulsating for him. Bridget was not at all the victim Bobby was expecting her to be. She was not a victim at all. Bobby was the victim there. He was being violated and he didn't like it. Not one bit.

Bridget's hands were roaming around Bobby's upper body. She was exploring his pectoral muscles through his heavy cotton work shirt, but he was not feeling anything. Touch sensation was not enjoyable to him at that moment. It was like he was watching her navigate the chest of another man. He was percolating anger from every pore of his body. Bobby did not want her to continue the assault. He would have done anything in that moment to have her stop, but she continued on with her unwanted aggression. Bridget quickly worked her way down to her knees and attempted to disengage the button that held his khaki pants loosely around his waist. He objected again to her advancements. His penis was disappointingly flaccid in spite of the firm rubdown. Bridget knew if she could only take him in her mouth, he would respond to the rise and fall of her soft lips around his cock. Bridget considered herself an expert and everyone, so far, had responded to her offer of oral pleasure. She didn't always make them cum, but that was of her doing. She just knew when to ease the pressure and slow her mouth down so that the sensation he was experiencing would temporarily abate. She could then be mounted and be finished off the way she liked it. That's exactly what she had planned for Bobby. She just loved bald men, especially those who were strikingly handsome and in good physical shape.

Bobby pulled back even further from Bridget, temporarily escaping her grasp. She expressed disappointment in her inability to engage Bobby for some free love. Bridget lit another joint and appeared rejected through her facial expressions and body language. "Just measure what you have to measure and get out," she cried out in tion. "Make sure someone else comes up to deliver the washer and dryer. Are you fucking queer or something?"

Bobby did not respond to Bridget's acquisition. He reached into a pocket on the outside of his right thigh to retrieve his tape measure and began to measure the width of the door to her apartment.

"The opening is thirty-five and three-quarter inches," Bobby said out loud. "Can you show me to the closet where the washer and dryer are?" Bridget rose from the seat at the kitchen table, donned her man-cut white tee shirt and proceeded to the hallway closet without a word. She pulled her joint out of her mouth with her right hand, holding it skyward as she exhaled the smoke in the same direction. The smoke waved behind her, separating, then quickly reconnecting, as she walked directly through its flight path. "Here it is, queer boy. Measure it and get the fuck out," she said harshly.

Bridget entered what Bobby knew to be her bedroom and slammed the door behind herself. Her high-cut shorts and tee shirt fell to the floor and she dressed herself in very unflattering pair of gray sweatpants and a sweatshirt. Her fashion statement was to no longer be a young, sexy, available, stoned, and horny woman. Bobby had rejected her in every possible way. She had offered him her marijuana to help him relax. She had basically offered him her breasts, her mouth, and everything else she had, and he rejected it all. She was not feeling high or sexy anymore, and for Bridget *being* sexy meant *feeling* sexy. It was hard to feel that way when you had been rejected like that. She was furious with herself and with the maintenance man.

When she finally opened the bedroom door, Bobby was standing there, blocking the path down the hallway which led back to the kitchen area. "Forget it buddy. It's too late to be interested in me now," Bridget said. She read Bobby's face the second she opened the door. She assumed that Bobby had reconsidered her offer and was now interested in her game. Maybe he wanted to get high or maybe he wanted to take her up on her offer of sex, but Bridget was already over that and as far as she was concerned, it wasn't going to happen. Bobby held his ground outside Bridget's bedroom door and wouldn't open the path to the living room. She tucked her right shoulder down and in toward her hip, grabbed her right wrist with her left hand, and hit Bobby one inch above the solar plexus. The shot knocked the wind out of him for an instant. He buckled, but did not collapse to the floor, nor did he clear a path for Bridget to pass. She was now trapped in a narrow hallway with no way out, except back into her bedroom.

Bobby immediately went for her throat upon rising from his slouched position. "That wasn't very nice, Bridget," Bobby said as he tightened his grip around her neck. Bridget raised to her tippy-toes trying to relieve some of the pressure on her airway. She punched and kicked, but could not gain enough air to scream. He pushed her backwards by the neck and back to the bedroom. Bridget managed to maintain her airway because she was sufficiently tall, but only when she elevated her neck away from Bobby's grip. Bobby pushed her back further until she lost her balance when the back of her knees connected with the bed. She fell back onto the bed in a submissive position. Her head had only hit the mattress when Bobby allowed it to come to rest with his hands still crushing her windpipe. "Bridget, you don't want to die here today, do you?" Bobby turned the statement into a question that Bridget could not answer. She tried to shake her head from side to side, but the movements Bobby allowed were minimal. Bridget was fading from oxygen deprivation, and she feared she would be put to sleep or die in his clutches. Bobby only released the grip on her neck periodically to allow a lifesaving breath or two at a time, then back to sealing off her trachea.

Chapter 30

Bobby had to slap her in the face two or three times before she was back in the game. A few well-placed knuckles, crushing her skin into her sternum, really did the trick. Bridget did not feel, nor was she aware, that Bobby had cut her shirt off with one clean slice down the front. Her sweatpants were thrown clear across the room and lay out of reach, hanging off the edge of her dresser. The knife remained imbedded in the white satin sheets, piercing straight into the mattress so that only the dark wood-and-brass handle protruded. Bobby was quickly naked from the waist down. Bridget could not comprehend what Bobby was doing to her. Why didn't he respond to her and have consensual sex with her just a few minutes ago? She had been high and willing at the time. What was he doing? Why did he choke her to the point of unconsciousness? Why did he want to kill her? What was he going to do with her? How was it that she was almost naked and did not remember a thing?

Bridget's thoughts blazed through her mind as she fought off the remaining marijuana fog which was now hindering her survival. She fought to clearly think about her situation and how to escape from the maintenance man who was viciously attacking her. Bobby Maseano reached for his Buck knife, removed it from the mattress that held it upright and in place. He thrust it horizontally into the subcutaneous tissue just below her rib cage, then pressed down on the center of her chest just two inches from her neck. When Bridget tried to scream, Bobby's hand slid down the contour of her chest and did not stop until her airway was effectively cut off again. She had no choice but to comply, because of the crushing force he applied to her chest and trachea. When Bobby allowed Bridget to speak, he made it clear that she could only speak and not yell. "Why are you doing this to me?" she cried.

"Can't you come up with something I haven't heard before?" Bobby asked. "Why do all of you bitches ask the same fucking question, all the time? It's getting a little old, ya know."

"I'll do whatever you want, just don't kill me."

"No promises, Bridget. No promises," Bobby replied.

Bridget felt the blood leaking out of the area just under her rib cage. Bobby hadn't pushed the Buck knife in any farther, but the blood was still exiting the wound in significant quantity. "If you try and scream, I will cut you like a slaughtered pig," he said with a crazy look on his face. She acknowledged his statement with an affirmative nod of her head. Bobby slowly eased the pressure from her chest. In an instant, and in a moment of clarity, Bridget chopped with expert precision at the area of Bobby's neck containing the jugular vein.

Bridget had learned this strike in the karate lessons she had been taking for almost a year. She had made the agreement with her father that if he supported her move to Kew Gardens, Queens from Rockville Centre, Long Island, she would learn how to defend herself by taking martial arts lessons. She never thought she would have to use any of what she had learned. She now wished she had been more committed to the lessons she was supposed to be taking every Saturday morning. She only showed up to the dojo on occasion, when she wasn't messed up from partying the night before. She had committed to the chop which she applied to Bobby's neck, more than she had committed to any other aggressive strike ever. The blow landed almost squarely on the intended target, maybe a fraction of an inch off dead-center of the vein. The strike was intended, as she had learned it, to shock the vessel into a spasm, effectively cutting off a majority of the blood and oxygen flow to the brain. But even if executed perfectly, the spasm would be only temporary.

The novice karate blow was executed, but not with expert precision. The connection of the blade of her right hand to Bobby's neck knocked him off her, causing him to fall to her left side onto the bed. Bobby rolled in pain on the now blood-stained sheets. It did not, however, render him immobile or unresponsive. Bridget grabbed at the knife that was stuck under her ribs and removed the blade. More blood flowed from the wound. She twisted her body as if to ride Bobby's back, then plunged the knife toward the center of his back. He rolled off the bed, anticipating the thrust of the knife toward him. The knife remained where it landed, piercing the satin sheets and mattress again. Bridget scooched her ass to the edge of the bed in an intense effort to escape her own bedroom and the madness that would certainly end in her death.

Bridget Jenkins launched her naked, bloody body toward the door, when Bobby grabbed her left arm by the wrist and swung her back violently across the room, back onto her bloody bed. Bridget's body flew nearly five feet, the perpetual motion halted only as the right side of her skull smashed into the solid oak headboard. The blood began to flow almost immediately from the three-inch laceration which opened instantaneously. "Now look what you've done, Bridget," Bobby said. "You've made another mess. This is not going to be easy to clean up, but I do want to thank you for putting up a fight. You've really turned me on now--look how hard I am now!" Bobby began to rub himself as he thought about how he was going to take her. "What's the matter Bridget, don't you want to fuck anymore?" Bobby said, with a lunatic grin on his foaming face. He wanted and needed something big. *This is going to be great*, he cheered himself on as he admired how much work he had done in such a short period of time. Bobby leaned across the bed to grab Bridget by the hair. He pulled her away from the headboard and lunged her forward, crashing into the corner post. She lay limp on the bloodied mattress, as still as if she were dead.

Bobby did not want to take the half-unconscious girl who was bleeding out before him. He realized that he did have time to bind and gag her. Bobby lanced the cord from her bedroom window shade. He wrapped his right arm under her body, then moved it just above her center mass line. This was the point which, when upward pressure is applied, causes her body to fold in half. She remained face down in a pool of her own blood. He pulled at her right arm, then twisted her left arm behind her back and effectively tied them tight with the cord. The slaps that Bobby slammed into Bridget's ass from behind left five-finger welt marks that quickly raised and reddened. The pain response brought Bridget back to a semiconscious state.

Bobby was waiting for her to gain back her mind. She moaned, but did not cry out. Each moan from the beaten girl was a moment of ecstasy for Bobby. He interpreted her moans of pain and agony as sounds of pleasure and passion. Bridget might be enjoying this more than him. He could not bear to be without her any longer. He mounted the bed where Bridget had collapsed and again raised her, lifting her midsection high enough so that she would not collapse on him again. Bobby entered her from behind while kneeling on blood-soaked satin. He punished her for the mess she had made smacking her ass, one cheek at a time, alternating sides with each strike. Bobby had planned on making love to Bridget for hours, but her cries were beginning to become problematic. Bobby had no intention of killing Bridget. After all, he did love her. He repeatedly told her how much he loved her as he continuously drove himself into her. There was nothing Bobby wouldn't do for her. All she had to do was ask for it and Bobby would give it to her, now that he knew she was a fighter. All she had to do was ask.

Bobby filled her up from behind, then leaned over and laid his sweaty head on the middle of her back. "Bridget, isn't it nice to be on this side of the tracks?" He asked. His penis was spent and unresponsive, but he remained inside her. He slid himself from his full mount and retreated to a kneeling position on the floor behind her. Exhausted from the preceding moments and thankful that Bridget was no longer screaming and crying, he took a well-deserved minute to collect himself. Bobby needed and earned a few seconds of rest.

Just as Bobby's muscles fully relaxed, Bridget, already having a locked and loaded knee from the doggie position he had held her in, released with all her might a devastating back kick that connected squarely with Bobby's nose, right eye, and mouth. The full force strike nearly exploded his face. His nose shifted a full inch to the left as the bones nearly disintegrated inside his head. His right eye was instantly closed and completely purple with engorged blood. Three teeth were lying on the floor, where spatters of his blood began to mix with hers. The kick, which was worthy of a second-degree black belt's expertise, probably saved her life. Bobby was stunned and she was on the move. Bridget, still with bound hands, bolted toward the bedroom door, then halted dead in her tracks. Bobby beat her there. Blood was leaving his body through his shattered and mangled face. Bridget slammed and locked the door to her bedroom as Bobby exited, leaving a trail of his own blood behind. She tried mightily to free her hands from the rope that bound them. It was no use to struggle with it anymore. The more she tried to free herself, the tighter the ropes became.

She sat down on her bed and knocked the phone from the hook with her foot. Bridget used her extended and firmed-up tongue to dial the emergency operator. She glanced at the phone dial, sized up the location of the nine and aimed the point of her tongue into the hole. She was able to turn the dial to the right until the metal tab stopped the travel of her tongue. Bridget repeated the same process for the number one and again for another number one. "Emergency Operator. What's your emergency?"

"Help me," Bridget cried. "Please help me. I've just been attacked, bleeding bad, and I'm bound up." The tears began to flow from Bridget's eyes as the prospect of the ordeal coming to an end was finally real in her mind. "Hurry, please hurry. I'm bleeding all over the place." Bridget held it together long enough to tell the emergency operator where she was located and was also able to give the operator her allergy information. She had severe allergies to many medications, and quickly recalled the anaphylaxis-type reaction she had experienced when she took a friend's Tylenol with codeine. It had almost killed her in a matter of minutes. Bridget wasn't sure she would be conscious when NYPD and FDNY emergency services reached her. She did not want to succumb to a medication allergy after all she had been through with that animal.

Bobby had no choice but to go to the nearest emergency room. His face was shattered from Bridget's enormous heel kick, and if he didn't get the medical attention he needed, he would surely bleed out and die. Blood was running out of his face like water coming from a garden hose. He expected the doctors to have to pull bones from his brain. He held the shattered pieces of his nose in place with his uniform shirt. The bones in his face rattled from side to side alarmingly as he ran from the building. The Corvair seemed to be a thousand miles away when he left the building through the same door from which he had entered. Blood was leaking out from beyond the edges of his makeshift bandage. He walked nervously to the Corvair, trying not to run. He knew that running would increase his heart rate as well as his respiration rate, causing the massive bleeding to speed up. He could barely see with his one functioning eye, because of the shirt he had compressed on his face. The short walk to the cemetery took forever, because Bobby was beginning to feel the woozy effects of the blood loss. He began to feel the same lightheadedness that he had felt when he was smoking pot, only he didn't feel any euphoria right now, only panic. He wondered if he was going to make it to the emergency room before he passed out.

Bobby raced away from the cemetery, nearly waking the dead as he floored the Corvair. It was a short trip to Queensboro Hospital, which he made faster by ignoring all the traffic signals. He parked the Corvair out of sight in a dark end of the parking lot. It was only a couple of hundred feet to the Queensboro Hospital emergency room entrance. He thought he could make it. He staggered down the five-step staircase just off the parking lot, trying not to collapse in an obscure location. Bobby almost made it under his own power. He collapsed nearly ten feet from the emergency room doors, with little blood volume left. Emergency room staff responded to the collapsed, unidentified white man who was hemorrhaging just a few feet from the doors. Bobby immediately became the number one priority for the emergency room staff. After a quick one-minute initial assessment, he was given two pints of typed and cross-matched packed red blood cells. He would require a third to improve his hemoglobin and hematocrit. He was not in the trauma bay for more than ten minutes before he was stabilized and sent to the operating room for corrective and reconstructive surgery on his shattered face.

Acknowledgments

On behalf of Nicholas, I wish to thank the efforts of Jonathan Sturak for his technical expertise in moving Nick's manuscript from Microsoft Word to a format ready for publication. My thanks also to Adam Hall who helped us create an intriguing cover.

And Dr. James Lenhart, you have no idea how grateful I am to you for all your help and all your hard work helping me get Nick's book published. I had no idea where to even start and you guided me the whole way. You told me we would get it done and here we are. We did it! You will never know how happy you have made me. Thank you!

About The Author

Nicholas Del Gandio was born October 23, 1968 in Brooklyn, New York and gained his street smarts in the shadows of New York City at an early age due to the family upheaval created by his father's vicious crimes. Although his father was arrested, found guilty and incarcerated well before Nick's 4th birthday, an unexpected and extraordinary societal backlash pervaded his early childhood and adolescence.

Throwing this off, Nicholas enrolled in St. John's University School of Pharmacy and graduated in 1991. He married the love of his life, Gina in 1998 and shortly after they moved to Las Vegas, Nevada in part to distance them from the lingering trail of Bobby Maseano.

Although a compounding pharmacist by profession, Nick was a man of letters and expressed much of his perspectives on life, love and happiness through poetry. However, in 2011 Nicholas was moved to tell his provocative life story so that others like him might gain insight and meaning into their own lives through his words. Unfortunately, Nick died suddenly and unexpectedly on May 9, 2015 before *First Victim* was ready for press.

The publication of this manuscript in its untouched form since his death, honors Nick, his loving wife Gina and their two children.

www.ingramcontent.com/pod-product-compliance
Lightning Source LLC
Chambersburg PA
CBHW020358030726
47496CB00007B/2198